First For Freedom

By

Maxville Burt Williams

authorHOUSE™

1663 LIBERTY DRIVE, SUITE 200
BLOOMINGTON, INDIANA 47403
(800) 839-8640
WWW.AUTHORHOUSE.COM

© 2005 Maxville Burt Williams. All Rights Reserved.

No part of this book may be reproduced, stored in a retrieval system, or transmitted by any means without the written permission of the author.

First published by AuthorHouse 08/31/05

ISBN: 1-4208-1895-3 (sc)

Printed in the United States of America
Bloomington, Indiana

This book is printed on acid-free paper.

I would like to thank the Department of Archives and History for all the information and illustrations that have been made available to me. The minutes of the meeting of the Fourth Provincial Congress were valuable to me and gave much information about what actually happened at Halifax.

This book should be read as an historical novel. It is primarily fiction with great authenticity given to those parts which are considered historical.

Special acknowledgement is given to Mrs. Mebane Holloman Burgwyn who gave me direction when I lost my way and made it possible for me to explore new avenues as a student in her creative writing class.

Dedication

I dedicate this book to four people, who more than others, have given me reason to write it. To my mother, Mrs. Ada Bell Williams; to my wife, Mary Lois Williams; to my daughter, Elizabeth Ada Williams; and to my son Maxville Burt Williams, Jr.

I hope it will serve as an enjoyable and meaningful experience to all who read it.

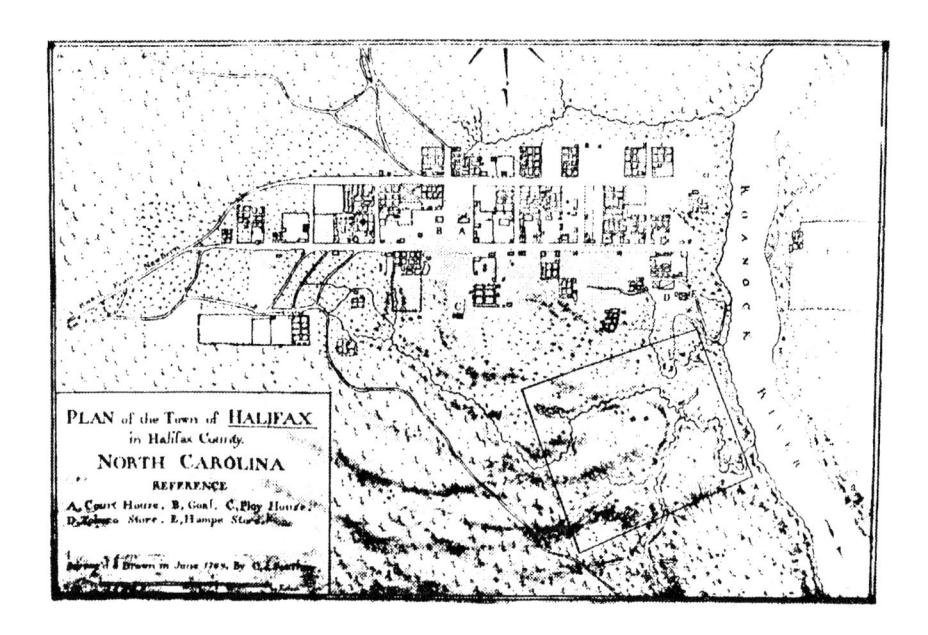

BOOK ONE

CHAPTER ONE

It was four o'clock when eighteen-year old Sam Pickett entered Halifax. It was a town of approximately one thousand people who made their living from the land and various activities of trade and commerce. There were several plantations and many small farms in the counties of Halifax and Northampton. The Roanoke River was the route that led to the coastal towns and was used by the people who lived in Eastern North Carolina.

He pulled his gentle bay horse, 'Jericho', up to the hitching post in front of Martin's Livery, dismounted, and walked across King Street to the town common. From here, his dark eyes surveyed the men in front of the courthouse. Market Street was perpendicular to King Street and was the place where people came to trade on Market Days. When people came to Halifax, they always came down King Street. It was the street that ran in a north and south direction. Other streets, such as St. David and Pittsylvania, branched off the main avenue and ran in an east or west direction.

Sam had been aware of an unusually large number of people in town as he had ridden down King Street, but now he especially noticed a small group of men talking excitedly in the courtyard across Market Street. His curiosity aroused, he headed immediately in that direction. He waited for a carriage to pass, then hurried across the street. He nudged his agile body through the crowd to the courthouse door and read the bold-lettered words printed on the notice: FOURTH PROVINCIAL CONGRESS, April 4, 1776. Sam turned to the men around him.

"That's tomorrow," he said, more to himself than to the group of men.

"It's about time we had the Congress here," said one of the men.

"There's gonna be some big decisions made at this Congress," said another.

"I say we ought to do something with them prisoners we got down the street. It ain't safe having them here in Halifax." Said a lanky, pointed-faced man, that Sam recognized as Jesse Turner.

Sam turned to face Turner squarely. He now realized that Jesse Turner, the town agitator, had already worked the men into a rebellious mood.

"You just hold on, Turner, these prisoners are being guarded. They ain't likely to harm anybody. Why are you always trying to rile people up this way?"

"We ought to left'em lying on the ground at Moore's Creek Bridge. That's what it's coming to---either them or us," came Turner's quick response.

There was a rumble of approval from the group.

"Most all the prisoners are Scotch-Highlanders. They've had their problems with King George, too," said Sam, trying to calm the men.

"Sam you've been in Edenton too long. Don't you know they all took the oath to fight for King George? Everybody here knows it." Turner's dark beady eyes flashed as he spoke.

The crowd began to get loud and boisterous in their support of Turner's statement. Their mood was almost ugly.

"I know what happened at Moore's Creek Bridge but these people don't really want no fight with us. All of you here know Jesse Turner well enough to know all he wants to do is to get somebody worked up over nothing," said Sam, firmly, as he moved nervously up the steps of the courthouse.

"What are you ---A Tory-Lover," asked Turner, not giving the men time to consider Sam's words.

"They killed some of our boys at that battle," added one of Turner's supporters.

The men began to move closer to Sam, who was now on the top step with his broad back to the door.

"Now you fellows calm down. You all know me. I'm a Patriot---just like the rest of you," shouted Sam. "We don't have any say in what's done with the prisoners."

Sam stepped aside and pointed to the poster.

"The Congress will convene tomorrow. We can wait another day to see what is decided."

From the edge of the crowd came a deep voice that caused all the men to turn around.

"Sam's right. Let's wait and see what the Congress decides. Them prisoners ain't 'bout to go nowhere," said Harry Bedlow, the town's blacksmith.

The crowd became more relaxed after Bedlow spoke. Sam felt more confident knowing that Harry was in the crowd. A two hundred-pound, burly man like Bedlow was one man whose words were heeded.

"Well, the main thing is to let the Congress know how we feel about them prisoners," said Jesse Turner

"We can say what we want about what we need to do but we can't do anything until the Congress has acted, " continued Sam.

With these words, Sam stepped down and moved through the crowd. From the courtyard, he crossed Market Street and was on his way to Dudley's Tavern.

Before he had been selected by Allen Jones to study surveying in Edenton, Sam had worked for John Hamilton at the general store on Saturdays and helped Dudley during the weekdays. The work at the General Store was not as demanding as the work at Dudley's Tavern. At the tavern, there was always too much to do and never enough time to get all the work done----four rooms upstairs that were let to travelers--meals to be served in the dining hall during the day; and a game room where cards were played nightly. All these facilities had to be properly tended. Sam had done it all. He had helped Dudley clean the rooms, serve the guest, bring in wood from the woodpile for the fireplace, mop the floors, clean the cellar, and anything else demanded by the rotund Christopher Dudley.

As Sam entered the tavern, he saw the round-bellied Dudley at the end of the bar. He was a jolly fellow, about fifty, with heavy sideburns and a thick growth of hair on his chin. The rest of his face was cleanly shaven. His bulging eyes and snubbed nose caused him to look almost comical. His happy disposition made him a most agreeable tavern-keeper.

Dudley was serving a mug of ale to one of the men at the counter but noticed Sam immediately. A big smile changed the shape of Dudley's fat jaws and his friendly blue eyes held a special welcome for Sam.

"Hey, Sam," yelled Dudley, "come on over here. I've got something for you."

As he walked to the empty stool at the bar, Sam noticed that most of the tables were occupied.

All who frequented the tavern had come to know each other as well as they knew members of their own family. The closeness of this group was strongly cemented by that constant craving for the spirits served by Dudley.

As Sam sat down on the stool, Dudley reached beneath the bar and handed him an envelope.

"One of the soldiers from Colonel Nicholas Long's Outfit brought it in here yesterday."

Sam quickly noticed that the envelope had already been opened.

"Dudley, do you always read everybody's mail?"

Dudley smiled.

"That ain't the first one of them letters I've passed out. I just checked to see if it was like the rest."

"It just don't seem right for you to read other people's mail."

"Well, you've got to keep up with what's happening. People have come to expect me to know. It is part of the good service I offer my customers. Most of the time I have to read the letters to the ones who don't know how to read."

Sam looked up from the letter.

"It says I'm to report to Colonel Long's Headquarters at Quanky next month."

"Yep, it's just like the rest of them letters," assured Dudley

Dudley reached under the counter and poured a mug of homemade wine for Sam. "Try some of this. It's the best I've ever made. I keep it for my special customers."

"Hey, Dudley, I almost forgot. Have you seen Uncle John around the last few days? Mama's been worried about him. He ain't been home for a week."

"Let's see, the last time John was in here was before Montfort's funeral."

"Uncle John has stayed away from home before, but never this long. How long do you suppose he'll mourn Montfort's passing?"

"Look at this crowd, Sam. They don't need no funeral to get them to drankin'."

Taking the mug of wine from the counter, Sam turned toward the men sitting at the tables. Conversations among these men had recently turned from talk of crops and trade to talk of war and independence. Some spoke of revolution and others listened because all knew that this was not idle talk. From the sound of the news from Boston, there could be very trying times ahead for the colonies. The battle of Moore's Creek Bridge was regarded by many as a clear indication that the North Carolina Colony was even now at war. The fact that the FOURTH PROVINCIAL CONGRESS was coming to Halifax had stimulated many questions that would soon have to be answered. It seemed that the men in Halifax were becoming more and more aware of some impending danger. Sam's thoughts of war and revolution were interrupted as Dudley touched his left elbow.

"I got some news yesterday that might interest you, Sam."

Sam turned around on the stool.

"What kind of news?"

"Did you know the Hamilton Family is coming back to Halifax this afternoon on the five o'clock stage?"

"You'd better not let John Hamilton know you've been reading his mail."

"Even when it was wrote to me? He asked me to have his carriage come for his family."

"It'll be good to see George. I haven't seen him since I left Halifax for Edenton."

"Well, you'll be seeing him any time now. It's already after five but you know the five o'clock stage don't ever get here until after six."

"I think I'll walk down to the common and watch for the stage."

"Look Sam, if you've got any extra time before you join up with Colonel Long's Outfit, I could sure use you. With all the folks coming to town I'll need all the help I can git."

"I'll help you when I can, Dudley. You know that. I can't make any promises though, -- the way things are."

"Any time you want to help, you know where to find your apron," said Dudley, motioning toward the kitchen.

"You know Dudley, reading other people's mail can come in handy at times," said Sam, as he walked to the door.

"I tell you Hamilton wrote that letter to me personally. But, to tell the truth---other people's mail is more interesting," added Dudley, throwing up his hand and laughing as Sam left the tavern.

CHAPTER TWO

Leaving Dudley's Tavern, Sam walked along Market Street toward the town common. He thought of the many Saturdays that he had spent working as a clerk in the Hamilton General Store. Mr. Hamilton had quickly realized that Sam was eager to learn to read and had brought books to the store for him to take home and had encourage his son, George, to help with the reading. Since George was the same age as Sam, the two had much in common. George would help Sam with his reading and Sam would help George with his fishing and hunting and learning about the outdoors. George had often said that the two were swapping education. They had learned much from each other over the years.

The Hamilton family was one of the first families in Halifax and had influence with other members of the aristocracy throughout the colony. Mrs. Abigail Hamilton always seemed concerned about proper association with other members of her own social standing, and at times Sam felt that she was resentful of his presence in her home. She was an aloof person, and Sam seldom saw her at the store. She always left the menial work to those whom she employed for such service.

George Hamilton was given all the proper advantages and had made the best associations. Abigail Hamilton had seen to that. George had progressed in his studies and was planning to travel to England to attend Eton in the fall. The daughter, Josephine, had always been a tomboy and had constantly pestered Sam and George during their childhood. She always wanted to be with the two boys, even when she was not wanted----which was most of the time.

Sam's thoughts quickly turned from the Hamilton family, as he became aware of new faces he encountered as he came to the town common. He assumed that many of these men were delegates to the Congress.

Since the convening of the Congress was imminent, the number of people in town had almost doubled. Many came to see the representatives from other counties and towns; others came because of the great excitement and concern about the present state of uncertainty that prevailed throughout the province.

The society of Halifax was as polished and cultivated as any in the colony. The aristocracy was composed of the large landowners and others who had accumulated great wealth. The shop owners, tradesmen, and small landowners made up the middle class. The poor white people and the slaves made up the largest segment of the population. There were as many slaves as there were members of all the other classes.

First For Freedom

The visiting delegates would bring with them a philosophy that represented the thinking of the people in the towns and counties throughout the colony. It would soon become evident to the delegates that the people of Halifax were as strong for independence as the people they represented, thought Sam, as he sat down on the wooden bench at the corner of Market and King Street.

He was convinced that now was the time for new ideas to be considered and old ideas be challenged. It was a time to side with those who believed and thought the same, and it was time to oppose those who thought differently. It was time for the divine rule of government to be put aside. It was time for loyalty and co-operation. It was time to take a stand.

On the town common, small groups of men stood talking and an atmosphere of excitement---tempered with uncertainty prevailed. The store-keepers and shop-owners were busy selling goods and giving advice to all who entered their establishments. The taverns and lodging houses were quickly being filled. The great influx of people would soon take all available accommodations, and it was evident that many of the delegates would have to inquire at private homes to find places to stay.

Sam turned to his left and looked down Market Street. There were people milling around as if they had no place to go. They seemed to be anxiously awaiting something to happen. He looked to his right and noticed a large crowd of men standing next to the gaol. The prisoners seemed to interest the men more than anything else in Halifax. Sam wondered if perhaps the Moore's Creek prisoners represented a threat to these men and if the prisoners were somehow symbolic of all that they hated.

His eyes shifted from the jail and he could see the stage coming down King Street. He stood and waited for it to make its turn onto Market Street.

As he walked back toward Dudley's Tavern, six passengers stepped down from the stage. He could see their expressions of surprise to find so many people in town. They looked toward the common as they gathered their baggage.

Sam recognized three members of the Hamilton family immediately. Mr. John Hamilton and George wore silk stocking of light blue; both had buckled shoes and silver buckles at the knees. Mr. Hamilton's suit was lavender and George's suit was shade of blue darker than his stockings. The laced ruffled wristbands and silk shirts were clear indications that they were men of high breeding. Sam, in his leather brown breeches and faded blue shirt, was a contrasting figure as he approached the family.

Mrs. Abigail Hamilton was busy dusting her light pink, silk dress with a rose-colored cambric handkerchief. Her dark pink, buckled shoes complimented her dress. She was a sophisticated lady who seldom met her equal in Halifax. Coming closer Sam recognized the familiar lilac odor that was always a part of Abigail Hamilton's person. She was a small lady with graying hair and her pale blue eyes looked tired. Abigail Hamilton always made Sam feel uncomfortable. Yet, there was something pleasant about the soft, penetrating fragrance that radiated about her.

It was the girl who caught Sam's eye. Her vivacious and striking beauty was evident even from a distance. Her dark, blue chintz gown fitted snugly over a perfect figure, and she wore a pretty apron of white that had large blue dots the size of two shillings. His eyes rested on the dark-lashed, blue eyes of the young girl and he looked no further.

"Look, Josie, it's Sam Pickett," said George, as Sam walked toward them.

Sam was unable to speak for a moment---then his words came slowly.

"You mean----you mean-----this girl is -----ah----lady-----is ---Josie."

Mrs. Hamilton stopped dusting her gown for a moment.

"We've been gone for three months and Josie and I have had some time to shop. They have such lovely things in Charles Town. We thought it was about time that Josie had some gown-up things of her own."

Sam, still not recovered from the shock of seeing the matured Josie, spoke slowly.

"It really is Josie. I----I didn't recognize you from over yonder. I wondered who you were when I saw y'all get off the stage. It's only been a few months and you're all grown up."

"Oh, Sam, I haven't changed that much," said Josie. Her manner was demure but there was a definite sparkle of pleasure in her eyes.

"You sure look different to me," said Sam. But he knew that the conversation was leading in the wrong direction--so he turned to Mr. Hamilton.

"How was your trip home, Sir?"

John Hamilton was a stocky man of fifty and had curls of graying hair about his ears. He would have been a handsome man, thought Sam, if his long nose were shorter and his thin lips were just a little thicker. His blue-green eyes were reddened, perhaps from the road dust, and his mouth had turned up corners that made Hamilton appear to have a slight smile.

"Oh, we're tired. Nothing tires you out like a long trip on the stage. I'm surprised to see you, Sam. I thought you were in Edenton studying to be a surveyor."

"I was, but Mr. Allen Jones called me back. Colonel Nicholas Long is trying to raise a town militia. He needs all the MEN he can get."

First For Freedom

"Well, if you have any extra time, there'll be work for you at the store, that is if want it," offered Hamilton.

"I'm afraid I won't be able to help you at the store anymore. I've been informed that my first duty is to our colony."

There was momentary silence, then John Hamilton spoke.

"You were the best help I've ever had. You can have your old job back any time you need work."

"So, you plan to join the cause that we've been hearing so much about in Charles Town," said Abigail Hamilton, fidgeting at her dress.

"Oh, yes. It seems we don't have much of a choice but to join. I reckon I'll have to give up everything I've been doing for a while."

"It does seem a shame. I'm sure you would have made a good surveyor," said Hamilton.

"It looks like the fighting will have to come first. Y'all plan to join the Patriots, I hope." Sam noticed that John Hamilton reacted as if he had been insulted. Perhaps he shouldn't have asked the question.

"What we plan to do is get some rest. Sam, I want you to tell everybody that I have purchased some fine merchandise that will soon be shipped from Charles Town. We'll have most everything that people will want to buy," said Hamilton, avoiding Sam's question.

"Most people don't have buying on their minds right now. Everybody around here is talking about independence. Since the Battle of Moore's Creek Bridge, about all the people are talking about is fighting. We've got General Donald McDonald and Colonel Allen McDonald, you know Flora McDonald's husband and her son Alexander McDonald, in the jail, along with all the other prisoners captured in that battle."

"It seems that you've become quite involved in the conflict," observed George.

For the first time, Sam looked at his boyhood companion. George possessed an air of pride that was quickly evident, a grace of manners that seemed completely natural and a handsome face that was immediately noticed---especially by the young ladies. He had a prominent nose and friendly, pale blue eyes----the same as his mother. He was a young man of charm and wit. His figure was slender and he only weighed about one hundred and forty pounds. George looked almost frail, thought Sam, as he picked up the conversation.

"Oh, I'm not even a soldier yet; but I've learned a lot about what's going on since I've been back in Halifax. There's a saying among the men at Camp Quanky that YOU GOT TO LEARN FAST OR ELSE YOU WON'T LAST."

Abigail Hamilton interrupted.

"I hear so much about fighting that it makes me weary. How is your mother's health, Sam?"

"Mama!" Sam was not thinking of his mother but was staring at Josie.

"Your mother's health, Sam. How is your mother?"

"Oh---Mama---She's full of energy. I just can't seem to do enough around the house to suit her."

"Well," continued Mrs. Hamilton, "you tell her I have a great deal of sewing I'll be wanting her to do for me. She's the only one I can trust with the material I've bought. I want her to have the work."

"I know she'll be thankful for it."

"Why are there so many people in town today, Sam," asked George, as he looked down Market Street toward the town common.

"I thought you all knew the Fourth Provincial Congress is being held here. I tell you big things are about to happen. This Congress will just about have to set some course for us to follow."

"Congress! My Lands! Where is the royal Governor Josiah Martin," asked Mrs. Hamilton.

Sam was eager to answer.

"He's down on the coast. The talk is that he's waiting for General Clinton to come for him. Most of the people are following the Provincial Congress now. There are still some highlanders around the coast who might rally to his colors---but most of the people are with this Congress. Everybody's listening to people like Cornelius Harnett, Samuel Johnston, Abner Nash and all the other Patriots."

Josie seemed confused by all the talk of fighting.

"And I suppose you're going to be one of the soldiers who will be fighting at their side, if war does come."

"If God gives me the strength," was Sam's quick reply.

John Hamilton turned to his wife.

"I see the carriage has come for the ladies."

As John Hamilton reached down for his baggage, he turned to George.

"Go by Dudley's Tavern and pick up my mail. I'll wait for you at the store."

"Let me help you, Sir," said Sam as he took two valises from John Hamilton and followed George to the carriage that had stopped in the middle of Market Street. Sam and George placed the baggage on the back of the carriage.

"Sam, why don't you come by the house tomorrow after supper. We'll catch up on all that has happened since we've been gone," suggested George Hamilton.

"I think that's a good idea," agreed Josie, looking at Sam as she boarded the carriage.

Sam felt a quickening of his heartbeat when he heard her words.

"I'll look forward to it, Joise---ah--George." Sam's eyes were on Josie, even though he was not talking to her.

Abigail Hamilton looked out of the window of the carriage.

"Don't forget to tell your mother that I'll be sending some cloth to her in a few days."

"Yes, Mam. I won't forget," yelled Sam, as he watched the carriage turn around.

Sam felt a certain weakness as the carriage departed down King Street. He was oblivious that George stood at his side but was suddenly aware that Josie had become a lady and, even though she was only sixteen, he could see maturity beyond those years. The young tomboy, the pestering shadow that had followed him in his youth, was gone forever. This feeling that Sam had for the young Josie was quite different from the feeling that he was now experiencing.

"Come on with me to get the mail. Father is already half way to the store," said George.

Sam and George bounded onto the plank sidewalk in front of Dudley's and entered the crowded tavern. George led the way and found two empty stools at the counter.

"Hey, Dudley, let me have father's mail," said George, as Dudley handed a mug of ale to a small bearded man at the bar.

"So you got back from Charles Town. Tell me about all the lovely ladies, George. Did you find one for yourself while you were gone?" asked Dudley, as he handed George a package of letters.

"Dudley, you know one would never be enough for me," said George, winking at Sam.

"How about Josie? Did she meet any young men in Charles Town," asked Dudley.

"Josie stayed close to mother. Several young fellows came to call but mother turned them away at the front door."

"Well, I say, your mother did just fine," Said Sam, secretly smiling to himself.

"What did you say, Sam," asked George who was observing the unusually large crowd.

"I said--ah--how about some homemade wine? Dudley give us two mugs of that wine you made. It's good, George. Nothing like that imported wine."

Even before George and Sam were served, Jesse Turner strolled up to the bar.

"I hear you've been called by Colonel Long, Sam," began Turner.

"Yeah, news travels fast," said Sam, looking at Dudley.

"You git a letter like Sam here got, George," asked Turner, placing his mug on the counter for a refill.

George thumbed through the letters.

"I don't have any letter from Colonel Long."

"There must be some reason for you not gitting one," Turner turned to the men sitting at the tables. "Maybe your old man don't want his little boy to be doing no fighting."

"When you don't have any enemies, you don't have anybody to fight," said George, turning toward Turner.

"You talk like we're already at war," interrupted Sam

"It's just a matter of time. Everybody knows that." Jesse Turner did not take his eyes off George as he spoke to Sam.

"What's your hurry, Turner. You talk like you can't wait to start a fight with somebody---anybody," George stood up to face Turner.

"I'm letting everybody know where I stand. Can you say that much for yourself?" Turner looked to the men in the tavern and several nodded approvals.

"I don't have to answer to you or anybody else," came George's quick reply.

"Now that ain't being friendly ---not with your hometown folks, Georgie, boy," said Turner, as he moved closer to George.

Sam stood up and stepped forward.

"What do you want from us, Turner?"

"I don't want nothing from you, Sam. I just want to know if George is a Patriot or a Tory," said Turner, not backing down.

"Yeah, speak up Hamilton. We all want to know," came a voice from a side table.

"Jesse Turner, if you don't beat all I've ever seen. Why can't you let people alone," said Sam.

"Sam, you know if he was a Patriot, he wouldn't have no trouble answering. What we need to do is to take him down to the Roanoke River and wash away any Tory sympathies that he contracted in Charles Town." Said Turner as he looked to the crowd for support.

First For Freedom

Several men walked slowly to the counter and George and Sam were pressed with their backs against the bar.

"You're not taking George anywhere," said Sam, as he pushed one of the men away.

"Jesse Turner, you ain't starting no fight in my place," yelled Dudley, coming from behind the counter.

Suddenly the men around Sam and George parted as if Moses were in their midst. The familiar figure of Allen Jones walked slowly up to Sam and George. He was a distinguished gentleman. He wore a dark, blue suit, buckled shoes, and a black cocked hat. His features were sharp and his dark eyes intently surveyed the crowd. His long, black hair covered his ears and was tied at the back. All the men in the tavern knew the owner of Mount Gallant Plantation in Northampton county. Allen Jones and his brother, Willie, were involved in politics and both were independently wealthy landowners. Allen Jones was known to be an independent thinker---often expressing his opinion though others disagreed. Yet, he was always held in high esteem by all who knew him---and the men at Dudley's Tavern knew him well.

"What is this shouting all about," asked Jones, standing next to Sam.

"Jesse Turner just got all these men stirred up and carried away with his wild talk," said Sam, looking intently at Turner.

"Well, from what I could hear it was George who was about to be carried away," said Allen Jones.

The crowd laughed at Jones' quip and their mood no longer seemed violent.

"Seems to me people ought to be proud of the fact that they are a Patriot. George Hamilton, here, won't even say if he's one or not," said Turner. His voice no longer sounded angry but rather calm.

"Yeah, if it was up to you--- you'd take all the prisoners from the jail and hang'em to the nearest tree," said Sam, looking at Jesse Turner.

Allen Jones turned from Sam and faced Jesse Turner.

"What's done with the Moore's Creek prisoners will be decided by the Provincial Congress---not by a crowd of men shouting at one another in a tavern. They will be protected while they are in our custody. If there is anyone here who thinks differently, he will have to answer to the Congress. Some of the delegates are already here. Now, how do you men think a visiting delegate would regard this kind of behavior. Since I am a delegate to the Congress, I'll give you one delegate's opinion. I think all of you need to leave the decision to those who have been elected to make the decisions. As for George Hamilton, all of us will soon have to decide about freedom from England but this is not the time nor the place---so I suggest that all of you be about your drinking and leave the boys alone."

The men began to murmur in low voices as they returned to their tables.

Allen Jones

"Well, I suppose they've got a right to feel the way they do. They just seem to let their feelings get the best of them," said Sam, as he looked toward the men.

"You boys have to be careful about what you say. These men aren't always so easy to handle." Said Allen Jones.

First For Freedom

"Who gave them the right to demand anything of anybody. I don't like what's happening here, Sam," said George.

"I thought the men in Edenton were against the King but these men seem ready to fight anybody." Sam sat down at the counter.

"Well, if there's a fight here, you'll have to handle them alone because I'm going home. Sam, don't mention anything about this to father. It would only cause him to worry. Come on by the house tomorrow and we'll talk." George walked quickly to the door and out of the tavern.

Allen Jones occupied the stool next to Sam.

"These are troubled times. That's the reason I asked you to come home. Have you any word from Colonel Long?"

"I'm to report for duty next month. I just got my letter this afternoon."

"What you boys just experienced is only a sample of how concerned and disturbed the people are becoming. The militia will soon be needed if we are to have any kind of law and order."

"I'm glad you came along. It seems I'm becoming more and more indebted to you. I don't know when I'll ever be able to repay you for all your kindness to me."

"I was well paid when you won that horserace last year. Willie made enough on his bets to pay for that racetrack. When you become a surveyor, I'll have enough work for you. You need not worry about that now. There is one thing I'd like for you to do for me. I've had my horse MIDNIGHT, stabled at Willie's for the past three months. I wish you'd go by and see how Uncle Louie is managing. I haven't had the time to check on him for some time now. This convening of the Congress has kept me so busy I've hardly had time to see about my work at Mount Gallant."

"I've been looking forward to seeing that horse ever since I've been home. He probably needs to be taken to the track."

"I want Cornelius Harnett and some of my friends to see a real race horse. See that 'Midnight' is properly groomed and exercised. Who knows, by Jove, we might have us a horse race before the Congress adjourns."

Dudley came to the counter.

"Some of the delegates are waiting for you in the game room, Mr. Jones."

"Oh, I almost forgot. Tell 'em I'm on my way. By the way, I'll be wanting a room when the Congress convenes. Sam you take care of my horse. You know I'm partial to that animal."

"I know, Sir. I'll be in touch."

Sam turned to leave the tavern as Allen Jones went to the game room.

The sun was setting as Sam walked to Martin's Livery to get his horse. There were fewer people on the street now. When he crossed King Street, he looked toward the Roanoke River and could see the butcher shop, the tannery, and Hamilton's General Store had closed the shutters for the day. Crossing King Street, he mounted his horse and rode toward Quanky Creek.

The loud clanging of the hammer against the anvil cause him to look to his right as he approached Harry Bedlow's blacksmith shop. Harry's day was longer than any other working man's day. Demands from the planters required prompt service----the members of the gentry were not to be kept waiting. Bedlow was a man to be trusted and Sam felt an unusual closeness to him that he had not realized before this day.

The shops and stores were behind him as he came to the residential section. To his right were small white, wooden, houses spaced along the streets that ran perpendicular to King Street. Silent black smoke curled lazily from the chimneys toward the sky as the people of Halifax prepared their last meal of the day.

Sam walked his horse and nodded to the people along the street and the few sitting on the porches. The large two-story home of John Hamilton on his left was about forty yards from King Street. Now the oak, maple and elm trees shaded the road and became more numerous. He had passed through the residential section .

As he crossed Quanky Bridge, Sam realized that he had noticed with new appreciation---things that had been familiar to him all his life. The houses that had been merely houses were now homes and dwelling places where friends and people lived. There seemed to be a new significance----a meaning ---a difference---that brought forth an awareness of other people----their hopes---their dreams and their destinies. He wondered, as he rode toward his home, if this new outlook on life was somehow related to the fact that Josie had suddenly changed the meaning of things---or the way he looked at life.

CHAPTER THREE

When Sam had finished his supper, he told his mother and Aunt Jenny all that had happened in Halifax. Sarah Pickett seemed worried that there was no word of the whereabouts of her brother, John. Aunt Jenny was especially interested when Sam had described the meeting with the Hamiltons. When he saw how pleased Aunt Jenny was, he made an extra effort to describe each detail as vividly as possible.

Now he lay on the top bunk of the double bunk bed. The bottom bunk was for his Uncle John and had been empty since Sam had been home.

The moon cast a brightness through the window at the foot of his bed and illuminated the large room that was in many ways two rooms---part was where he and his uncle slept and the back part was the kitchen. Midway along the opposite wall was a huge fireplace where three black pots hung on swinging cranes. Close by the fireplace was a spinning wheel that had hummed many times to the rhythm of his mother's foot when she pressed the treadle.

Shadows fell about the room on furniture set sparingly here and there. Three simple homemade chairs held together by wooden pegs and a rough table against the opposite wall to the left of the fireplace were seldom used since most of the living was done in the back part of the room. On the front wall and next to the door was a long board with six wooden pegs spaced about four inches apart for hanging clothes. Clean bright, yellow curtains of linen on the front and side windows seemed to absorb the moonlight and cast an efflorescence throughout the room.

Sarah Pickett and Aunt Jenny were by this time asleep in their room adjacent to the kitchen. Now the house was quiet---it was a good time for thinking. A disturbing thought entered his mind as Sam considered how the spirit of the people in Halifax had changed during the time he had been in Edenton.

He had heard rumblings of discontent at Horniblow's Tavern in Edenton but somehow had not expected the disturbed atmosphere he had witnessed upon his return. The climate of opinion in Halifax seemed volatile. Wild talk and quick reactions to touchy questions caused the men to separate into small groups to seek out those who shared common opinions. Sam had noticed these groups at the town common and in Dudley's Tavern. They seemed at times boisterous when there was a receptive audience. Then again---they would withdraw to themselves as if they shared some hidden secret.

It had been only a few days since his return to Halifax. Now that he thought about, it seemed that he had been home much longer. It even seemed as if had never really left. The day of his return had been a memorable day, one of mixed emotions and sadness. He closed his eyes and retraced all that had happened from the moment that he had approached Halifax by boat.

A crisp March wind was blowing across the Roanoke River that day and had caused Sam to pull his frocked coat collar up closer around his neck. The clapping of the oars had seemed to punctuate his thoughts as he lay under the canopy of the thirty-foot boat headed up the Roanoke to Halifax.

His cocked hat and frocked coat made him feel important and caused others to regard him as a gentleman. He sat at the side of the boat and smiled to himself as he remembered how the boatman called him 'Sir' when he boarded the boat in Edenton. Clothes made a big difference---especially his fine clothes. His mother had spent many days sewing the material for the clothes he wore. All the material had been selected by Allen Jones at Hamilton's Store in Halifax and brought to his mother. Sarah Pickett had followed each instruction sent to her and had taken special pleasure in making the different articles for her only son. It wasn't easy sewing for Sam. There weren't many men in Halifax who demanded so much cloth to outfit. He was almost six-foot tall and weighed one hundred and seventy-five pounds. Born and raised on the Nicholas Long Plantation, his work there had demanded much strength and his young body had grown to meet those demands.

Sam leaned over the side of the boat and looked down at the water that cast his reflection. He was handsome with a ruddy outdoor complexion and had thick, dark brown hair that was neatly tied at the back with a riband. His eyes were large and so brown that they seemed black when there was not much light. So clear and bright were they---so alert---so much his most dominant feature. The image in the water smiled back at him and seemed as pleased as he.

Sam's mind quickly turned to his affairs. He thought of the time he had stayed at Horniblow's Tavern and was glad his benefactor, Mr. Allen Jones, would pay his expenses. He hadn't especially wanted to stay at Horniblow's since it was the most expensive tavern in Edenton, but Mr. Jones insisted that he stay nowhere else.

Reaching inside his coat, Sam withdrew the letter of credit, knowing he would need it when the boat docked. He had been given this letter by Mr. Jones to show in order to establish his credit, and it had brought a great change in his life, suddenly promoting him to the society of 'gentleman'.

Sam had been continuously astounded at the immediate response from all who beheld the seal of Mr. Allen Jones.

Along with the letter of credit, he had been given a list of instructions including the names of people he was to contact in Edenton and how he was to pursue his apprenticeship as a surveyor. There was a great need for a good surveyor in and around Halifax, and Sam was glad that Allen Jones had recognized that need and had selected him to be that surveyor.

He had contacted Mr. Charles McCrackin and had worked successfully under his supervision. His studies, however, were suddenly interrupted when he received a letter from Mr. Allen Jones. The letter did not go into details about his studies or about what was happening in Halifax. The most important thing about the letter was that his studies were to be put aside temporarily, for there was great unrest among the people in Halifax. Allen Jones had given Colonel Nicholas Long orders to form a militia. There was urgency in the wording of the letter that had caused Sam to pack immediately.

Sam had known how well the people of Halifax regarded Mr. Allen and Mr. Willie (Wylie) Jones, but the visit to Edenton had added new meaning to the character of the two gentlemen. Most of the gentlemen of Edenton thought that Willie was not as steady as Allen. From all he had learned in Edenton, Mr. Willie had one great weakness that seemed to be known to all who knew him---that weakness was gambling. Cock--fights and horse races and cards were his favorite pleasures. Winning at either seemed to give Willie that extra excitement he demanded of life.

Sam had heard a rumor at Horniblow's that Willie had asked for the hand of Miss Sukey Cornell. Her father, knowing of Willie's love of gambling, would not consent to give his daughter unless Mr. Jones agreed to give up gambling. Of course, Willie would not let anything like marriage change his way of life, so Sukey was left sulking. Sam thought this was a wise decision since Mr. Willie's name had recently been linked to the name of Miss Mary Montfort. Sam did not know what Mr. Willie Jones would have to give up if he married Miss Montfort, or if he would have to give up anything, other than his freedom. From what he knew of Willie Jones, freedom was something that this man deemed precious---especially his freedom.

Sam was glad to be associated with the more stable of the two brothers.

His eyes slowly closed as the rhythm of the oars struck the water at monotonous intervals as they were approaching Halifax. Sam was aroused to quick attention as the boatman yelled----

"Willie Jones' dock just ahead."

The oars were drawn into the boat and the four oarsmen heaved a sigh of relief as the boat slid up to the dock.

Reaching for his baggage and following the boatman, who stepped onto the dock, Sam handed the man his letter of credit and was given a bill for his passage from Edenton.

"Thangs look mighty dead here," said the boatman, as he looked toward the bank.

"I was getting ready to say the same thing. I wonder where the men are who tend the dock." Sam's dark brown eyes were alert as he noticed the strangeness of these familiar surroundings.

"I'll find out what's happening," he said, walking to the steps that led to the bank.

"Good luck to you, Sir. I hope you find all is well." The boatman waved as he yelled.

As Sam walked up the steps to the bank, he could hear the motley boatman shouting curses to his men and he thought how fortunate he was to be regarded as a gentleman.

He walked along the road that ran parallel to the river. The wind from the Roanoke nipped at his ears and was blowing harder now.

Turning off the river road onto King Street, he walked up the well-worn road which was the main avenue of Halifax. Just ahead and to his left were several warehouses that held goods and produce until it was time for shipment down the Roanoke to the coast.

There were barrel staves neatly stacked and tied with hemp and several stacks of green lumber on the platforms. The pungent odor of naval stores caused Sam's nose to burn slightly.

The Roanoke River served as an important artery of trade with the coastal towns and since Edenton was so near the coast, most of the produce was shipped directly to that town. The river was gentle enough for sloops, schooners and flatboats to venture as far as Halifax. There was virtually no movement of vessels beyond Halifax. The rapids in the Roanoke were too numerous.

Sam looked back over his left shoulder at the warehouses. There was no one tending them. Strange, he thought, there was usually limited activity this time of year. Yet, there was always someone tending the docks and warehouses, even during the slack season.

His footsteps quickened, as he became more aware that something was wrong. He had walked almost half-a-mile and had not encountered a single person along the road to the river. To his right, the tannery, and the butcher shop had closed shutters, and it was only mid-afternoon.

Hamilton's General Store was just ahead. As he approached the store, he noticed there were no horses---no wagons out front. He bounded onto the porch and went quickly to the front door. It was locked. A paper hung from a nail next to the door. CLOSED: JOSEPH MONTFORT'S FUNERAL---OPEN TOMORROW.

Not believing what he read, Sam read it again. Joseph Montfort dead? The great Joseph Montfort-----dead? The man on whom all relied, in one way or another? Why, Joseph Montfort was in so many ways Halifax, itself. He was as an institution among the people of Halifax. Clerk of the Court, Colonel of the town militia, first Masonic leader of the Royal White Hart Lodge. THE FIRST GRAND MASTER OF THE MASONIC LODGE OF AMERICA. The undisputed leader of the people. Sam briefly recalled how Montfort had stood against Governor Tryon when the Governor had drafted funds from his account to arm the militia against the Regulators in Orange County. The same Joseph Montfort-------dead?

Sam looked down King Street and saw a great gathering of people at the cemetery. As he walked toward the crowd, he felt an emptiness----a loss-----as if something had been taken from him personally. He slowly approached the crowd and sensed that there were many who shared his feelings.

He could not get close enough to see what was happening, so he stood on a bench at the edge of the town common and removed his cocked hat. Standing there, he could see over the crowd. There was Reverend Ford and several members of the Royal White Hart Lodge waiting near the coffin. Sam strained to see better. Then-- he heard the deep voice of Reverend Ford, as his words boomed out loud and clear. Even the wind from the Roanoke seemed to be calmed by the sound of his deep voice.

"Friends of this beloved man---'ahem' ---we are here today giving witness to the passing of a man who has dedicated his life to the betterment of his fellow man. 'Ahem' a man whose life has touched every living soul here. He was a father to many of you. There has been no man among us who has given more. I have here a note from a man who considered him to be more than a father."

Reverend Ford reached inside his black coat and withdrew a folded paper.

"I was asked not to reveal the man who penned these words. Let us all bow our heads and hear this elegy.

OLD FRIEND, CAN IT BE THAT THE ANGEL OF DEATH
HATH STROKED THOU SWEET BROW WITH ITS PITILESS BREATH?
AND SLAIN WITH THAT CRUEL AND UNMERCIFUL TOUCH

THAT HEART WHOSE AFFECTION WE CHERISHED SO MUCH
OLD FRIEND, I AM LONELY AND LONG FOR THAT REST
THY SOUL HAS'T NOW FOUND IN THE ISLES OF THE BLES'T
TO THE DAY WHEN THE TIES, SO RUDELY THUS RIVEN
SHALL BE JOINED BY THE HANDS OF THE FATHER IN HEAVEN

May God be his judge and may Joseph Montfort's spirit continue to be with us----as strong in death----as it was in life, Amen."

Sam stepped down from the bench and put his cocked hat on his head. He watched the crowd disperse. There had never been a funeral such as this in Halifax. He watched the people walk past him. The men had blank expressions and the children looked to their crying mothers and could not understand.

Now, thinking of these things, Sam breathed deeply with a sense of sadness. Joseph Montfort was needed in these troubled times. He closed his eyes----, floating on the edge of many confused thoughts that crowded his mind. Montfort---Congress---Hamilton----Josie-----Josie-----

MASONIC LODGE

The Royal White Hart Lodge, No. 2, was established in Halifax on April 18, 1756.

CHAPTER FOUR

Much to Sam's amazement, time did not stop with the death of Joseph Montfort. Ironically, the town seemed more alive than he had ever remembered it to be. There was talk of independence everywhere, and he felt a part of all that was happening.

He had worked hard during the morning so he would have the afternoon free to visit Allen Jones' horse 'Midnight'. He had finished in the barn and was getting a drink of water from the well in the front yard when he heard his mother call.

"Sam, come on and get something to eat."

Sam looked over the bucket.

"I'll be right in."

He put the bucket on the edge of the well and started toward the cabin.

As he was walking, he momentarily wondered what skills his father had known about carpentry. His father, who had hewn the logs, notched them into locking joints at the corners; then mortared the open spaces between the logs when he built the cabin. Along the left side of the house was a large chimney of mortar mixed with rocks that varied from the size of Sam's fist to the size of his head. At the front, a porch running the length of the house extended about twenty feet from the front wall. Two large rough-looking chairs with knotted legs and woven hemp bottoms guarded the front door.

Life on the Long Plantation had been hard but good over the years. Although the home place was only a small three-room log structure, his mother had made it comfortable. From her, Sam had learned to appreciate many things that other boys his age would have taken for granted. They had worked hard on the farm but the work had never been enough to satisfy the needs of the family. The untimely death of his father when Sam was only seven causes him to have to mature early in life. During his early teens, Sam had found work at Dudley's Tavern and Hamilton's General Store. This, along with the sewing done by his mother, was enough to satisfy the needs of the family. Since Sarah Pickett was regarded as the most accomplished seamstress in Halifax, much work was required of her. The LADIES of Halifax, who wanted expert work done, brought their cloth to the Pickett house.

Sam walked through the front doorway to the kitchen and sat down at the place that was usually occupied by his Uncle John. He had grown accustomed to this routine whenever his uncle was away. Sitting in his uncle's place somehow made him feel more important, for it temporarily made him head of the family.

Looking up from his plate, Sam notice his mother had walked to the front door. She was looking down the road as if she were expecting someone.

The cornbread, eggs and side meat quickly disappeared from his wooden plate.

Sam closely observed his mother as if was the first time he had seen her since his return. The homespun dress had faded from the original dark blue. Her hair was in bun and tied behind her head. Standing in the doorway, her stout frame looked somewhat muscular. As he watched her, Sam thought that perhaps others would regard her as being quite plain---but -----not he. Beauty was not just something that one beheld at a glance. It was something that had a deeper meaning----something that involved character---and Sarah Pickett had more character than anyone he had ever known.

"Don't worry about Uncle John, Mama. He'll come home when he's ready."

"It seems that he stays away more and more, here, lately. I can't help but worry."

Sam frowned slightly, thinking about his uncle. John Thompson had for years been known to drink too much and many time Sam had to take over the work on the farm that was usually his uncle's responsibility. During his younger days, Sam had to ride to Dudley's Tavern each Saturday night to bring his uncle home. He respected his uncle, however, and always did whatever John Thompson asked him to do---that is---when John Thompson was sober. When John was drinking, Sam stayed away from him as much as possible.

Sarah Pickett, being the dutiful sister, accepted John's drinking and always seemed willing to believe him when he promised that he'd never touch the bottle again.

"Where's Aunt Jenny?" Sam asked, trying to make his mother think of something else.

"She's out back. I think one of her cats has found kittens."

"Agin!"

"Agin."

Aunt Jenny was his father's oldest sister and had been living at the Pickett house when Sam was born, so she had always been a member of the family as far as he was concerned.

During the last few years, his aunt had become quite childish and at times would do strange things that Sam did not understand. When he asked his mother about Aunt Jenny's behavior, Sarah Pickett told him that Aunt Jenny was getting to a time in her life when these things could be expected. Aunt Jenny had one great love and that was a special affection for her cats. She had cats in the house, cats in the barn, cats in the yard, and whenever a stray cat come to the house, she would always give it a home.

Sam got up from the table and walked to the kitchen window. He took a towel from the rack and began wiping his hands and mouth.

"I'm going by 'The Grove' to check on Mr. Allen Jones' horse like I promised him. When I get to town, I'll ask about Uncle John. Don't worry about him, Mama."

"I don't suppose it does any good to worry." Sarah Pickett began clearing the table. "I just can't understand why some of the men folks have to drink so much every time someone passes away."

"I heard about a funeral at Tarboro that lasted for a month. Some of the men had to make two trips to Enfield to get enough liquor to see them through their time of mourning," said Sam.

"I think that's the crowd that John got up with."

"That's the only reason some of 'em go to funerals---some of"em don't even know who's being laid to rest," said Sam, as he picked up his cocked hat from the side table.

"Oh, Sam. I almost forgot. I've got some pillowcases I've done up for Mrs. Long. She wants them taken to 'Grove House'. They're a wedding gift for Miss Montfort. She's having all her gifts delivered there."

"When is the big wedding suppose to take place?"

"Sometimes in June, I understand, or whenever she can catch Willie at home."

Sarah Pickett handed the bag of pillowcases to Sam.

"You be careful and don't soil them."

"I'll be careful. You just stop your worrying," said Sam, as he walked out the door.

A short while later, Sam was on the road to Halifax. As he rode 'Jericho', he thought of the many times he had traveled the road. He remembered the times he had been to the Roanoke and watched the barges; sloops and the schooners come to dock at Halifax. His favorite time for remembering was his early teens, when he and George Hamilton would fish from the banks of the Roanoke and then parade through the town with their catch---as if they were advertising that they had fish for sell. They were good days. He and George had been close during those years. A quick smile came to Sam's face and he laughed out loud as he remembered the time when the boys of Halifax had played a trick on George.

George had been fishing on the Roanoke and several boys had approached him with the idea of playing an Indian game. George was delighted because the boys had never before asked him to join them. A new Indian game was something that George couldn't resist. As the game progressed, the boys tied George to a pine tree--took his clothes and left him. When George did not come home for supper, Mrs. Hamilton sent for Sam. So, he went to the Roanoke to bring George home. When he found George tied to the tree---stark naked----he laughed the whole time he was untying him. Sam remembered saying, "that must have been some Indian Game, George. You look like old Chief Blunt has had a hold of you."

He had taken George home that day through the woods to the back of the Hamilton home. Sam laughed again in his remembering. It was one of the funniest experiences he had ever had. George standing before his prim mother with only Sam's shirt to cover his naked body. However, Mrs. Hamilton was not amused. She vowed that the ruffians would be punished. But she never did find out who the boys were---George never told---Yes, Sir, those were days worth remembering. Sam felt a little sad now that they had grown older and had drifted from that close relationship.

Coming to the lofty, wooden bridge that spanned Quanky Creek, Sam looked down at the creek that flowed about fifty feet below the bridge. Many times he and George had explored along the creek for miles in both directions. About three hundred yards west toward Willie Jones Plantation was a cave that he and George had dug out of the bank of Quanky Creek during their 'Pirate' days.

Crossing the creek, Sam turned left and took the road that led to 'Grove House'. This road was always in good condition. Mr. Willie Jones would not have a bad road leading to this home. A rider could hurry along and not have to worry about his horse's footing. Trees thickly grew on both sides of the road and the limbs permitted shafts of sunlight and tiny specks of light to dart among the deep shadows.

As he entered the shaded tunnel, his mind recalled the most glorious day of his life. He walked 'Jericho' so he could enjoy his remembering in the cool shade.

It was the day he had sat on Allen Jones' horse 'Midnight' in the mile 'Heat' against Nathaniel Duckenfield's 'Golden Boy'. Duckenfield's supporters from Edenton and Allen Jones' supporters from Northampton and Halifax County had bet heavily on their favorite horses. Sam had worked with 'Midnight' at Willie Jones' racetrack in Halifax and knew the horse's temperament. There seemed to be an understanding between 'Midnight' and him. Sam could tell when 'Midnight' wanted to move and he also knew when to keep his horse in check. 'Good communications' is what Allen Jones called it.

That was some day----that day. It had been only a year since the race and Sam could remember each detail as it happened. He had relived the events many times and each time he remembered them more vividly.

The park at 'The Grove' was teeming with spectators who had brought picnic lunches. Some special friends of Willie Jones had been staying at 'Grove House' for several days prior to the 'Big' race. Notices were posted in all the surrounding towns announcing the event.

A mile 'heat' was an unusual distance for any horse to run. Four times around the quarter-mile track was demanding too much of any horse, so Sam had heard from the quarter-horse owners. The quarter-mile races were held in the morning and many good horses were shown.

The main event, the mile 'heat', was scheduled for the afternoon. That race was the reason for the crowd. Small bets were placed on favorite horses and fellowship prevailed among the men from both towns. However, just before the main event, the Halifax crowd had assembled on the side of the racetrack next to 'Grove House'. On the opposite side of the track, the Edenton crowd anxiously waited for their horse to appear.

There seemed to be something magnetic about the way the crowd polarized for the coming event. Fellowship was quickly forgotten as shouts and jeers were heard coming from both sides of the track.

Sam was with Uncle Louie at 'Midnight's' stall, but 'Midnight's' rider was nowhere in sight.

"Where's Johnny Turnbill?" Sam asked. "The race will be starting before he's given 'Midnight' his warm up." He looked among the faces for Turnbill.

"Don't know but Marster Allen will reckon wid him. Dat's fuh sho." Answered Uncle Louie.

Sam looked again and could see Allen Jones walking briskly toward them. 'Midnight's' owner was dressed in different shades of green that day. His pants were light green and complimented his darker green coat. No one could mistake the striking figure of Mr. Allen Jones. Many avid supporters, including his brother, Willie, followed him. People stepped aside and made way for them. Sam saw a troubled look in Allen Jones' eyes and knew immediately that something was wrong.

"We need a rider," began Allen Jones, "Johnny Turnbill was at Dudley's last night and part of this morning prematurely celebrating his victory."

"Call the race off, Allen," suggested one of his supporters, who had perhaps bet to heavily on the race.

"We cannot let our supporters down," came the quick reply from Allen Jones.

"Is he able to ride at all, Sir," asked Sam.

"He's in a drunken stupor. He'll never race again. I'll see to that. I've warned him about his drinking. I shouldn't have placed so much trust in him."

"What can we do now, Sir?" Asked Sam.

There was no answer.

Sam looked at the downcast faces of the men around him. They were dejected and had no suggestions. Sam looked to Uncle Louie, but the old man looked away. Turning again to Allen Jones, Sam saw a gleam of hope that suddenly lightened Jones' eyes.

"There is but one hope. Sam, you must ride 'Midnight'. It is the only solution. There has always been an understanding between you that horse. Maybe your feelings for 'Midnight' will be enough to compensate for the skill of the Duckenfield rider. You're heavier than Turnbill but 'Midnight' can carry you. You've ridden him enough and he's a strong horse." Allen Jones made the statement as if all were settled.

"That boy's thirty pounds heavier than the other rider. He'll never make the last lap," said one of the men.

"I say-- I know my horse --and I say we race," said Allen Jones, emphatically.

"Well, I'm not betting my money on that kind of odds," said the man, as he walked away.

Allen Jones turned to his supporters.

"You all do what you think is best with your money. I'll take all the bets you men want to change, if you have doubts about the race."

Willie Jones had not voiced his opinion but now he stepped forward.

"What bets my brother does not see fit to cover I'll gladly take."

He turned to the men who were no longer avid supporters.

"You men spread the word through the crowd and if anyone wants to change his bet ---send them to me."

The men scurried through the crowd to tell the people of the change that had been made in the race. Those who were not willing to risk their money on the race suddenly surrounded Willie Jones.

"Cover any bets and I'll settle with you after the race, Willie," yelled Allen Jones.

Sam knew now without any doubt that the race was on. That moment---oh, that moment---the world suddenly began to whirl. As if by an act of God, he was thrust from a mere stable boy to that glorious position on

First For Freedom

'Midnight's' back. A lump came to his throat. He swallowed---the lump remained.

"Mr. Jones, I love that horse," the words seemed inadequate, but Sam could muster nothing more at that moment.

"Well, let us hope that love conquers all," philosophized Allen Jones, as he turned to Uncle Louie. "Get 'Midnight' saddled and make ready for the race."

"I'll do my best and pray that it will be good enough," said Sam, not really knowing what to say.

"Uncle Louie, get the boots and that light blue jacket for Sam," ordered Allen Jones.

Sam sat on a stool, pulled the boots on quickly and stood for Uncle Louie who was holding the blue jacket.

Uncle Louie cupped his hands and Sam was catapulted onto 'Midnight's' back.

Allen Jones inspected the bridle and the saddle.

"Let him have his way when you come to the last lap. Don't hold him back---just let him have his way. He knows the way home."

The world had not stopped whirling, whirling. Sam let 'Midnight' trot to the track. There was a great roar from the Halifax side of the track, and Sam slowed 'Midnight' to a walk. 'Midnight' pranced haughtily as they waited for the Duckenfield rider. The strong body between his legs gave Sam confidence that his horse was ready. He pulled reins and held his horse. He wanted 'Midnight' to feel peaked by the time the flag was dropped. Sam felt there was an anxiousness beneath him that he had not experienced before with 'Midnight'. Perhaps the race had excited his horse too much. He spoke softly, and it seemed to calm 'Midnight'.

'Golden Boy' was brought to the track and a swell of cheers came from the Edenton crowd. The great chestnut had a professional rider. The cheers were deafening, as the yellow jacket rider trotted 'Golden Boy' before the Edenton supporters.

Two riders on lead horses came to the track and led the two racehorses to the starting post. Sam could feel a nervousness in himself as well as the unsteadiness of 'Midnight'.

Before Sam could get 'Midnight' settled for the start, the flag was down and 'Golden Boy' was off. Sam tightened his legs and was off. It was a poor start for 'Midnight'. The chestnut was ahead. To his right, Sam could see blurred faces, flying hats and waving arms. They were galloping through the backstretch. Sam could feel the flowing power beneath him as he stared at the hindquarters of 'Golden Boy'. A hail of gravel pelted Sam's face. He was temporarily blinded. He had not expected this. They were to the far end of the track and Sam's blurred vision cleared enough for him to see the black faces of the slaves at the turn of the oval track. He sat steady with a firm grip on the reins.

"Three more laps," came a yell from the rail near the starting post.

Sam forgot his nervousness and leaned forward.

"Not yet, not quite yet. I'll tell you when----."

He was moving, riding----hurling through space. 'Midnight' pulled at the bit. Sam restrained him. He knew his horse.

"Go easy, boy. Go easy. We've got a long way to go."

"Two laps to go," came a yell from the side, as they rounded the track for the last half of the race.

The chestnut began to put more space between them at the beginning of the third lap. Sam thought that 'Golden Boy' was at top speed. He hoped 'Golden Boy' was at top speed. The gap between the two horses lengthened and Sam was a good four lengths behind.

The faces of the people were blurred as Sam looked intently at the yellow-jacket rider ahead.

"One lap to go." He had passed the starting post for the third time. They were beginning the final lap.

Sam let the reins loose and yell to his horse.

"Now, 'MIDNIGHT' now----NOW."

He felt a surge beneath him and the space between the two horses began to diminish. Sam leaned forward and let 'Midnight' have his way.

"Homestretch," someone yelled as the horses rounded the turn.

The chestnut ahead was gathering speed as the yellow-jacket rider began whipping his horse. 'Midnight' was gathering more speed. Sam was riding---riding----then---closing -----closing. Then, the two horses were side by side. 'Midnight' continued to gather speed. Sam had never ridden so fast. The two horses were straining for the lead. The two riders were straining----straining. The professional and the amateur were side by side and straining. Sam suddenly felt his horse ease forward. There was a quick look of surprise on the face of the professional as 'Midnight' moved ahead. The great 'Golden Boy' was a good length behind as the horses finished the one-mile 'heat'.

When he rode 'Midnight' to the Halifax side, George and Josie came from the crowd and seemed even happier than he as they ushered him to the Halifax supporters. The spinning world seemed to gain momentum as he was boosted on the shoulders of two men and held above the cheering crowd.

A blast of sunlight quickly made Sam realize that he had passed through the cool shaded tunnel and that day of glory a year ago. Reality displaced his recollections of the past. Yet, in his reflections, he realized that it was on that day in his past that Allen Jones first came to regard him as more than a stable boy. It was on that day that he was given his first horse, 'Jericho'. Allen Jones had given him a choice of any horse he had stabled at the 'Grove' other than 'Midnight' or his other breeding stock.

It was not until later that Sam realized what an impact that wonderful day would have on his life. In so many ways, it was the time in his life that changed him from a boy to a man. People treated him differently after that race and he had friends among the people who were previously unknown to him. Allen Jones became his benefactor and even acted as a father toward him in many ways.

Sam could see the stately 'Grove House' in the distance. Giant oaks grew along the road that led to the house and the lawn was beginning to show hints of spring growth. As he approached the yard, he looked toward the front door where six majestic oaks and two sycamores grew in balanced harmony. The front yard had well-groomed shrubbery and on each side of the porch were limbs of crepe myrtle interlaced with "Rose of Sharon" and Mock Orange. Six large white columns supported the gabled roof. Two giant, green rockers were on the front porch one on each side of the large front door

Sam had heard his uncle speak of the work that had been done by Willie Jones and how the old 'Castle' in Northampton County had been dismantled. The timbers had been brought from the old home place and were used in the construction of 'Grove House'. He had also been told that the brick and all the materials used for finishing the inside had been shipped from England. The steps were red sandstone and had been brought from Scotland. This was, no doubt, the finest home in this part of the colony.

He rode past the large white house toward the stables and came to the part of the plantation that interested him more than anything else. The racetrack was an oval track on the eastern side of 'Grove House'. There was a large bay window on this side of the house facing the track from which spectators could view the races.

Sam pulled 'Jericho' up to the hitching post at the back of the house and walked to the stables.

As he crossed the road, he could see Uncle Louie leaning against the railed fence just beyond the carriage house. The white-haired old slave's strength was not what it once had been and Willie Jones had taken him from the fields so he could tend the stables. He was a faithful servant and Sam knew how Willie Jones depended on Uncle Louie for information about the overseers and the other slaves. It was common knowledge that

Uncle Louie could determine the kind of punishment a slave would receive at the hands of the overseer. If a slave was to be punished, Uncle Louie was informed and often consulted. There had been slaves sold because of some infraction of Mr. Willie Jones' rules and there was no man on the plantation who knew the rules better than Uncle Louie. Therefore, Uncle Louie held a respected position among the other slaves at 'The Grove'.

Grove House

Uncle Louie did not see or hear Sam come up behind him.
"Hey, Uncle Louie," yelled Sam.
Uncle Louie jumped to the side, then leaned with his back against the fence rail.
"Marster Sam. ----How come you come up behind me lack dat. Ah thought you was up to Eden Town learnin' to lay de line."

"Oh, I was at Edenton but I'll be home for a while now. How's our horse, 'Midnight'?" Sam pointed to the black stallion in the pasture.

"He's rearin' to run. Ah never did see sech a hoss. All he wants to do is run de race."

"Have you had him on the track lately?"

"Naw, Suh. Ain't been to de track since you last took him. Dat was before you left for Eden Town."

"It's been too long. He needs more time on the track."

"Marster Allen don't let Turnbill work him no more."

"When is Mr. Willie coming back to 'Grove House'?" Sam looked toward the large white house as he asked.

"Ah don't know, he took anuff blankets and trinkets and sech wid him to satisfy all dem Indians in Georgia."

"Those Indians and settlers can't seem to get along."

"Marster Willie can deal wid dem. If any man can handle dem, hit's Marster Willie."

They watched 'Midnight' run the length of the pasture. As the horse reached the far end, his stride was broken and he wheeled and ran back toward them.

"Dat hoss is got to be raced. Dis pasture don't give him no room to git up no speed at tall. Ah thank he's gittin' tard of stayin' away from the track."

"When Mr. Willie returns, I'm sure we'll have another race. He likes the horses as much as Mr. Allen Jones and he knows how to get the people out to the track. I'll come back in a few days and we'll take him out to the track for some real runnin'. He needs to stretch his legs."

"Dat hoss sho needs dat. He done started thankin' dat he lost de last race he runned."

"Maybe we'll get that Edenton crowd back down here this summer for another race."

"Dey ain't comin' back heah. Naw, Suh, dey ain't comin' back heah," laughed Uncle Louie.

"We gave them a good race last summer, didn't we, Uncle Louie?"

"De utter side of the track was as quiet as Marster Montfort's funeral de utter day. Dat crowd crept away lack they waren't heah at tall. Marster Allen sho took a lackin' to you after that race."

"You know, I was thinking about that day on the way over here. That was some day. That day changed my whole life."

"Hit changed de lives of de people from Eden Town, too. Some of dem come heah rich and some of dem left heah po."

Both laughed at what Uncle Louie said, as they watched the horses in the pasture. Sam promised Uncle Louie again that they would have another race soon.

Sam waved goodbye to Uncle Louie as he was untying 'Jericho' from the hitching post.

As he mounted his horse, he saw Aunt Grace come from the kitchen. With plump, tanned fingers, she handed Sam some food wrapped in a blue linen cloth. She was a middle aged, light-skinned servant who had grown too plump from her own cooking.

"Aunt Grace, Mama told me to give you this present. Will you see that Mrs. Mary Jones gets it? Sometimes I feel like you know me as well as my Mama," continued Sam, as he took the blue linen cloth.

"It don't take much knowing to know when you're hungry. You always hungry." Aunt Grace stepped back from the horse.

Aunt Grace came to 'Grove House' when Willie Jones moved from Northampton and was perhaps the most valuable household servant on the plantation. Her value lay in her ability to manage the other servants and her knowledge of her master. She knew how to please Willie Jones and had long-standing confidence that came from many years of faithful service. It was told that Willie Jones gave her a free hand to run the house and merely made suggestion on special occasions when he had some friends visiting 'Grove House'.

"I think you just give me food so I'll tell everybody you're the best cook in Halifax."

Sam complimented Aunt Grace whenever he had the opportunity and spoke highly of her to other people, and it always paid off when he needed food. It was something understood between them.

After thanking Aunt Grace, Sam turned his horse toward Halifax. He wanted to stop by the Hamiltons before he rode to Dudley's Tavern. He walked his horse along the lane and immediately opened the linen cloth. As he munched on the ham and biscuit, he was glad that Allen Jones was not his only supporter. Having friends in high places was a comforting thought-----but the ham and biscuits were satisfying his growling stomach. Having friends in low places was more than comforting----it was downright filling.

CHAPTER FIVE

Sam, being very concerned and dedicated to the cause of the Patriots, wondered how the Hamiltons would really regard the strong feeling for independence that was so evident throughout the colony. Which side would they choose, if they were made to take a stand? This question had preoccupied all his thinking since he left 'Grove House'.

It was late afternoon when he pulled 'Jericho' to a halt in front of the large two-story Hamilton home. Walking from the hitching post, he could see George sitting on the front steps and John Hamilton seated in a large, dark, green rocker on the porch.

It was a regular routine of John Hamilton to rest for about thirty minutes after the evening meal. He would sit and take his pouch of tobacco from his coat and fill the long stemmed clay pipe. His servant, Josh, would bring a coal from the fireplace. He would settle back and enjoy the rich smoke.

Shadows from the large oak trees fell across the walkway that led to the front of the majestic house.

Sam nodded as he sat down on the porch and leaned against the post at the top of the steps.

"Y'all about got settled?"

"We've still got things to do. We're just relaxing, you know, trying to put the work off as long as possible," said George.

"Is there anything I can do to help?"

"We don't have that much left to do, Sam." John puffed at his pipe as he spoke, then leaned forward.

"I hear Willie Jones has gone to Georgia to try to deal with the Indians."

"I just came from 'Grove House' and Uncle Louie said he didn't know when Mr. Jones will be coming home. He'd better be home soon 'cause Miss Mary Montfort is planning a wedding when he returns."

"Well, in that case, he might just take his time." John Hamilton smiled as he spoke of his friend.

"If I were Willie Jones, I would take the fastest horse I could get and be waiting at the church," said George, winking at Sam.

"I'd be there before the preacher," agreed Sam.

"What do you two know about marriage? If Mary Montfort ever cast an eye in either of your directions, you'd run off and hide somewhere."

"Maybe George would, but I don't know about me. If I was to run off---I think I'd take her with me."

The amused look on John Hamilton's face changed as he looked intently at Sam.

"I've heard a lot of talk at the store today and I've thought at some length about what you had to say yesterday. Do you really think a complete break with the mother country is forthcoming?"

"Well, Sir, it seems to me that most everything has been tried and nothing seems to be acceptable to the King. I heard talk that the Parliament has declared the colonies in rebellion and the King has hired Hessians to fight against us. We don't have any other way to go, since the King has declared us outside his protection."

"But it seems that there is still hope, if the Colonials would only obey the laws that are set to regulate the colonies," said George.

"There's no hope left, George. We aren't even thought of as citizens with our own voice. We can't stomach the idea of royal rule without some say in the way we're treated." Sam's voice rose in excitement, as he emphasized the seriousness of the issue.

John Hamilton became irritated.

"Sam, if you knew anything about government, you'd realize that, if we didn't have any laws, we would have nothing but anarchy. We all owe allegiance to our King or there would be no safe place for any of us. I thought you would have learned something from your reading."

"I don't think the answers are in the books. We'll have to look for the answers in the actions that men take in the months to come."

"Sam, perhaps you need to read more," said George, siding with his father.

"I know it's not my place to try to convince either of you of anything, but what about the people in Mecklenburg? They refused to obey any laws of the King. They made it clear that they would not be subjects of any Royal rule. So, it seems to me, it just depends on who you want to be loyal to---either the King or the Provincial Congress."

"Oh, we know all about the Mecklenburg people. Nobody paid any attention to what they did," said John Hamilton, making little of what Sam said.

"They had no right to act so independently. Those people didn't have any authority to act the way they did. Even the Provincial Congress admitted to that, Sam," added George.

"I admit that's true and the Provincial Congress didn't agree with what they did, but it was the way the people felt. A whole lot of people now feel the way those people felt a year ago. Things have really changed this past year. Maybe there was nothing official about the Mecklenburg Resolves, but when the Fourth Provincial Congress acts and something is done, then that will be official----that's for sure."

"I heard at the store that only about one-third of the elected delegates came to the meeting today," said John Hamilton.

"Some of them have a long way to travel," said Sam. "They'll be here. Just give'em a little more time."

"Since the Battle of Moore's Creek Bridge is the only open conflict so far, I don't see why the people can't resolve their differences," stated Hamilton, in a matter of fact tone of voice.

"It's the only big fight we've had, but the feeling for independence is the same throughout the colony. That's what I'm trying to get y'all to understand. The people in Rowan, Tryon, and all over now have the same desire as the people in Mecklenburg had a year ago."

"I still have faith in the good judgment of the people hereabouts. I feel sure they will consider the great odds against them and determine that they will remain loyal to the King," continued John Hamilton.

"I don't mean to dispute you, Sir, but I doubt that. I really do doubt that."

John Hamilton stood.

"I see you've have come to doubt YOUR LOYALTIES to the King. Sam, you'd better start thinking about how much you owe England."

"Our debt has been paid, Mr. Hamilton. We want only what is rightfully ours---mainly---our freedom."

John Hamilton leaned over the porch railing and violently pounded his pipe against his palm, then threw the ashes in a large clay pot to the left of the steps.

"Sam, you know that no people have freedom to do what they want to do. People must always obey the law."

"Even when the laws are unjust and unbearable?"

"That's a matter of opinion. You've been to Edenton studying to be a surveyor and now you've come back to Halifax telling me what the law is and how I'm suppose to regard it. You must be confused about what you've been studying. What right do you have to speak of the King this way? You'd better mind your tongue."

"My words are no different from what you'll hear from the rest of the people. The planters are the leaders. You'll lose more friends and customers than I will."

"Sam, I'll not listen to idle talk about the King."

"You have to cover your ears because that's all the people are talking about. I'm no different from any of the rest."

"Well you're different from us and until you find some respect for the King, I think you'd better find other company. These men who are speaking against the King are not my friends----they are traitors----that's what they are."

George moved from the steps and stood next to his father.

"Sam, I think it's time for you to leave, if you're so bound to argue with father."

"I was about to suggest that, George. It seems that our young friend has turned rebel since our visit to Charles Town."

Sam had seen the desire for freedom among the men in Halifax. Now he saw a devout loyalty to King George. It was the first time he realized that John Hamilton was so devoted to the King. Hamilton believed in his King as strongly as Allen Jones believed in the Provincial Congress.

It was good that Josie came out to the porch at that moment. Sam started to speak but hesitated when he saw her. Josie had changed from her traveling clothes to a pale green, housedress and she looked more like the Josie that he remembered before she went to Charles Town. She held a tray with three glasses of water.

"I thought you all would like to have some cool water. It sounded as if you were having a hot discussion. I'm sorry we don't have any tea."

Josie passed the water to her father.

"Tea has put a bad taste in so many mouths lately, I think most all the people around here find the taste a little bitter," responded Sam.

John Hamilton took his glass and turned to George.

"George, we've still got to unpack the trunks that arrived on the stage this morning."

He opened the front door; then looked furtively at Sam.

"I'll not expect to see you here again unless you change your way of thinking."

Sam walked quickly toward his horse; Josie placed the tray on the porch and hurried after him.

"Your father is a hard man to convince, Josie." Sam turned and looked back at Josie who was now behind him.

"Father has always been devoted to the King. It's just his way. Slow down, Sam."

"I hope he realizes what's happening before it's too late. The Congress is headed for independence and your father is siding with the British."

"Well, father doesn't seem too worried about it."

"That's what bothers me. He and all of you need to be worried."

"Oh, Sam, what could possibly happen?"

First For Freedom

"Y'all don't know how the people around here feel about Tories. The congress has the power to order this house and everything your father owns to be taken----if they find out that your family is loyal to the King."

"But that's tyranny."

"I don't know about that. It all depends on how you feel about all that's happening. But whatever happens, I don't want you to go away again unless you let me know where you're going. Maybe things will be different after we settle our quarrel with England."

Josie smiled and didn't seem too concerned about the quarrel with England.

"I don't think you have to worry about that, Sam. Things have a way of working out. You'll see."

They were almost to the hitching post and Sam turned abruptly as his dark eyes looked directly into the blue eyes of Josie.

"Now you sound just like your father. I know you need to help your mother and I need to be getting to town. It's good to have you back in Halifax. You know-----I missed you more from yesterday--'til today---than I missed you the whole time you were in Charles Town."

"I never realized that returning home would be like this. I can truly say that the trip was worth it. I'll look forward to seeing you soon. Sam, don't let father discourage you from coming."

"You know I feel like what's happening to this colony is kinda like what is happening to me. I'm growing up to be old enough to know what I want. How your father feels about me doesn't mean so much so long as I know how you feel. This new feeling of freedom that's runnin' through the colony makes me feel as important as just about anyone else. It's not going to mean so much who you are as it's going to matter how you believe."

Josie took Sam's hand as they stood in front of the hitching post.

"No one could feel as happy as I do at this moment, Sam."

"I would argue with you about that, but you Hamiltons are so hard to convince, I feel I might be fighting a losing battle. So, I will say goodnight." He took Josie's other hand.

"Goodnight, Josie."

"Bye--Sam."

Sam was sure of it----there was no doubt in his mind---Josie had squeezed his hand when she had spoken, and there was a softness in her eyes. It left him with a good feeling----a feeling that he did not completely understand--a feeling that had gone directly to his heart. It had by-passed all reason. Thoughts and doubts that he could ever have her for his own had suddenly vanished.

With a lively leap to the saddle, Sam was astride 'Jericho' and turning his horse onto King Street.

As he walked his horse toward Halifax, he felt a new time of his life lay before him that he would one-day share with Josie. But as distance separated them, this new feeling that he had for her was suddenly clouded by the shadow of the impending conflict that he felt was inevitable.

CHAPTER SIX

The twilight shadows had changed to shadows now cast by the light of a full moon as Sam rode down King Street toward Martin's Livery. Riders always tied up a Martin's Livery if they had business on Market Street. All the people in Halifax understood that Market Street was a place for people and no hitching posts were available. Through traffic was allowed and the stage stopped in front of Dudley's Tavern, which served as the local depot.

It was only a short ride to Martin's Livery and Sam was soon tying 'Jericho' out front.

Knowing that his Uncle John always tied his team to the hitching post at the back of the stable, Sam walked in that direction. The cemetery was to his left and Sam noticed a freshly dug grave beside the road. He turned to his right and immediately saw his Uncle's team. He walked up to the horses; placed his hand on the rump of the black mare and could tell from the moist feeling that the horses had recently been tied to the post. His Uncle John was back in Halifax.

He glanced toward the open grave as he returned to the road that led to King Street--- then across King Street to Market Street. As he walked along Market, he decided he would enter the tavern from the back and get an apron in the kitchen---then surprise Dudley when he entered the tavern. This had been the routine he had followed when he had worked for Dudley. He was pleased with the idea and eager to see how Dudley would react when he walked in---all prepared for work.

Coming to the back of the tavern, Sam heard a rustling sound among the large, wooden, trash boxes. He stepped in a shadow and peered in the direction of the sound. From behind the pile of trash emerged a shadowy silhouette. He knew immediately that it was Looney Oney. Scratching and plundering in the trash was Oney's reason for being in Halifax. What was Dudley's trash was Oney's treasure. She was collecting what she could find and quickly stuffing her burlap bag. Looking to her left and right, she lightly stepped from the pile and hurried to the side road. Sam moved from the shadow and could see the sprite-like Oney looking back as she skipped along the path. There was no other person who moved like Looney Oney. She did not run nor did she walk, but had a gait in between these two paces that was uniquely hers. She seemed to lean to her right as if she were about to topple over, but her forward inertia kept her to her path.

Willie Jones had brought Oney to Halifax when he moved to 'Grove House'. She was known to conjure up spells and concoctions to cure rashes, snake bites, fevers and she could talk the devil out of people who were possessed by that evil spirit. Her powers were highly respected among his slaves and were well known to the people in Halifax.

Since Loony Oney's powers were causing some problems among the slaves; Willie Jones gave her an old hunting cabin in the swamps of Quanky Creek. The recesses of Quanky were considered and often referred to as 'Oney's domain.'

As he watched the darting spectre fade into darkness, Sam recalled the first time he and George Hamilton had explored Quanky Creek and had stumbled onto the little cabin where Oney lived. The footpath they following that day crooked and twisted through undergrowth so thick the trail often became obscure.

Both had watched from the bushes and remained quiet until Oney emerged from the one-room, log hut. The front door swung open and was held clear of the ground by two leather hinges. The small, bronze-skinned woman wore an old homespun black felt hat that looked as if rats had gnawed its edge. The hat covered her ears and was pushed back on her head to reveal two muddy looking eyes arched with heavy brows. A long pointed nose dominated her face. Long, silky, black hair hung about her rounded shoulders. She was unlike any other person Sam had ever known. The characteristics were so mixed in her that she did not belong to any given class or race of people. Sam could not see into her past any more than he could see beyond her cloudy eyes.

Oney moved quickly from the doorway to a small black pot hanging from a thin iron rod held in place by two forked limbs. Squatting beside the pot in front of the cabin, she blew hard and a tiny flame licked timidly at the twigs that Oney placed over the fire. The fire evidently had been burning earlier for it was quickly revived and soon the black pot was hissing.

"She's making a brew," said George, tugging at Sam's sleeve.

"She's only cooking something to eat, George."

"I've heard how she brews up all sorts of concoctions. Uncle Josh was once cured of high fever and swears by Oney's medicine. Father says it's some kind of voodoo."

"She's got to eat, too, George. Now be quiet. Let's see what she does."

"Look she's putting some roots in the pot."

"Just to add some flavor to what she's cooking."

Oney stood and swept her hands over the small black pot, flitted around the pot three times, then mumbled some words that were not clear but were loud enough for Sam to know that they were not words known to the English tongue.

"You hear that, Sam?"

"Yeah, I heard it----but --I don't know what I heard."

"What did she wave her hands over the pot for, Sam?"

"George, I think you're right. That ain't food she's cookin'."

"I'm going to the cave. I'll feel safe there!"

George ran over a mile back to their secret cave. When Sam arrived, George was sitting at the back of the cave sobbing. His knees were buckled up under his chin and he did not look up when Sam entered.

When George calmed down, he began talking and sobbing at the same time about the day Looney Oney had come to doctor their servant, Uncle Josh. It was something that weighed heavily on George's mind and he would not continue until Sam promised by a sacred oath that he would never reveal what was being passed between them.

George related that he had been playing with two flint rocks behind the Hamilton's smokehouse. He had made a small fire behind the smoke house and when a sudden gust of wind blew the fire into leaping flames, the smoke house had caught fire and burned to the ground. All the meat was reduced to a smoldering heap before the fire could be brought under control. When John Hamilton had come running from the house, he saw Looney Oney coming from the servant's quarters. George seemed almost hysterical as he told of the dreadful experience.

"Oney did it. I saw her behind the smokehouse. Oney did it. Oney did it. Oney did it, father." George remembered.

"Get my whip from the buggy," ordered John Hamilton.

George began to cry even more as he told of the beating Looney Oney received from the strong right hand of his father.

"If I ever find that cabin of yours. I'll burn it to the ground the way you burned my smokehouse," said Hamilton, as he stopped the whipping.

"Dat boy lies. Dat boy lies. He de one to pay fuh Oney's beatin'. He de one to pay fuh Oney's pain. Oney got ways to make people pay."

John Hamilton relentlessly whipped Oney until she was off his property. George had followed his father to the edge of the yard and had continued to shout, "Oney did it. Oney did it."

Returning home late that afternoon, Sam told Sarah Pickett about Oney's cabin in the swamp and all that he had seen there. Somehow he hoped that she would quickly dispel any fears he had perhaps imagined. Upon hearing what Sam told her, his mother had said "Leave Oney be."

Sarah Pickett seemed to know more than she told Sam. There was a strange look in Sarah Pickett's eyes when she spoke of Oney. Her reaction frightened Sam more than what he had experienced in the dank recesses of Quanky.

As he had grown older, Sam came to realize how strong the powers of witchcraft influenced the thinking of the people of Halifax. The people speculated about Oney and servants and slaves relied on her for relief from uncommon illnesses.

Sam felt a cold shiver creep over his body as he thought about Looney Oney. Sam knew that Christopher Dudley believed that Oney had 'the power'.

Now, as he moved to the back door of Dudley's Tavern, Sam was careful not to make any noise. When he entered the kitchen, he found an apron inside the linen closet. Then, he carefully made his way to the door that led to the taproom. He pulled the door ajar and could see Dudley standing behind the counter. Wanting his timing to be just right, he waited to seize the right moment to make his entrance. With the door slightly open, Sam could hear the conversation of a group of men at the table near his door. He had heard the loud voice of Jesse Turner many times but what he was saying this time was interesting and quickly caught Sam's attention. He pulled the door open a little wider and sat in a chair beside the door to listen.

From what he could hear, Jesse Turner was trying to develop a scheme to make John Thompson give up drinking. Sam thought of the many pranks that had been played on his uncle in the past and it seemed that Jesse Turner had always been the instigator. Since his uncle was regarded as a worthless, no-good drunk, his character lent itself to the rationale of the cronies.

Even Looney Oney had once been one of Jesse Turner's victims. Several years had passed since the incident, but Sam never forgot what happened that night at Dudley's. Jesse had caught Oney selecting scraps of food from the trash pile and had dragged her inside the tavern. He had held her before the cronies and would not release her from his grasp until he made her sit down at one of the tables.

"Dudley, I found her eating food from your garbage pile---so I brought her in here to get something to eat." He looked at the cronies. "You know what I told her? I told her to go inside and eat. You ain't no better than nobody else."

The cronies thought that was the best joke that Jesse had ever come up with and had talked about the incident many times. What Sam remembered most vividly was Dudley's reaction to Turner's prank. Dudley had walked from behind the counter and lifted Jesse Turner from the floor with his strong right hand grasping Turner's collar.

"One day, you'll get what's coming to you, Turner. If you ever pull another stunt like that, you'll have to find somewhere else to go."

Dudley was kind to Looney Oney that night and told her to take what she could find. He even gave her some scraps from the kitchen.

That Jesse Turner would play a trick on the devil--if the devil didn't know him so well.

Sam peeked through the opening of the door and listened. Turner stood up at his table. His beady eyes looked intently at his companions. Sam had often thought how Jesse's face resembled a possum's face. He was tall with long dangling arms that seemed loosely attached at his shoulders. Dudley had once remarked that Jesse Turner was the ugliest man in Halifax, and just as mean as he was ugly. Dudley's once stated that Jesse Turner could do what no other person in Halifax could do---and that was to overlook his long protruding nose. Turner's face was flushed from drinking and his small eyes were a little glassy.

"Did y'all know John Thompson has been drinking ever since Montfort's funeral, and he's been layin' out at Long's hunting cabin on Quanky Creek for over a week?"

"He's a disgrace to the rest of us----who ain't allowed to git away with that kind of drankin'," said one of the men.

"Well, John Thompson is back in Halifax. I saw him come in on his wagon a while ago. If I know John, he'll be in here before closing time," said Jesse.

"You know, if I thought I couldn't handle my drankin', I'd give it up," said the cronie whose elbow slipped from the table as he spoke.

"All of you know how John gits every night. He ain't likely to ever quit drankin' unless we help him. It's for his own good. We've got to help him help hisself," encouraged Jesse.

"It's the only Christian thing to do. Hey, Jesse, what is it we're about to do?" The man to Jesse's left seemed baffled by all the talk.

"Y'all know where that fresh dug grave is at the side of the road that goes past Martin's Livery?"

"Yeah, we all know. Old man Taylor's suppose to be laid out there tomorrow at four o'clock," said one of the men.

"John'll have to go right past it on his way to git his team before he leaves Halifax. I'm gonna git in that open grave and when John comes by, I'll make him thank a dead man is after his soul. He'll turn cold sober right dead in his tracks," said Jesse, stepping aside to make room for Dudley.

Dudley placed a tray of mugs filled with ale on the table.

"John Thompson will be so drunk by closing time, he'll walk right by you and never bat an eye," said Dudley as he walked away from the table.

"Y'all come to the edge of the cemetery and git behind them bushes and I'll show you what it takes to make a man give up drankin'. If it works, it'll be for the good of John Thompson and the whole town." Jesse was not at all discouraged by what Dudley had said.

All the men agreed and it was settled. They took up their mugs to drink to the success of their scheme.

What an hypocritical gesture---drinking to a scheme to make a man quit drinking---thought Sam. It would be interesting---if for once---Jesse Turner was made the fool instead of John Thompson. This thought was quickly interrupted as Dudley came into the room. He walked to the cabinet; placed his candle on the table and put some fresh mugs on a tray. Turning to go back into the taproom, Dudley saw Sam and nearly dropped the tray of mugs.

"What are you doing back here, Sam:"

Sam held his finger to his mouth and spoke softly.

"I was going to surprise you. Then, when I heard what Jesse Turner was planning--I just sat back here and listened."

"So, you heard it all. That Jesse Turner is about to make me lose my best customer, Sam."

"I know Uncle John's drinking is a problem. But those fellows don't really want to help him. They're in as bad a shape as Uncle John. They just want to make fun of him---like they always do."

"Jesse needs to be taught a lesson. I wonder how he'd feel if somebody pull a trick like that on him?"

"Dudley, you just gave me an idea. I think I'll be waiting in the dark part of that grave when Jesse comes to scare Uncle John."

"Good boy, Sam. That'll serve him right. I've been thinking about a way to get that scheming scoundrel. Take that black cape of mine and pull it over your when you get in the grave. This is the best idea I've heard yet. He'll be the victim of his own scheme."

"You don't think anybody will get hurt, do you?"

"I say whatever Jesse Turner gets is long been due him. You stay quiet until closing time," said Dudley, as he left the back room.

It was only a short while before John Thompson came into the tavern. The cronies welcomed him back to town and even bought him a mug of ale. The next hour passed quickly and the men were careful not to say anything that would cause John to become suspicious.

When the time was right, Sam grabbed the black cape from the coat rack and quietly left the tavern by the back door. It was darker now and he could see huge black clouds passing the full moon and he felt a lively wind blowing from the Roanoke. As he hurried down Market Street, he became concerned that the storm would interfere with his plans.

Sam skipped across King Street onto the path that led to the back of the stables. Approaching the open grave, he could see that even when the dark clouds passed the moon there was still a shadow in the corner of the grave. He quickly jumped into the opening, pulled the cape over him and concealed himself in that black shadow and was completely out of sight.

Soon he heard the men coming. Jesse Turner was giving them instructions.

"Here he comes. Y'all git behind them bushes," ordered Jesse, as he came closer to the grave.

Jesse then slipped into the opening at the opposite end of the grave. His back was toward Sam.

Sam pressed his back flat against the wall of the grave so Jesse would not touch him. Jesse stood and peeked from the grave as John came staggering along the path. When John was near enough, Jesse began moaning.

"Oh---Oh------Oh----I'm sorry I drunk all that ale. I wouldn't be here it won't for drankin' all that ale."

John Thompson stopped a bit unsteadily and turned toward the open grave. "What wash that?"

"I SAID --drankin' caused me to be in my grave. REPENT----REPENT----JOHN---REPENT-- JOHN THOMPSON," came the voice from the grave.

John took a careful step toward the grave.

"Who said that?"

"This is the dead soul of a departed drunkard---warning you to stop drankin'----Repent----JOHN THOMPSON.

Sam felt that he must---at this moment make his presence known. He spoke in a very deep voice that sounded as if it came from the other side of eternity

"GIT----OUT---GIT---OOOOOOOOOUT ---OOOF ---MY GRAVE----"

A sharp bolt of lightning followed by a clap of thunder that shook the earth gave extra meaning to the words that came from the dark corner of the grave.

Jesse Turner did not bother to look back. With one single bound, he was out of the grave. As he struggled to get to his feet, he knocked John

Thompson down, fell down himself, crawled to the path---gained control of his feet and ran down the path toward King Street.

The men behind the bushes heard the deep voice from the grave and followed Jesse's lead.

After several unsuccessful attempts, John got to his feet and staggered to the grave and looked down. Sam sat still and looked up at his weaving Uncle.

"Dish grave ain't been filled. Thash how come that departed drunkard come up,"

John reeled back to the path and Sam could hear him yelling---

"Come back Spirit and let me cover you up----COME BACK DEPARTED DRUNKARD----COME BACK".

Sam climbed out of the grave and could see his Uncle stumbling across King Street in pursuit of Jesse Turner.

Walking to the front of Martin's Livery, Sam looked up and noticed that the clouds were dissipating. The elements were now calm and Sam became uneasy as he thought about the sudden burst of lightning. Perhaps the SPIRITS were at work tonight.

Sam mounted 'Jericho' and had to hold his horse to keep him from breaking into a trot. 'Jericho' seemed eager to leave Martin's Livery. It was not like his horse to be so skittish.

About half way down King Street, Sam loosened the reins and 'Jericho' walked at a steady pace. Considering all that had just happened, Sam amused himself with the thought that his mother just might be the only person for miles around who would be happy to know the Uncle John was back in Halifax.

First For Freedom

CHAPTER SEVEN

The sun was setting and Sam had waited for an hour outside of Dudley's Tavern. From the bench he could see the courthouse. He had waited there in hopes of seeing Allen Jones when the Congress adjourned. He wanted to tell him that 'Midnight' was in fine form but needed to be taken to the track. Even more important was the letter he had just received from Horniblow's Tavern in Edenton. This letter included a bill for three months room and board and Sam was eager to settle the account. Allen Jones would need the bill before any payment could be made.

Waiting outside the tavern, Sam realized the business that now occupied Allen Jones' time was more important than anything else, so he decided to wait until another time to see his benefactor.

He got up from the wooden bench and walked inside the tavern. Dudley was standing behind the bar looking disgustedly at the small crowd.

"Hey, how come some of you don't git outa here and git me some business off the streets? Tell some of them new folks in town about Dudley's place."

Dudley came from behind the counter and walked to a table occupied by two cronies. He grabbed a small man by the arm and started toward the door with him.

"See if you can find Zeb Joyner out there. I saw him go by a while ago with his guitar," said Dudley, as he helped the reluctant small man out of the tavern.

Dudley looked at Sam as he walked back to the bar.

"I git a pain lookin' at so many wall-eyed men all the time. If it won't for the money, I think I'd go into the ministry."

"Dudley, if you ever went into the ministry, you'd win a heap of souls for the devil," said one of the men.

"I'm doing a good job of that now, so I might as well stay where I am," responded Dudley.

"Hey, Dudley, what's happening at the courthouse? Mr. Allen Jones is still over there," said Sam, as Dudley came from behind the counter.

"The just broke up. It's a little early for any of 'em to be coming in here. If he's on one of them committees, it's no telling how long he'll be over there. Oh, by the way, He stopped in here before he went to the courthouse and asked me if I would be willing to help with collecting silver from all the people in and around Halifax. He says that's the only way they'll be able to get any gunpowder. I'll be needing you to help me if the Congress decides that I'm the one for the job.

Why do you want to see him---you expecting some kind of appointment," teased Dudley.

"I've got these bills from Horniblow's that I wanted to get to him." Sam reached inside his coat. "Will you put them inside his box?"

"He usually comes in for his mail in the morning." Dudley took the envelope from Sam. "I'll see that he gets it----and since you've told me what's in the envelope, I won't even need to read it."

Dudley turned his back to Sam and placed the envelope in the pigeon hole box behind the bar. Turning around, he looked toward the table where three ill-clad cronies sat.

"Hey, you fellows, you all know Sam Pickett, here. He's going to join up with Colonel Long's men soon. He's been to Edenton studyin' to be a surveyor---so if any of you want your plantation laid off---well, now's the time to git some free advice." The men looked to each other as if they did not realize that Dudley was being sarcastic.

Before the men could make any sense of what Dudley had said, Zeb Joyner entered the Tavern. Several men, including the small man who had been sent to fetch him followed him.

Zeb was a regular at Dudley's and one of the most popular men in Halifax. Playing the guitar and making up songs on the spur of the moment caused him to be in great demand at the tavern. He was well liked by all who knew him and those who knew him best were the regular customers at Dudley's. Zeb's slender body looked even thinner when he was seen with his robust wife, Jezebel---which was not too often. There was not a woman in Halifax as large or as strong as Jezebel Joyner. Sam thought the reason Zeb came to the tavern so often was because he hated to go home.

His work at Willie Jones' gristmill kept him busy during the day, but when the sun was low, Zeb could usually be found at the tavern. Some of the men had said that Zeb had to come to the tavern to drink up enough courage to go home and face his wife. There was one thing that he loved more than playing the guitar--and that was playing cards. He seemed to be a chronic loser and stayed in debt to those who would extent credit to him.

He had been married the last ten of his thirty-five years and Jezebel had tried desperately to change Zeb's habits but seemed to be fighting a losing battle.

Zeb's dark eyes and thick brows were his most attractive feature, and it was easy to look on this man whenever he entertained the cronies.

Dudley saw Zeb and yelled, "Hey--where've you been?"

"I've been over to the jail talking with Flora McDonald's husband. I've been working on a song. I heard about that lady Flora McDonald might be coming to Halifax and I needed some information. Then, I stopped at the common and brought some joy to the people there."

"Well, I think we need some uplifting in this place," said Dudley, looking at the crowd.

"From the looks of this crowd, I think I got here a little too late." Dudley smiled as Zeb spoke.

"There's still hope for what you see sitting at those tables. They just need to be revived," said Dudley.

"Where's Jesse Turner? He's always trying to revive somebody." Zeb shook his head as he surveyed the group of men.

Dudley cast a quick surreptitious look at Sam and replied--

"Jesse Turner had hisself a vision and I hear he took it as an omen from the great beyond. He's been telling everyone that it was a revelation that was sent to him personally. He ain't been in here the last few days."

"He was at the town common yesterday telling people about some kinda miracle that took place at the cemetery---nobody paid him any mind," added one of the men.

"Maybe he's going to give up drinking---," said Sam smiling sheepishly at Dudley.

"That would be a blessing to all of us. Now, Zeb come on, do that song you wrote about the 'Gambler'," encouraged Dudley.

"Dudley, you know I can't do a song without some kind of refreshments to help my throat. I've been out there singing and picking and my throat is as dry as shucks." Zeb gently touched his throat as he spoke.

"I know what's ailin' you, Zeb." Dudley turned to Sam. "The onliest way to git him wound up is to give him a mug of ale."

Zeb overheard what Dudley said.

"Sam, you know he's right. It's the only thang I git for all the business I bring him." Zeb then turned toward the men in the tavern.

"Gentlemen--ah---I mean friends---ah---Hey what is it you call a bunch drunks? Y'all thought I was going to say fellow-drunks, didn't you? Sam, you need to learn the words."

"I've been standing here wondering when I'm going to get the chance to hear it. I'll have to hear it before I can learn it," said Sam.

"Well, I don't blame you for being so impatient. 'Cause what you're about to hear is worth waiting for," bragged Zeb.

Dudley, like Sam, was eager to get the song started.

"Will you all hold it down so the musician can begin his perfomance. I hope this song is half as good as all the talk I've been hearin' about it."

Zeb was quick to respond.

"If the song's not good, it'll be because my throat is so dry."

Zeb made himself comfortable on one of the tall stools at the bar. He strummed and tuned his guitar momentarily and then looked up at his audience.

"Well, here's what y'all have been waiting to hear. This one is called my Tavern Song."

I held my horse's reins,
And kissed my love farewell
I climbed upon Old Betsy
And started down the trail.
I was going after that crooked crook,
Who gave me a crooked deal.
He dealt my cards from the bottom of the deck,
And my money from me he did steal.
I had bet my horse, I had bet my house,
I had even bet my land.
On the cards that I was to get from that crook
Which was to be the last hand.
Then the candles went out,
And there was a shot and a shout.
And when the candle was lit,
Alone I did sit,
And my money was nowhere about.
But tonight was the night
And if that crook was in sight,
I promised myself he'd be found.
I knew if I would look,
I could track down that crook.
For I heard that he was in town.
In the tavern there were few,
But as I entered, I knew,
There was a gambler I'd met before.
Then, he threw back his chair,
But, I didn't care,
For I had come to even the score.
Like a flash of lightning,
That gambler did move,
And his pistol let out a wail.
And I twisted and turned.
And my stomach it burned,
And then to the floor I fell.
You may wonder why,

I chanced to stop by,
A spirit with a story to tell.
But I've heard it said,
"Mong those who are dead,
That a tavern's where spirits do dwell.

As Zeb finished the song, Sam slapped him on the shoulder and said, "Zeb, you sure have got a way with words. How do you come up with your ideas?"

"When the spirit moves me. I just sing it the way I feel it. Some people have just naturally got to make music," said Zeb.

Dudley leaned across the bar.

"Zeb, I'm the one with the spirits that move you. You know, I'll have a heap of ghost hanging around here when all of you pass on. Most of you think this place is heaven. So, when y'all go to your just reward--I just might be the one standing at the door to let y'all in."

"We'll more than likely die from this stuff we've been drankin'. Dudley, you've shore got some soul killin' spirits. Where do you git this ale? ---from the British," asked a big freckled face man at the bar.

Dudley quickly replied.

"The way people are talking--you all might not have to drank yourselves to death. You might git a chance to do some fightin' before you all pass on. But, to tell the truth, I don't think we'll stand much of a chance---if we ever do have to fight the British."

Zeb put down his mug and made a face that would scare the devil.

"Hey, I've got an idea how we can whip the British---if we have to fight'em. Here's the plan. We just invite them to come to Dudley's Tavern and when they start drankin' this stuff, (Zeb picked up the mug) they'll start dropping like flies and when they hit the floor all we'll have to do is haul them off. It won't hurt us 'cause we're use to it---but for the British, it would be sure death."

The crowd laughed. There were few who could joke about Dudley's business and get away with it the way Zeb could. The laughter quickly subsided as three well-dressed gentlemen entered the tavern. Sam immediately recognized Samuel Johnston, the President of the Fourth Provincial Congress, who walked just behind Allen Jones. The man who came in behind Samuel Johnston was one of the most popular delegates of all---Mr. Cornelius Harnett. The three walked by the bar and sat down at a corner table.

Dudley reached beneath the bar and withdrew a bottle that Sam knew to be a special brandy reserved only for Allen Jones. With a towel folded across his left arm, Dudley walked quickly to the corner table.

Maxville Burt Williams

Sam watched the three men and thought of the seriousness of their work. Here it was the first Monday in April and planting time at Mount Gallant and Allen Jones was needed at his plantation in Northampton. Pressing business at the Congress had caused all the delegates to forego many of their other responsibilities.

Samuel Johnston pulled a chair from the table and sat between the other two delegates. He was an imposing figure. His large form sat erect and his handsome features were familiar to most of the men in the tavern. A white powdered wig gave him an air of distinction. He was held in high esteem by all who knew him and there seemed little doubt of his ability to conduct a Congress. His skill had been proven by experience, for he had been the President of the Congress since the death of John Harvey and the place left by Harvey was no office for a lesser man than Samuel Johnston.

Samuel Johnston

Sam's eyes moved to the small man to Johnston's left. There was charisma about Cornelius Harnett that made Sam want to keep on staring until he could determine what attraction held his attention. Harnett's hazel eyes seemed to penetrate the depth of one's soul. He was not a handsome man---yet there was a magnetism that made Sam want to know even more than he now knew about this small giant. Harnett's leadership among the Patriots caused even the leaders to seek advice from him. His experience in government was well known. He had been Chairman of the Committee of Safety at Wilmington, Chairman of the Provincial Council, and had headed more important committees than any other delegate in the new government. Being a wealthy merchant, Harnett had led the opposition to the Stamp Act on the Cape Fear and it was told that the Royal Governor, Josiah Martin, considered Harnett his main source of opposition in the colony.

Dudley returned to the bar and leaned toward Sam.

"You've got business with Mr. Allen Jones, Sam. He want to talk with you just as soon as they finish their drinks."

"Did he say what he wanted?"

"I didn't ask. You know I'm not one to interfere in other people's business. You can tell me all about it later."

It was obvious that Harnett and Johnston were hurrying their drinks and soon Allen Jones stood as his fellow-Patriots left the table.

As the two delegates walked past him, Sam nodded, then he walked to Allen Jones' table.

"Sir, Dudley said you wanted to speak with me."

"Sit down, Sam. I don't know how aware you are of the workings of the Congress but I've come to realize that more work has to be done outside the courthouse than is done on the inside. President Johnston feels strongly that we need more order in our meetings. He wants a guard at the door to make sure there are no unnecessary interruptions. I knew you were signing up for the militia, and I thought maybe you could handle the job."

"Sir, you know how interested I am in what's going on inside the courthouse. I would consider it a great privilege and honor."

"When you see Colonel Long, tell him of your assignment. We'll expect you there on Friday."

"What are your feelings about the Congress, Sir? Are we moving toward independence?"

"We're moving, Sam. We're moving faster than I had anticipated. President Johnston appointed a select committee today to consider all the usurpations that have been brought against us by the mother country. Harnett is in charge of the committee and has asked us to meet at Mrs. Eelbeck's Boarding House tomorrow night. We'll make our recommendations to the Congress on Friday."

"How do the other delegates feel about independence?"

"I feel certain independence is what the rest of the Congress wants."

"There seems to be no choice left to us, Sir."

"I know, I know. But an act for independence must be carefully considered. There are still those among us who have close ties with England."

"I know what you mean." Sam quickly thought of the Hamiltons.

Allen Jones then motioned to Dudley who came from behind the bar.

"Dudley, you know I mentioned that we need somebody in Halifax to collect silver so we can buy gunpowder for the militia. I told President Johnston that you were in contact with more people than any other person, so I offered him your services. What do you think of that?"

Dudley seemed especially pleased to be held in high esteem by Allen Jones. "I'll do what I can, Sir. You know I'm as involved as anybody else. Our boys can't fight without gunpowder. I'll start collecting what I can in Halifax and then we'll spread the word throughout the countryside." Dudley looked around the tavern then leaned down closer to Allen Jones.

"Sir, I don't want you to tell me nothing you wouldn't tell anybody else but I've had people ask me every day what's going on inside the courthouse. What can I tell them?"

"You can tell'em, they'll know something by the end of the week. The only thing I've heard since this Congress convened is talk about independence and I'm sure the people have been listening to the same kind of talk. I think we'll soon know how eager the people are to fight. Plans have already been made for a recruiting program and a training camp right here in Halifax."

Allen Jones stood and looked toward Sam.

"Sam, you come on by Mrs. Eelbeck's about eight-thirty Friday morning---and we'll go to the courthouse together."

Sam walked along with Allen Jones as far as the front door. Jones tipped his cocked hat to several men as he left the tavern. Sam watched him leave and realized that he had completely forgotten to mention the bill from Horniblow's Tavern and had failed to inform Jones of his horse 'Midnight'.

Dudley leaned over the counter.

"According to Mr. Jones, the Tories around here might as well pack their baggage. By the way, Sam, what do you hear about the Hamilton family."

"Yeah, I hear you're pretty close to that family, Sam," added Zeb, leaning over to hear Dudley's question.

"That family is mighty undecided about what to do right now," Sam spoke softly.

"I hear John Hamilton's business ain't what it has been. Fact is---most of the people don't want to do no trading with no Tory," said one of the Cronies.

"They don't all think the same way. Josie don't think the way her father thinks," Said Sam.

"It ain't her place to think. John Hamilton does the thinking for that family," said Dudley.

Zeb picked up his guitar and walked to a table where three men were seated. "Y'all talk about fighting and I'm losing money talking when I ought to be playing cards. Who wants to play some cards." Three of the men nodded and got up from the table to go to the game room.

Dudley spoke more seriously now.

"You'd better come into a fortune, if you've got any ideas about Josephine Hamilton. 'Cause John Hamilton ain't about to let her go to nobody that ain't got as much money as he's got. That family don't do thangs that-a-way."

"Josie is different from the rest," Sam held his ground.

"I say you're asking for trouble with that Hamilton girl, Sam. She's a Hamilton ---if you know what I mean." Warned Dudley.

"I know what you mean--but things are changing and they're changing fast."

"If thangs are changin' so fast, why weren't you invited to the Hamilton's tonight? I sent a good supply of Madeira wine over there this afternoon for the big social they having."

"I won't invited, but I think I'll go by there anyway. It won't do any harm just to go over. I don't have to go inside."

"You're just going to stand outside and look in. That's as far as you'll ever get. You'll always be on the outside looking in, Sam"

"Now, you can't tell about that, Dudley. One day I just might be on the inside looking out. Like I say---things are changing," retorted Sam

"You'll always be on the outside looking in.".

"Oh, I know how things are now. I know how the Hamiltons feel about social standing and all that. John Hamilton has even asked me to stay away from his house.---but you don't know how Josie feels."

"Sam, with the ambition you've got, you might just be a general before you get outa the army," teased Dudley.

"I'll be back in a while to help you close up," said Sam, as he glanced back at Dudley.

"You be careful, Sam. Remember what I told you about stayin' in your place. It's always better to make a good leaving than have a bad stayin'," warned Dudley, as Sam left the tavern.

CHAPTER EIGHT

Sam walked along Market Street to the corner and turned right onto King Street. He had stayed at Dudley's longer than he had intended. The sun had been down for about an hour and the shadows from the tall oaks fell across the road. He had not told Dudley that he thought Josie loved him. He had not mentioned those incidental moments that had brought new purpose to his life---the tender and meaningful words that Josie had spoken.

Tonight was the first time he'd had heard about the party at the Hamiltons. Sam knew, when the Hamiltons gave a party, all the members of the most prominent families would be invited and he also was well aware that he was not included in that select group.

As he approached the spacious yard of the house, he could see a number of carriages and horses out front. Sam walked to the edge of the yard and sat on a stone bench; he could see shadowy figures inside as they moved past the large windows. The music from the fiddler playing a minuet was loud and clear. Sam was not able to discern several couples, as they moved to the rhythm of the music. Once, he thought he saw Josie, then decided he was not sure.

He considered what Dudley had said at the tavern. Dudley knew the Hamilton family as well as anybody in Halifax. Maybe he was right when he said the Hamiltons would never accept him. At Edenton, he had been accepted by the gentlemen of the gentry, but in Halifax, he was still regarded as Sam Pickett. Here, he was too well known, his background was common knowledge. Here--- he had no place among the gentry. Sam wondered if he would ever be accepted. The more he thought about it, the more absurd it all seemed. When would people ever be accepted for who they are, acceptance into the gentry was based on wealth---that was the only requirement.

Then a feeling of shame caused Sam to realize that this was no place for him--for he was lacking anything that vaguely resembled wealth. It bothered him to be ashamed. There was no justification for it. People shouldn't be judged by wealth. People should be judged by character and he was not ashamed of his character, but the shame was still there. Then--he thought of Uncle Louie, Aunt Grace, and the hundreds of slaves in and around Halifax. Slavery-----bondage----buying and selling of human life---never had seemed civilized to him. There were voices speaking out against slavery, strong voices, but these voices were few and the sound was not audible to the deaf.

He decided to leave, but as he glanced once more toward the house, he saw Josie and a gentleman coming to the front yard. He wanted to leave before he was discovered but it was too late--Josie had seen him.

"Hello----Sam----Hello---Sam Pickett," called Josie, as she ran toward him.

Sam hesitated, not knowing how to respond.

"I had to see George, Miss Hamilton. Is he at home?"

Josie looked at Sam questioningly.

"He's inside, Sam. Oh, Mr. Lawson, this is Sam Pickett, one of our very close friends. Sam, this is Mr. Jonathan Lawson. Mr. Lawson is one of father's partners. He's in charge of the warehouse in New Bern."

"I'm very pleased to know any friend of the Hamiltons," said Jonathan Lawson, as he extended his right hand.

Sam looked at the tall figure dressed in very fine purple silk. The shirt had ruffles at the wrist and a pair of fine black leather shoes with silver buckles. He was a man who would be welcomed at the Hamilton home, thought Sam.

"I'm happy to know you, Sir," said Sam. He grasped the hand of Lawson, trying not to show any hint of jealousy.

It was an odd feeling handshake. There was something in the feeling that was different from any handshake that he had ever felt. When he withdrew his hand, Sam quickly noticed that the middle finger of Lawson's right hand was missing.

"Do you think George could come out here for a while?" Sam quickly turned to Josie as he spoke.

Josie looked at Lawson.

"Mr. Lawson, will you please see if you can locate George. Sam seems so anxious to see him. I'm sure it must be important."

"I'll tell him you are here," Said Lawson, as he turned and walked toward the house.

"Why are you here, Sam?"

"I heard about the party----I thought I'd come by to see what it was like---I suppose this is about as close as I'll ever get to knowing."

"I know how you feel, Sam, and I'm sorry."

"I don't like to feel that I'm anywhere I'm not wanted."

Josie sat on the bench and extended her hand for Sam to sit by her.

"Sam, you know I don't like the way things are any more than you do."

"That's the only thing that keeps me from giving up. I think how you feel means a lot. But it's not enough. It's really not enough, Josie."

Josie and Sam turned to watch the moon as the light came through the tall oak trees that grew at the edge of the yard. He slipped his arm around her and she leaned toward him submissively. His rough hands touched her fine silk dress. As he held her, he wondered if Josie could possibly feel the way he felt at that moment. Would this be a fleeing moment in his life, or could it be something more lasting---deeper and more meaningful.

Josie lifted her head from Sam's shoulder. She turned her face up to his, her lips parted as Sam leaned down and pressed his lips against hers. He kissed her hard and passionately. Then----for the second time in his life the world was whirling----whirling---spinning---and he was flying through space and time.

Unbeknown to either Sam or Josie, George had come from the house and had walked slowly and softly up behind the two lovers. Now standing directly behind them-----he spoke in a deep voice that sounded like his father's voice.

"SAM PICKETT---what is the meaning of this kind of behavior?"

Sam and Josie were startled, and both jumped from the bench. They turned and saw George holding his hand over his mouth to smother his hysterical laughter. He could speak exactly like his father and had many times played pranks on his mother and Josie by using the resemblance. Sam and Josie did not join him in his laughter.

"George---George, you scared the life outa me." Sam was not amused by the prank.

"Why do you do things like this, George," asked Josie.

"It was my understanding that you came to see me. I suppose I'm just disappointed, that's all," said George as he calmed down.

"Oh George," said Josie, petulantly.

"Will you be telling your father about us," asked Sam.

"I would have told him before now, if I were going to tell him. Do you think that I didn't know how you two feel? I would suggest that you keep it that way," advised George.

"I don't know if we'll be able to hide our feelings forever," said Sam.

"That seems evident, since you two are becoming so bold. Well, like they say, nothing remains the same. Maybe father will come to understand. You two will just have to give him more time."

"We'll wait as long as we need to wait." Josie was willing to accept the fact that her father was not yet willing to accept the relationship.

"Josie knows father too well to think that he can be told anything. By the way, what is it you wanted to see me about, Sam?"

"Oh, it wasn't important. Whatever it was---you scared me so bad---- I've completely forgotten."

"I somehow have the feeling that you didn't come to see me at all," said George, sounding disappointed.

"There's no need denying it. Your know me too well, George."

"I'm glad you understand, George. You know---all's fair in love and war," said Josie, as she turned to go back to the house.

George looked back at Sam.

"From what I saw a moment ago, I'd say it sure wasn't war."

Josie grabbed her smiling brother by his arm.

"Oh George, you're such a tease."

She looked back at Sam and tenderly said, "Goodnight, Sam."

Walking back to Dudley's Tavern, Sam felt his confidence in two members of the Hamilton family had been restored. George seemed more like the old George, and Josie---well---she was so completely different---so warm---so tender--so beautiful.

When he arrived at the tavern, the crowd had dispersed and Dudley had started cleaning. Dudley looked up from the table he was wiping.

"Sam, how about you finishing up with the tables. I want to check in the cellar. I don't think I've got enough ale to last through the week."

Sam found an apron under the bar and got a cloth from the table and began wiping the tables. When he finished a table, he extinguished the candle, which was in a bottle at the center of each table. He could tell that Dudley had already swept the floor---so there was little left to be done before the tavern was closed for the night. The tavern had become quite dim now that Sam was wiping the last table.

Dudley came up from the cellar and immediately began wiping the bar.

"Hey, Sam, how's your Uncle John?"

"He's been staying close to home the last few days. He's trying to find some way to get his hands on some money."

"Well, I can expect him back in here before too long. He always finds a way to get money."

"You know Dudley, when you think about it---you're about the only man in Halifax---that I know of---who can really depend on Uncle John."

Sam began extinguishing the candles in the sconces along the wall as Dudley finished wiping the bar. Both stopped what they were doing and looked toward the door as a gentleman entered the tavern.

"Are you preparing to close," asked the gentleman as he walked to the bar.

"We usually close around ten o'clock," said Dudley.

"I was at the Hamilton's party and the Madeira was superb. I believe Abigail said you ordered it for her. Do you happen to have another bottle?"

Sam immediately recognized Jonathan Lawson.

"I'm staying at Martin's Ordinary, but I doubt he has anything in his cellar to compare with the Madeira I had at the Hamiltons." He walked to the bar.

"That was a special order, but I usually have some extra bottles for special occasions. The meeting of Fourth Provincial Congress is a special occasion and I ordered two extra cases."

"Could you spare a bottle?"

"Whenever a gentleman wants to purchase a bottle of Madeira--that's a special occasion."

Dudley reached under the bar.

"You left the party early, didn't you?"

"Yes, as a matter of fact, I did. I need to get an early start for New Bern tomorrow."

Sam put out the last candle along the wall and walked to the bar.

"Good evening, again, Mr. Lawson."

"Oh, it's you----ah--Sam ---isn't it? I hardly recognized you. The light in here is not fit for seeing."

"We were closing and we usually put out the candles after we finish cleaning," informed Dudley.

"Mr. Lawson is from New Bern and is here on business with Mr. Hamilton. Mr. Lawson, this is Christopher Dudley---my employer and my friend."

As the two shook hands, Sam wondered if Dudley sensed that there was a missing finger."

"What kind of business are you in?" Dudley released Lawson's hand and placed an empty mug on the bar.

"We store merchandise in our warehouses. We handle almost anything that can be shipped by wagon or boat from New Bern."

"I understand that Colonel Nicholas Long is in need of some gunpowder. Do you know anybody in New Bern who has any to sell," asked Dudley.

"Oh, we have an ample supply in our charge."

"Well, it looks like we'll be needing all we can git our hands on," said Dudley

Lawson held up the bottle of Madeira and examined the label.

"I'm sure the price of powder will double in the next few months."

"I hope you plan to use it for the cause of the Patriots," said Sam sitting on the stool next to Lawson.

Lawson poured a mug of wine and took a large gulp.

"I plan to let the powder go to the man with the best offer."

"What is you price, now," asked Dudley.

"My latest offer was four shillings a pound."

"We just might do some business. I'll pay you five shillings a pound if you'll guarantee delivery. How much can you let me have?"

"Oh---I can let you have---say a fifty pounds---I'll require ten per cent down before shipment."

"We don't have the silver ---yet---but I feel certain we can strike a bargain."

"Why don't you see if you get the down payment. That way you'll be assured of delivery."

"I'll be right back." Dudley looked toward Sam who nodded approval.

"Don't you have to get John Hamilton's approval," asked Sam.

"I'm in charge of the warehouse. You just leave John Hamilton to me."

Sam was not satisfied with the answer.

"You know as well as I that John Hamilton sympathies are with the crown."

Lawson was getting a little frustrated with Sam's questions.

"Yes, --John Hamilton is quite loyal ---and that Josie's a striking beauty-----a man would be most fortunate to gain her hand? What a pleasant and easy way to come into a fortune---eh--- Sam? One does not always marry for love, Boy."

Sam was not about to be talked down to.

"The Hamilton's money does not interest me in the least, Mr. Lawson."

"Come---Come now----Sam. You need not protest. I understand. I saw how you looked at her. It does amuse me that you think Miss Josie would be content with a mere tavern boy----what she'll need is a man."

"Like you?" Sam questioned.

"Possibly!"

It seemed the more they talked the more Sam felt his anger rising.

"What are your intentions, Lawson?"

"I'd say that's a personal matter," came Lawson's quick response.

"Call it what you may----I want to know." Sam moved closer to Lawson.

Dudley came from the cellar just in time to hear the last part of the conversation and he sensed the anger and stepped between the two rivals.

"Hey, you two listen---I've got twenty shillings and I'll pay myself back when we've collected the silver. I'll need your signature on this receipt, Mr. Lawson."

"Hand me your quill." Dudley placed the paper on the counter and Lawson signed the agreement. He then handed the paper to Dudley.

"Here you are, Mr. Dudley."

"Then the deal is completed." Dudley reached out and shook Jonathan Lawson's hand as he handed him the twenty shillings.

"Well I must be going. Sorry to have kept you from your closing, Mr. Dudley. Sam --here has been entertaining me." He held up the bottle of Madeira. "The Maderia?"

Dudley looked at Lawson and said, "Consider it a part of the bargain."

Lawson started for the front door.

"Thank you Mr. Dudley. Oh, Sam ---I'll be around for a while if you care to finish our little---conversation."

"You can depend on it, Lawson." Sam moved toward the front door.

Dudley stepped between the two rivals.

"Let it be Sam." Dudley then turned toward Lawson. "Lawson our business is finished. Why don't we leave well enough alone?"

Lawson stepped back from Sam and suddenly drew a blunderbuss from inside his coat.

"Now, boy stand back or you'll not see the light of day when the sun comes up tomorrow."

Suddenly Sam lunged toward Lawson and Lawson struck Sam with the butt end of his gun. It was a hard blow to the head.

Dudley rushed to Sam. He realized that Sam was not conscious---so he hurried back behind the counter and brought a wet towel, which he placed on Sam's head. Dudley gently slapped Sam's cheeks briskly and then spoke.

"Hey-----Sam ----Sam come on boy."

Sam's eyes began to flicker as consciousness slowly returned.

"I suppose you know I should have listened to you, Dudley."

"Come on, Sam. Git up. Sit in that chair for a while."

"I'll be alright. That was a silly thing to do. It seems that I've been doing a lot of silly things lately."

"You said it, Sam. I'm just listening. Can you make it home by yourself?"

"Well, I promise you one thing," said Sam, as he stood.

"I may not get the hand of Josie Hamilton--but I pledge to you here and now---one day-----I'll get the hide of Mr. Jonathan Lawson."

"You go on home and git some rest. Your head will clear tomorrow. You can think about that when you're able to think." Dudley helped Sam to the door.

Sam walked slowly to Martin's Livery and climbed on 'Jericho'. His head was reeling; he walked his horse down King Street toward Quanky Creek. When he passed the Hamilton house, he could see that the party was still in progress. He thought about the great confidence he had only a while ago and how Jonathan Lawson had teased it into uncertainty.

As he approached the bridge at Quanky Creek, 'Jericho' suddenly shied from the bushes to the left of the bridge. Sam did not understand what had caused his horse to jump and before he could determine the cause, a gun shot shattered the silence of the night and caused 'Jericho' to lurch forward onto the bridge. He could not gather enough strength to restrain 'Jericho' and the horse galloped wildly across the bridge. Just as he reached the opposite bank, the saddle slipped and Sam was hurled to the ground. He rolled with the fall, and was fortunate to have made it across the bridge. 'Jericho' turned and ran back across the bridge and turned onto the road to 'The Grove'. 'Jericho' had been out of stable several times in the past year and always went back home to the stables of Willie Jones.

Sam quickly sat up and could see a rider hurrying down King Street. The night was too dark to distinguish any features of the rider. That was not important---Sam know the rider. He also knew that he could not pursue him on foot and 'Jericho' was by this time half way to the stables at 'The Grove'.

Sam's head was aching and his arms did not seem to have the strength to pick up the saddle and lug is all the way home. He turned the saddle over and examined the girth. He had expected what he now confirmed. The girth had been cut. He dragged the saddle to the side of the road and concealed it behind a clump of bushes. He would come for it tomorrow.

Walking slowly down the road toward his home, Sam thought how complicated his life had become since he had returned to Halifax. Then, he thought of the things that he would have to face tomorrow and tomorrow---and the thought compounded the aching in his head. As he walked along the road, the sound of that gun shot echoed in his head. That was no ordinary sound----but more like the unique sound of a blunderbuss.

CHAPTER NINE

By mid-morning the next day, Sam and John Thompson had finished loading the wagon with corn. Now they were on their way to Willie Jones' gristmill to get the corn ground.

John sat beside Sam on the wagon seat. Sam held the reins in his left hand and felt behind his right ear. There was a slight swelling but the aching was gone. Thoughts of revenge had occupied his mind during the morning and he could think of no way he would ever be able to get even with Jonathan Lawson. This disturbing thought was as bothersome to him as the ache had been the previous night.

Sam looked at the small man sitting next to him. John Thompson never shaved. His clothes were wrinkled and worn and there was still an unsteadiness in his hands. When he returned home from his long absence, John had the 'shakes' for two days and was not able to get our of bed. Sarah Pickett had nursed him back to health, as always, and, as always, John had promised that he was through with liquor.

Sam spoke as he observed his uncle.

"Uncle John, I'm signing up with Colonel Long's outfit tomorrow. I've been given a duty at the Court House while the Congress is in session, and I won't be around much longer to help with the work on the farm."

"Well, it won't take too much work to tend the few acres we've got."

"I've been thinking that Mr. Long might send over some help now that its 'planting time'," suggested Sam.

"Long's always been obliging---ever since he gave your Ma the few acres she's got. He ain't 'bout to let your Ma want for nothing. There's been hard times before----Like when your Pa died---he furnished the family then---fact that's when he gave your Ma the land she's got now."

"I just don't feel right about leaving right at 'planting time'."

"Sam, you know that you've got to do what you've got to do. Sometimes a man ain't got no choice."

Sam thought about his uncle's drinking and wondered if he really had any choice. Some men drank so much that they no longer had a choice. The craving sometimes was stronger than the will to resist the temptation. The cronies at Dudley's had proven that---there were many men in Halifax who suffered the same weakness as his uncle.

Sam pulled the team left after crossing the bridge at Quanky Creek. Willie Jones gristmill was on the south bank of the Roanoke River and they would have to pass 'Grove House' to get there. It was a closer route this way than it was going through town and then along the river road.

Soon they were passing the large house and coming to the servant's quarters where Aunt Grace waved to them from the steps. She set the routine at 'Grove House" and it ran as smoothly as Willie Jones' grandfather clock.

To his right, Sam could see Uncle Louie down by the stables. The older slaves who answered directly to Uncle Louie tended all the cattle, horses, sheep, hogs and chickens. 'Planting time' demanded much hard work from the rest of the slaves but the old slaves' routine remained the same the year round.

Beyond the stables and opposite the racetrack stretched a row of twenty-five simple, two-room, log huts. The logs were cemented by red clay mixed with straw and had chimneys of the same substance. Small, black, half-naked children played about the yards and were being minded by old, wrinkled slave women dressed in gray homespun; their heads bound with colored cloth. As the wagon slowly moved by the huts, the old women looked up and watched as they reprimanded the children who played too close to the road.

Behind the slave quarters was a large orchard where pear, apple, peach and other fruit trees grew in abundance. Along the white rail fence that encircled the orchard, were several well kept grapevines---each producing a different grape. From this orchard came jellies, jams and preserves. The better grapes were pressed of their juice, which was put in the wine cellar for fermentation while cider and brandy aged in this special place at 'Grove House'.

The entrance to the orchard was at the back of 'Grove House' where a huge, iron double gate permitted only those who were allowed the key. When the fruits were harvested and all that was needed at 'Grove House' had been gathered, the gate was opened to the household servants who salvaged the remaining fruits. This was a special privilege allowed the household servants.

As the wagon rounded the curve at the far end of the racetrack, Sam looked toward the large expanse of open land now occupied by field hands. To his left and in the distance, the slaves were planting corn. Six male slaves followed horse-drawn plows that scratched the furrow. Stooping women walked in the furrow with burlap bags filled with corn, dropping the kernels at regular spaces. Young slaves boys and girls kicked the dirt over the grain with their bare feet.

In an adjacent field and beyond the planting slaves was a cluster of about thirty slaves weeding a field of potatoes. In this field, the slaves moved along so slowly that their progress could not be noticed from the road. The hoes moved up and down to the rhythm of a song that floated across the field. Sam was too far away to hear the words but the sounds that reached him were vibrant, melodious intonations of joy. Here the lowest from of human life in Halifax found a joy in living. Thinking of all that's good and bad in life depends on how one regards life, thought, Sam. Realizing that happiness was as much a state of mind as it was a condition suddenly caused him to feel fortunate with his station in life.

Several of the slaves at 'The Grove' had worked hard to buy their freedom and had stayed on to work for wages. Over the years only a few freed slaves had left to find work elsewhere. Freedom was something relative. This intriguing thought caused Sam to wonder what forces now moved the members of the aristocracy, who had more freedom than any others, to want even more. The slaves seemed to care less about freedom than their masters, and the slaves were the ones who were totally without it. Rationalizing as he rode along. Sam concluded that this thought was beyond his learning and he would understand it later when he had more time to think about it----yet he wondered if freedom could be a companion of happiness and as much a state of one's mind.

At the edge of the woods, several male slaves were clearing away brush from fallen trees----making new ground. With each group of laboring slaves, was an overseer who sat on his horse and occasionally shouted to some of the slaves who were moving too slowly.

Beyond the racetrack were many log buildings. First: a blacksmith's shop, a tannery, a cooper's shed, a weaving house, and then the many storage barns that lined the road to the river. Only the blacksmith's shop was being tended, now that it was planting time, and all the slaves were needed in the fields. Sam thought of the many interwoven relationships that held the people together at 'The Grove'. Young slave girls and boys imitated their parents and learned from them. The adult slaves, who had issues, were expected to teach the young all the skills and labors that they had learned from their parents. When the learning time was over, as much work was required of the young as was demanded of the adults. The overseers had to know the talents and abilities of the young slaves so that added responsibilities could be given the young. In many ways, the overseers were the ones who determined when the young slaves became an adult. Thus, the educational cycle continued from generation to generation.

Four overseers, who reported to Mr. Jones periodically, supervised all the work at 'The Grove'. While they were given great authority, they knew what was expected of them and therefore demanded strict obedience and hard work from all the slaves. Willie Jones judged them even as they judged the slaves. The overseers were mindful of their jobs and knew that they must produce the labor necessary to get all the work done on schedule. Willie Jones was a man who would not tolerate indolence from either the slaves or the overseers.

Very little had to be purchased at the plantation. The many crops, vegetables, and fruits grown for shipment up the Roanoke were also used for consumption at the 'The Grove'. The storehouses were filled in the fall but by mid-summer were empty again. Salt and different metals, mostly iron and copper, were shipped directly to Willie Jones' wharf.

The salt house ahead was about mid-way between the river and the racetrack and was always kept under lock. When the first cold weather came in November, time for killing hogs and salting meat kept all the slaves busy. Much salted meat was shipped but the smokehouses behind 'Grove House' were filled before any meat was sold. Smoked hams, sausages, bacon and fat meat were issued sparingly to the slaves---only two meats a week.

Life at 'The Grove' depended on bountiful harvest each year. If there was a shortage of corn, flax, wheat, tobacco, or cotton, the slaves were the first to suffer. Even though tobacco was the 'money crop', it was corn that gave substance to life for it provided the slaves with their main source of food. It was used for cornbread, mush, hominy, hoecake, ashcake; the slave women had their special ways of preparing different meals using corn as the main ingredient.

The shucks from the corn were used for matting inside the mattresses, the leaves were used for fodder, and the grain was the most important feed given the animals. The corncob was used for making homemade pipes.

Whenever Sam saw anyone smoking a corncob pipe, he always thought of the first time he had tried tobacco. He was twelve years old and had made himself a pipe with the reed stem and had quietly sneaked off to his and George's secret cave on Quanky Creek. He had been inside the cave for about thirty minutes and was puffing away trying to master the art of smoking, when George came inside the cave holding his hat full of water from the creek. Sam was choking from the dense smoke and when George heaved the water in his face, he almost drowned.

"I thought the cave was on fire," George had said. "Sam this cave looked like an erupting volcano."

When George understood what Sam was doing, he became angry that he had not been invited to share the experience. So, George then proceeded to teach him how smoking was suppose to be done. George knew about smoking and explained how he had learned to master the technique by watching his father. Later, that day, the two emerged from the cave with reddened eyes, a dizzy head, and an upset stomach. Neither of the two would have been able to climb the steep incline alone since the smoking had made them almost too weak to walk. For two days he and George were unable to get out of bed. It was a rare disease that they suffered; only they knew the demon that had invaded and conquered their young bodies.

When Sam told George that Looney Oney just might have a cure for their sickness, George immediately started to feel better. Sam smiled to himself as he recalled how he had taken up smoking and had quit smoking all in one day.

They were now coming to the slave cemetery on the right side of the road and just ahead of Willie Jones' gristmill and wharf.

It was late morning when they arrived at the mill. Zeb Joyner was sitting on the porch picking his guitar. He told Sam that he was behind schedule, but there was nothing to do while the wheel was grinding.

Sam and his Uncle John unloaded the corn in an empty bin at the side of the mill. When they were finished, Sam encouraged Zeb to do his 'Dead Horse' song. Zeb told Sam that he had been working on a song about Flora McDonald and he wanted to get some of the men at the tavern to help him with the chorus later when the song was finished.. Zeb said he would do his 'Dead Horse' song if John would stay and give him some help---meal had to be put into bags and more corn had to be moved from the bins. When Zeb told John that he would make it worth his while, John became interested in making some spending money.

Zeb made himself comfortable on the steps of the mill and strummed and tuned his guitar. "Well, here it comes, Sam. I'm just going to talk this one to you. I've got to save my voice for my audience at the tavern."

I bought me a horse from a man named Ned,
But Ned never said that the horse was dead.
Then Ned took off for I don't know where,
But I paid him in Continental money, so I don't care.
What Ned don't know, but he'll soon learn,
Is continental money ain't worth a durn
I'll bury that horse and pay the cost
'Cause a dead horse is worth more
Than the money I lost.

"I'll remember that one Zeb," Yelled Sam.

He sang the words to the 'Dead Horse' song as he walked back down the road to 'Grove House'. Just as he had expected--- his horse 'Jericho' was in the stall and contented to be back at his original home. Sam found a girth on the stall and tied it around his body as if it were a belt. He rode 'Jericho' bareback until he came to Quanky Creek where he stopped to retrieved his saddle from the bushes. He threw the saddle across 'Jericho's' back and tied the leather strap to the saddle, mounted his horse and continued on this way home. He knew his uncle would get enough money from his work to go to Dudley's before he came home. But------ 'some time a man just ain't got a choice'.

As he rode to the yard at his home, Sam saw the familiar Hamilton chaise. Josh, the driver, sat erect waiting for whoever was inside. After riding to the hitching post at the barn, he tied the reins and ran to the chaise, stopping only long enough to ask Josh whom he had brought. When he was told that Josie was inside---he hurried to the house.

Now standing in the doorway, Sam could see Josie sitting at the kitchen table with his mother and she seemed to be giving instructions about the large pile of silk and satin on the table. He noticed Josie's light green dress that hugged her shapely figure. Folded across her arm draped a silk cape of the same color. That must be the latest casual clothes from Charles Town, thought Sam, as he stood for a moment and looked at her. Josie looked beautiful and her blue eyes seemed to hint that she had come to the Pickett house for reasons other than to bring the cloth.

For a brief moment they were aware of no other person in the room--- then both suddenly became conscious of the presence of Sarah Pickett.

"Afternoon, Josie," said Sam, as he walked to the kitchen. "Would you like a cool drink of water?"

"That would be nice. It is hot today," said Josie.

Sam dipped a gourd into the wooden bucket that was on the small table beneath the kitchen window. "I'm sorry we don't have any tea." Sam smiled at Josie as he thought of his visit to her house earlier.

Sam handed the water to Josie. Aunt Jenny came into the kitchen through the back door. Her homespun brown dress was faded from many years of wear. Her small frame was erect. There had been no bending with age. The wrinkles that overlapped smaller wrinkles on her face told her age. Aunt Jenny did not know her age, but she could remember; Sam had traced her memory back beyond seventy years. She could seldom remember what happened the day before but she could describe vividly the days of her youth. She walked to the table and looked at the pile of material.

"Mighty fine---I say---mighty fine cloth." Aunt Jenny touched the cloth as she spoke.

"Mother picked it out when we were in Charles Town," said Josie, smiling at Aunt Jenny.

"You must be a-plannin' a weddin', child. ----Mighty---fine cloth---I say ----mighty fine."

"I hardly think that's in my plans------now." Josie glanced at Sam as she said 'now'.

"Well, I should have the sewing done in about two weeks. I don't have too much work on me now so I can get to it right away," said Sarah Pickett, as she folded the red cloth in her hands.

"As long as it's finished before Willie Jones' wedding---mother wants something new to wear that day. I think I've gone over all that mother told me, so I'd better be getting on home." Josie stood as she spoke.

Aunt Jenny stepped between Josie and the front door.

"No need of hurrin', child. You like kittens, Miss Josie? Sam, why don't you show Miss Josie my new kittens? I put'em in the barn yesterday."

"Would you like to see Aunt Jenny's kittens, Josie?" Sam looked at Sarah Pickett as if he was talking to her.

"I would like that very much, Sam." Aunt Jenny was not to be ignored.

"I always know what the young people like. I was young once myself. Some people don't think so, Miss Josie. Why---when I was to Joseph Montfort's funeral---that sorry Jesse Turner told me that it won't no need for me to go home---beings I was so old."

Aunt Jenny was reluctant to move from Josie's way and wanted to continue the conversation.

"Why that was an awful thing to say, Aunt Jenny," sympathized Josie.

"Well, I say, that Jesse Turner is jist one of that sorry bunch that hangs out at Dudley's Tavern," continued Aunt Jenny.

Sarah Pickett took Aunt Jenny's arm and encouraged her to move from Josie's way.

"I agree with you ---and Sam's been spending too much time in the tavern---but Miss Hamilton needs to be going."

Sam and Josie walked outside and talked as they passed the carriage. Josie looked up and told Josh that they would be back in just a few minutes.

"George told me what happened at the tavern last night. It's just a matter of time before father hears about it, too."

"News travels fast. Jonathan Lawson will pay his debt to me."

They came to the barn and walked inside. The pungent odor of hay and manure permeated the barn. To their right---a basket of kittens nestled on top of a large pile of hay caused them to walk to the corner of the barn. Josie took her cape from her arm and laid it on the hay; then sat down just below the basket. When she was settled, Sam lay on the hay beside her and took a small black kitten from the basket and handed it to Josie.

"Sam, I don't know what Mr. Lawson told you last night that caused you to get so mad, but I can't abide that pretentious man."

"I reacted too quickly, I suppose."

"I'm glad you felt that strongly about us, Sam."

"I haven't told anybody about this, Josie----but someone cut the girth of my saddle before I left Dudley's. I'm sure it was Lawson. He's the only one who would have a reason to do such a thing."

"George didn't tell me about that," said Josie.

"That's not all. When I rode up to Quanky, somebody fired a shot that cause my horse to bolt. I barely made it across Quanky Creek when my saddle slipped and I was thrown to the ground."

"Do you think it was Lawson? He must be mad."

"There's no doubt in my mind. Don't mention this to anyone. I don't want Mama to hear about it. It would cause her to worry and she's got enough to worry about right now. I'll settle with Lawson later."

"Father says he's one of the best swordsmen in New Bern. You must be careful when you're dealing with him."

"Maybe I'll have a chance to work with the soldiers at Camp Quanky and learn to use the sword. Then I'll be ready when the day comes to settle my debt with Lawson."

"I'd better get back to the carriage. I don't know what Josh tells mother." Josie handed the black kitten back to Sam.

"Look, why don't you and George meet me at the common tomorrow. I'm going to town after I sign up with Colonel Long. We can wait for the Congress to adjourn. We might hear some news."

"Will you be staying in Halifax after you join up, Sam?"

"This is just a town militia. We won't have to leave town. Will you and George come to the common tomorrow?"

"I don't think so, Sam. Mother has given us strict orders to stay away from the courthouse. She and father are both so upset about all that's happening." The words that Josie spoke did not seem to reflect the thoughts that lay behind her eyes.

Sam looked at her---so close---so beautiful. He longed to hold her----to protect her---to make her his own. To take her and escape to another time----to another place---so they could share their love without having to be afraid.

Josie's eyes seemed to invite him to that time and place and he moved closer to her. Sam gently took her in his arms and held her close.

"Why are our lives so complicated, Sam? Why aren't things simple for us? I wish we could re-shape these troubled times and make our lives different. It seems that everything is against us."

Josie lifted her head from Sam's shoulder and looked up. There were tears that clouded the blue of her eyes. Sam tenderly brushed the tears away and kissed her waiting lips. The hay beneath them suddenly became a magic carpet that hurled them through space. Josie clung to him as if she were afraid to let go. Spinning from a planet that could not hold them-----defying gravity-----denying the times---forgetting all-----clinging to each other---longing for this moment to last forever but------this new world was short-lived for there was instantaneous realization that they were again two troubled lovers--back on earth

"Miss Josie---Miss Josie----time to be leavin'," came Josh's voice from outside the barn.

"I'm coming, Josh," shouted Josie, as she stood brushing the loose hay from her dress and cape.

They left the barn and talked as they walked to the carriage.

"Josie, try to keep your hopes alive. There'll be a better time for us."

"Things are happening so fast. It's hard to know what to expect from one day to the next. I heard Father tell Mother that we might have to move if things get any worse."

"I wish your folks could understand what is happening."

"I'm sure I, too, do not understand. I suppose it's meant for men to know about these things. I'll never lose hope for us though, Sam."

Josie placed her hand on Sam's arm and stepped up to the carriage.

Sam moved back and watched the chaise turn around in the yard and start for Halifax. Thoughts of the future danced in his head-----uncertain thoughts---lurid by the troubled times.

CHAPTER TEN

Sam ate his lunch early the next day and went to Colonel Long's headquarters at Camp Quanky. After signing to join the militia, he was told to report back at camp when he had completed his duty at the Courthouse. Colonel Long had told him that there were no uniforms to be issued and that he would have to use his own hunting rifle if he wanted a weapon.

It had been hot during the morning and now at mid-day, it was even hotter. As Sam walked his horse from Quanky Road onto King Street, he saw several young boys hurrying by him. All the boys were yelling in unison and Sam kicked his horse to catch up. As he rode by the boys he heard one of them yell---"Flora McDonald----Flora McDonald---she's coming across Quanky Bridge."

He moved quickly ahead of the boys and rode to Martin's Livery. He knew Flora McDonald must have been coming to see about her husband and her son. After tying 'Jericho' to the hitching post, Sam ran across King Street to the town common. He looked to his right and could see that the Congress was still in session. Turning toward King Street, he could hear the shouting of the boys as they came nearer. Immediately behind the boys ran excited men, women and children. As the throng came closer, it grew in numbers and by the time they reached the common it was a huge crowd. Sam noticed Colonel Allen McDonald standing at the window of jail that faced King Street. Evidently McDonald had heard the shouting boys, too, for he was waving to the large black carriage coming down the street.

Realizing that Allen Jones would want to know about Flora McDonald, Sam turned toward the courthouse and could see that the Congress had adjourned. The delegates were leaving for the mid-day recess. He ran across Market Street to the courtyard and approached Allen Jones at the courthouse steps.

"Sir, it's Flora McDonald---she's coming down King Street. I think she's on her way to the courthouse."

Allen Jones noticed the large congregation at the town common.

"Sam, get over to Dudley's and tell him to send a messenger to Colonel Long. Tell Long we want the militia here immediately. We might need them before she leaves town."

Sam moved quickly through the delegates toward Dudley's Tavern. After delivering the message, he rushed back across Market Street and waited in the courtyard. Soon he could see the huge black carriage turn off King Street and come to the front of the courthouse.

There were six men who accompanied Flora McDonald. Four men were on horseback---two rode in front of the carriage and two rode behind the carriage. There was the driver of the carriage and a gentleman inside who sat opposite her.

When the carriage stopped, the gentleman stepped out and held his hand for Flora to step down. She was very beautiful, graceful and elegant-looking---with a perfectly formed oval face and high cheekbones. Her complexion was somewhat pale, but her dark, lovely eyes showed strength and vivacity. Her hair was graying a little but seemed to enhance her appearance. She was dressed in purple which seemed an appropriate color for her, thought Sam. She surveyed the crowd and then looked straight ahead.

The crowd became reverently quiet as Flora McDonald walked toward President Johnston and the other delegates. She couldn't have been mistaken for anybody else. She was the only Flora McDonald. Sam heard that she was middle age --but she looked much younger. She commanded the attention of all who looked upon her. There was silence now as she stood before the President of the Congress.

"Sir, I would consider it a great privilege if you would give me a brief audience regarding the welfare of my husband and son." Flora looked at President Johnston as she spoke and then to several of the other delegates as if she employed their support.

All the delegates turned their attention to President Johnston, who like the rest seemed to be taken by her beauty and charm.

"I have no authority to give any information regarding the welfare of your husband or your son," said Johnston.

"Would it be possible for me to speak with them? I have traveled a great distance in hope that I would at least get this opportunity," said Flora, again looking to the other delegates.

Cornelius Harnett stepped forward.

"Mr. President, I can see no harm that would come from a brief meeting. These Scotch people are not our true enemies."

President Johnston looked to several other delegates. They nodded. He then turned to Flora.

"You shall be escorted to the jail and have one hour to visit with your husband and son. Then you must leave quickly ----so as not to cause any disturbance among the townspeople. Mr. Allen Jones will see to your safety during the time you are visiting your husband and son."

Allen Jones nodded and led Flora McDonald from the courtyard. As they walked down Market Street, many people joined to follow the well-known lady.

Sam felt nervous about the crowd. There were many who hated the prisoners and anybody else who had any regard for their welfare.

While Flora McDonald was visiting with her husband and son, the crowd at the common became loud and began shouting jeers toward the goal. A group of about ten men were more boisterous than any others and seemed ready to storm the jail. This group had started moving toward the jail when Sam noticed Colonel Long and the town militia speeding toward the common. Word had reached Colonel Long in time and upon his arrival, order was quickly restored.

When Flora McDonald had concluded her meeting with her husband and son, the Town Militia escorted her across Quanky Creek.

Sam was among the many who followed her to the edge of town. He was glad he had seen her but felt relieved that she was not staying the night in Halifax. Flora McDonald was a legend among her own people but in Halifax she was not the great heroine of the past. Yet, she was greatly admired and respected---and had been given consideration due a lady of her statue---at least by the members of Congress.

The sun was setting as Sam walked with the crowd back to Halifax. The men, women and children talked excitedly among themselves and all seemed to realize that they had experienced something rare. Something that could be told to later generations----something that was uniquely theirs to share.

When he turned onto Market Street, Sam saw a small group of men outside Dudley's Tavern. Zeb Joyner was in the mist of the men and seemed to be giving instructions. Zeb saw Sam as he approached the gathering.

"Hey, Sam, we're gittin' ready to go over to the jail and serenade Colonel Allen McDonald. I've got this here song that me and the boys are going to sing to him. These fellows have finally got up enough spirit to go over there with me."

"I can see they've got the spirit. Where'd they get if from Dudley's Tavern?"

"Aw, come on Sam. We need a good voice in the crowd," employed Zeb.

"What kind of song you got, Zeb?" Sam was sure it would be good if Zeb had anything to do with it.

"Oh, it's about Flora, Sam. It's good," said one of the cronies.

"I don't know if its safe to be seen with you fellows or not. I think I'll just go along and listen," said Sam as he looked the men over.

"Aw, they'll be alright. That is if they don't git arrested. When they git wound up the way they are now, I'd be afraid to make any promises about what they might do."

Zeb motioned for the men to follow him.

Since Sam was the only one in the group who was completely sober, he decided it would be better if he lingered a little behind the serenaders.

When the group turned right on King Street, several men staggered all the way across the street---then---correcting their course, continued toward the jail.

They stood outside the jail and Zeb began to call. "Hello-----oooooo----oooo. Mr. Colonel Allen McDonald----hello----ooooo."

One of the cronies yelled, "Hey Zeb, do you think that maybe there ain't nobody at home?"

A prisoner inside the jail came to the window.

"You blasted drunks get away from this jail. Colonel Allen is sick with the fever."

"We got somethang to make him feel better. We got a little song we want to dedicate to him. It's about his lovin' little wife----Florie," said one of Zeb's men.

"Colonel McDonald doesn't feel like hearing any song.---GUARD------GUARD-----Where is that blasted guard," yelled the prisoner.

One of the men in Zeb's group began mocking the prisoner.

"Colonel McDonald doesn't feel like hearing any song.---GUARD----GUARD------Where is that blasted guard?"

The cronie continued, "I ain't never heard sech talk. He talks lack some ole maid. I bet if you'd sneak up on him in the dark when he's talkin' to hisself----he'd talk just lack the rest of us. We want to dedicate this song to the whole McDonald clan. Zeb here's done got us some words and we aim to sing it. Is everybody ready?"

"I'm all tuned up," said Zeb.

The men had been taught the refrain and Zed was to put all the words in that came between. Zeb began strumming his guitar and led off with the refrain.

Flora, Flora, you git on home,
And leave our people here alone.
You helped Prince Charlie at Culloden,
To escape the wrath of the government men.
And the tow'r of London could not hold you,
But there's nothing here for you to do.
So, Flora, Flora, you git on home,
And leave our people here alone.

Colonel Allen McDonald is our prisoner now,
And he can't be with you nohow.
At Moore's Creek Bridge, your husband was caught,
By a band of Patriots that he fought.
So, Flora, Flora, you git on home.
And leave our people here alone.
Git back to Scotland until we're through,
And Allen will be kept here safe for you.
So----make your plans and put to sea,
This is not place for a lady to be.
Oh, Flora, Flora, you git on home,
And leave our people here alone.

Some of the members of Harnett's select committee had worked late at the courthouse and had stopped to listen to the song. They only heard about half the song but seemed fascinated with what they had heard.

When the song was finished, Samuel Johnston called to the group.

"Hey, fellow-Patriots. I assume you are all Patriots. You sang that song like you think Colonel Allen McDonald will be with us for a long while. You all must remember that General Donald McDonald and Allen McDonald are not common prisoners of war, and they are to be treated with respect while they are in our custody."

Zeb turned to President Johnston.

"Well, it seems to me that you can't be any more HOSPITAL than to serenade the visitors with an original song. They wouldn't get this kind of entertainment in England."

"Yeah! Ah heard they might even put you in the Tower of London," offered one of the cronies.

"You all know that General McDonald has been given the privilege to walk the streets of Halifax, don't you?" asked Harnett.

"Did you know that the General has refused that privilege," Allen Jones was evidently telling Harnett something that he had not previously known.

"Colonel Allen is sick with the fever and the General probably feels that he needs to stay close by," explained Johnston.

"That was a good song you fellows were singing. Who wrote it," asked Harnett.

"Zeb made it up. He's gifted that way. You ought to hear his DEAD HORSE song," added one of the cronies.

"Well, how about you fellows doing that song about BARBARA ALLEN. That one of my favorites," said Samuel Johnston.

"We don't feel up to no more sangin'," said Zeb. "Seems like some people don't appreciate good music----when they hear it. Come on men let's go back to Dudley's."

They walked at an unsteady pace across the town common toward Dudley's. The men joined in the chorus of FLORA as the delegates watched them meander toward the tavern.

Sam stayed behind and listened to the conversation of the delegates.

"That jail is too crowded for the prisoners," said Samuel Johnston.

"Just the ranking officers are held there ---the rest are at Camp Quanky under guard." Came Allen Jones comment.

"Well, they won't have to stay here too much longer. We're sending them to Philadelphia along with the troops we'll be sending to the Continental Army," informed Samuel Johnston.

"Colonel Allen will have a tough time of it if he doesn't get better. It's a long walk to Philadelphia," added Thomas Burke.

Harnett looked toward the jail.

"These things are to be expected in time such as these. We have to consider the welfare of our fellow-Patriots before we get too concerned with the welfare of the prisoners. Tomorrow the Congress will make a decision that will affect the lives of all the people in this colony. We must consider these things first."

The delegates began to part company and go their separate ways. Sam walked to catch up with Allen Jones.

"Sir, I'll be by Mrs. Eelbeck's tomorrow morning at eight o'clock."

"Fine, Sam. I'll see you then." Allen Jones walked inside Martin's Livery as Sam untied 'Jericho' from the hitching post.

As he mounted his horse, Sam felt that he would soon know what the congress was going to do. He would be inside the courthouse tomorrow to confirm or dispel rumors, speculations, and fear that seemed to cloud his thoughts.----Tomorrow---he would know.

CHAPTER ELEVEN

It was half past eight in the morning and unseasonably hot for the second Friday in April. There was no hint of a breeze and Allen Jones had taken his frocked coat off and now carried it on his arm as he walked at Sam's side. It was only two blocks from Mrs. Eelbeck's Boarding House to the courthouse, so Sam and Allen Jones decided to leave their horses in the stable and walk the short distance.

Sam, dressed in his best clothes, had to walk faster than his usual pace to keep up with the rapid stride of Allen Jones.

"You know, Sam, I'm going to have to give up my work as a delegate to this Congress."

"I know you've got plenty to do at Mount Gallant, Sir."

"I'm not talking about my work there. The Congress yesterday voted to employ a military force for defense against domestic and foreign invaders. I'll just be one of the many delegates who will have to assume military duty. I'll be placed in charge of recruiting and training here in Halifax."

"You said that things were moving fast and we'd know something by the end of the week. Do you think the Congress will take a stand?"

"You know I spoke to you about Harnett's 'select committee'. Well, we met Wednesday night until after midnight. When the committee adjourned Harnett and I worked until early morning, adding and deleting until the "RESOLVES" finally took shape"

"Are you asking for independence, Sir?"

"You'll soon know, Sam. You'll soon know," said Jones as they turned off King Street and walked across Market Street to the courthouse.

"The courthouse has grown small now that all the members are here," continued Jones, as they walked up the steps of the courthouse.

"What do you want me to do, Sir?"

"Sam, you just stand here at the door and when you hear the gavel, don't let anybody in---unless he's a delegate or unless there's an emergency."

Allen Jones hung his coat on a coat rack at the entrance and walked inside. Not knowing what to do, Sam took off his coat and hung it next to Allen Jones' coat.

Sam stood at the door and watched as the wooden tiers on each side of the courtroom were being filled. The delegates were all well-dressed in clothes fitting to their station. Here is where the wealth and the authority of this colony lies, thought Sam, as he sensed an air of excitement that he felt was shared by the delegates. It was as if a strange anticipation of some culminating effort was about to take form and shape.

Directly in front of the President's platform were two rows of wooden benches about thirty-feet long and wide enough for the delegates to sit on with their backs to those sitting behind them. Today they would have to sit close---and the heat would only add to their discomfort. From the President's platform and to the right of the center was where Allen Jones took his seat.

All the windows had been raised to permit any breeze that might bring relief. There were two very large windows on each side of the courtroom and one window on each side of the front door where Sam stood. At the opposite end of the room was the president's platform. Directly behind the platform was a large window. If any breeze came from the Roanoke River, the President would be the first to know it.

Soon all the delegates were in their places and the tall, broad-shouldered Reverend Ford walked to the platform and took a seat. His thick, black hair was the same color as his suit.

Sam recalled the many times he had heard Reverend Ford preach in the small church behind Martin's Livery. They were good sermons but the Reverend had an irritating habit that was bothersome. Each sentence seemed to be punctuated with an 'Ahem'. When Sam was twelve years old, he once counted twenty 'Ahems' during one of Ford's sermons and had been severely reprimanded by Sarah Pickett for keeping count. Perhaps Reverend Ford's greatest contribution to the people was his sincere desire to visit his congregation and serve them in their daily spiritual needs. He was constantly moving among the people and available when needed

Reverend Ford stood before the Congress with outstretched arms. All the delegates responded and stood in silence.

"Almighty God---- 'Ahem'--we come to Thee for spiritual help and guidance. We are experiencing troubled times, Oh God----and we beseech Thee to be our guiding spirit. We have met the enemy and shall continue to fight for the many freedoms we hold to be --God-given. 'Ahem' ---we are cognizant of our weaknesses and know that only through Thy---divine providence shall we endure the many oppressions that we now face. Guide us in our endeavors and we shall give the glory to Thee--Amen"

Well, just two 'Ahems' in the entire prayer----but then it was a short prayer, thought Sam.

"This Congress will now come to order." Johnston pounded the gavel before he continued.

"We will have reports from the several committees that were appointed earlier this week. First, we will hear from the committee regarding certain merchandise that we deem useful to the service of this colony as was exhibited by Mr. John Wright Stanly. Mr. Abner Nash, are you prepared to give your report?"

Abner Nash walked quickly from his seat, which was across the aisle from Allen Jones. He represented the town of New Bern and had been instrumental in the removal of the Royal Governor from the colony. His large, brown eyes surveyed the delegates. He was a handsome man with a somewhat square shaped face, thin lips, and a perfectly formed nose.

"Mr. President, your committee has examined the goods imported by John Wright Stanly of New Bern and we are of the opinion that 500 pounds of gunpowder offered by Mr. Stanly at 4 shillings a pound is, at this time, a reasonable price. The gunpowder along with the other goods amount to 4848 pounds proclamation money which your committee is of the opinion may be allowed and paid for this merchandise on delivery at New Bern."

Samuel Johnston stood.

"We need this powder and merchandise for purposes we will not need to mention. All of you who favor the purchasing of said goods, let it be known by a show of hands."

President Johnston waited for the count.

"It seems that we are in agreement. So let it be purchased,"

As Abner Nash returned to his seat, Sam thought of the great need for gunpowder and how fortunate they were to get it---but wondered how Mr. Stanly would consider payment in proclamation money. Some merchants were beginning to refuse any payment in proclamation money--now that its value was not holding.

President Johnston then proceeded to call for the next committee's report. A certain Joseph Wood and partners had asked the Congress for permission to dispose of the late Royal Governor's effects now that he had left the province. Cornelius Harnett, Chairman of the committee, was asked to make a report.

Harnett's seat was at the front and he only had to stand and turn to face the other delegates.

"Mr. President, I have here a petition of Mr. Joseph Wood and Partners who are requesting the right to dispose of the effects of his Excellency, Josiah Martin, Esquire."

"The Royal Governor himself," came a voice from the back of the courtroom.

"You mean the late Royal Governor. He doesn't have enough power now to rule his horse," added another delegate, in quick response.

Sam joined in the laughter that spread throughout the room.

President Johnston pounded the gavel and the laughter subsided. Harnett continued----"Mr. Wood requests that he and his partners be reimbursed the loss that they have sustained by the capture and detention of their sloop JOSEPH and the cargo on board. It seems that Joseph Wood and his partners had loaded the sloop with goods and merchandise bound for Georgia. This vessel was captured by an armed vessel called GENERAL GAGE and brought to the Cape Fear. The late Governor Josiah Martin did violently seize this vessel and cargo to the use of the enemies of America. Joseph Wood and partners lost 1500 pounds currency money over and above the profits they would have made. You committee feels that Joseph Wood and partners should be allowed to dispose of the late Royal Governor's effects and be justly compensated for their losses."

Sam watched as the Congress concurred with the committee on the proposed resolution by Harnett.

Throughout the day, Sam was continually amazed at the many issues, petitions, and requests that came before the Congress. He was especially impressed by the great facility of the President in his handling of the business. He had never realized that there was so much to be done and now had a new appreciation of the great labor and long hours of preparation required of the delegates.

It was late afternoon before President Johnston heard from the last committee. He stood to introduce the chairman of the committee.

"We have one final committee report from the committee that was to take into consideration the USURPATION AND VIOLENCE ATTEMPTED AND COMMITTED BY THE KING AND PARLIAMENT AGAINST AMERICA. Let me make all of you aware of the grave undertaking of this committee. The resolution that is about to be put before you is by far the most important business that this Congress has yet had for consideration. Let us all be mindful of our responsibility but let us not be reluctant to act on this with resolute determination that what we do is right and just for the future welfare of this colony. Mr. Cornelius Harnett is the chairman of this select committee. Let us now hear the recommendations, Mr. Harnett."

Harnett stood and withdrew a copy of the RESOLVES from inside a large brown envelope; placed the envelope on his seat and held the paper in his right hand.

"Mr. President, your committee is aware of the far reaching consequences of what we are about to propose here and upon careful consideration of the many oppressions that have been forced upon us --- feel that the resolution could not be otherwise stated.

Sam completely forgot his duty at the door and became as involved as any delegate in the room. He listened as Harnett read a list of the many oppressions that had been brought upon the colony. Looking at the delegates' reactions, Sam could see there was awareness for they nodded

First For Freedom

to accent the seriousness of each listing. The mood of the delegates was somber, as Harnett spelled out the abuses with emphasis on those he considered most meaningful. Looking again to the speaker, Sam began to realize that he was witnessing a moment that would forever be as dear to him as life itself. Harnett slowed his words as he terminated his------RESOLVES-----"YOUR COMMITTEE IS OF THE OPINION THAT THE HOUSE SHOULD ENTER INTO THE FOLLOWING RESOLVE, TO WIT; ----THAT THE DELEGATES FROM THIS COLONY IN THE CONTINENTAL CONGRESS BE EMPOWERED TO CONCUR WITH THE DELEGATES OF THE OTHER COLONIES IN DECLARING INDEPENDENCE AND FORMING FOREIGN ALLIANCES, RESERVING TO THIS COLONY, THE SOLE AND EXCLUSIVE RIGHT OF FORMING A CONSTITUION AND LAWS FOR THIS COLONY, AND OF APPOINTING DELEGATES FROM TIME TO TIME-UNDER THE DIRECTION OF THE GENERAL REPRESENTATIVES THEREOF---TO MEET THE DELEGATES OF THE OTHER COLONIES FOR SUCH PURPOSES AS SHALL BE HEREAFTER POINTED OUT."

There were stunned looks on the faces of many delegates while some few quietly smiled and nodded in solemn agreement. The sound of silence was all that was heard for a brief moment.

President Johnston was the first to stir.

"Well, gentlemen, you have heard the resolution of Mr. Harnett's committee. Are there any questions?"

The delegates began to talk among themselves. They turned and seemed to be seeking answers from other nearby delegates. The murmurs swelled into loud conversations and President Johnston pounded the gavel.

"ORDER-----ORDER---We will have order in the courthouse."

As soon as quietness prevailed, a young delegate to Sam's left stood and spoke before he was recognized.

"Mr. President, is THIS COMMITTEE proposing that we declare our independence without knowing what the other colonies plan to do?"

"That's the proposal, as I understand it, " said Johnston, looking toward Harnett who nodded.

"The committee feels that it is time to take a stand. If we are to be the first for Freedom---SO BE IT," said Harnett, quickly following Johnston's statement.

"Suppose the other colonies do not follow the example we so BOLDLY set here today! We can not hope to stand against the British alone," added another delegate, in quick response to Harnett.

"We'll have no more comments unless the chair recognizes the speaker. Mr. Allen Jones, I believe you want to be heard."

Allen Jones stood but did not speak immediately. He looked toward two young delegates on the top row to his right who quickly terminated their conversation.

"There is no time left for waiting. We are the ones who are held responsible for the lives of our people. We can only look to the other colonies for support. From all we hear, other colonies will soon be moving in the same direction. We cannot always wish for our burdens to be lighter---there are times when we must pray for a stronger shoulder. All the colonies need to be preparing for the coming conflict."

Several delegates reacted but their poor efforts were futile as the sound of the gavel quelled any opposition to Jones' statement.

Laying the gavel on the table, Johnston looked intently at the young delegates who were not as convinced as the others.

"Most of us have close associations with many members of the government that supported the late Royal Governor, and we have much to lose if we support these 'Resolves'. However, ----I have a firm belief that unless we do support this resolution----then we stand to lose everything. I can bear the thought of losing my property ---I can bear the thought of losing my money----I can even bear the thought of losing my life. What I cannot bear is the thought of losing my liberty and freedom to determine the future of my children and their issues. In this Congress, you now have the right and the duty to determine what you think is the best course to follow. If you have doubts about this resolution----then let those doubts bet known through your vote. Let me see the hand so those who concur with the proposed RESOLVES."

Sam held his breath as he noticed that some of the younger delegates looked to the older, more experienced members, who held their hands up high. The young delegates were quickly influenced, and their hands went up.

The count of hands was made.

"I see that this Congress is in accord. The vote is unanimous. The RESOLVES are adopted. Since there is no time left for any further business---I declare this congress adjourned."

Even as the gavel sounded, several delegates hurried to Harnett's bench to offer congratulations for the work done by his committee. There was much rejoicing and loud comments by members who felt that the resolution was the thing most wanted and needed by the people they represented.

The men huddled around Harnett were the last ones to leave the courthouse and even as they walked past Sam, they still talked excitedly about what had just happened. When the courthouse was cleared, Sam locked the front door and ran across Market Street to Dudley's Tavern.

News of the HALIFAX RESOLVES had reached Dudley before Sam arrived. Dudley was making the announcement to the people in the crowded tavern when Sam walked through the front doorway.

It was a busy night at Dudley's. Many members of the Congress joined with the regular crowd to celebrate the DECLARATION OF INDEPENDENCE of the North Carolina Colony. There was not a dissenting voice to be heard among the many people---if there was a Tory in the crowd, no one knew it.

Sam knew it would be several days before the news reached all the people in the colony and there was no certainty how well the RESOLVES would be received; if the reaction at Dudley's Tavern was a hint of things to come----there would be no dissent.

Adjourning of the Provinical Congress

April 12, 1776

HALIFAX RESOLVES, April 12, 1776

The feeling of dissatisfaction grew in the colonies, though hope for reconciliation with England continued throughout 1774 and 1775. The Battle of Moores Creek Bridge on February 27, 1776, made many realize the inevitability of independence. North Carolina's fourth Provincial Congress met at Halifax on April 4, 1776, where a committee was appointed to consider the grievances the colonists had against British rule. On April 12 this group submitted a report - the first expression by a colony in favor of full and final separation from Britain - which the Congress adopted. The resolves also recommended that the Continental Congress, as the representative of all the colonies, should declare independence. The date of April 12, 1776, is shown on the North Carolina State Flag.

REFERENCES
Lefler, *North Carolina History Told by Contemporaries.* 103-104.
Lefler and Newsome, *North Carolina,* 204-205.
Hugh F. Rankin, *North Carolina in the American Revolution* (Raleigh: State Department of Archives and History, 1959), 21.
Saunders, *Colonial Records,* X, 512.

North Carolina   In Congress 12th April 1776

The Select Committee to take into Consideration the Usurpations and Violences attempted and Committed by the King and Parliament of Britain against America, and the further Measures to be taken for frustrating the same, and for the better defence of this Province, reported as follows, towit.

    It appears to your Committee that pursuant to the plan concerted by the British Ministry for subjugating America, the King and Parliament of Great Britain have usurped a power over the persons and properties of the people unlimitted and uncontrouled. And disregarding their humble petitions for peace liberty and Safety, have made divers legislative Acts denouncing War, Famine and every Species of Calamity against the Continent in General. That British Fleets and Armies have been and still are daily employed in destroying the people, and committing the most horid devastations on the Country.   That

First For Freedom

That Governors in different Colonies have declared Protection to Slaves who should imbrue their hands in the blood of their masters. —

That the Ships belonging to America are declared prizes of War, and many of them have been violently Seized and Confiscated. —

In Consequence of all which, Multitudes of the people have been destroyed, or from easy Circumstances reduced to the most lamentable distress,

And Whereas the Moderation hitherto Manifested by the united Colonies, and their sincere desire to be reconciled to the Mother Country on Constitutional principles, have procured no Mitigation of the aforesaid Wrongs and Usurpations, and no hopes remain of obtaining redress, by those means alone which have been hitherto tried, Your Committee are of Opinion that the House should enter into the following Resolve,

Resolved that the Delegates for this Colony in the Continental Congress be impowered to concur with the Delegates of the other Colonies in declaring Independency

Maxville Burt Williams

> Independency and forming foreign Alliances — reserving to this Colony, the sole and exclusive right of forming a Constitution and Laws for this Colony, and of appointing Delegates from time to time (under the direction of a General Representation thereof) to meet the Delegates of the other Colonies for such purposes as shall be hereafter pointed out.
>
> The Congress taking the same into Consideration Unanimously Concurred therewith
>
> By order
> Ja^s Green jun Sec^y

NORTH CAROLINA DOCUMENTS, 1584-1868
State Department of Archives and History, Raleigh
FACSIMILE NUMBER VIII

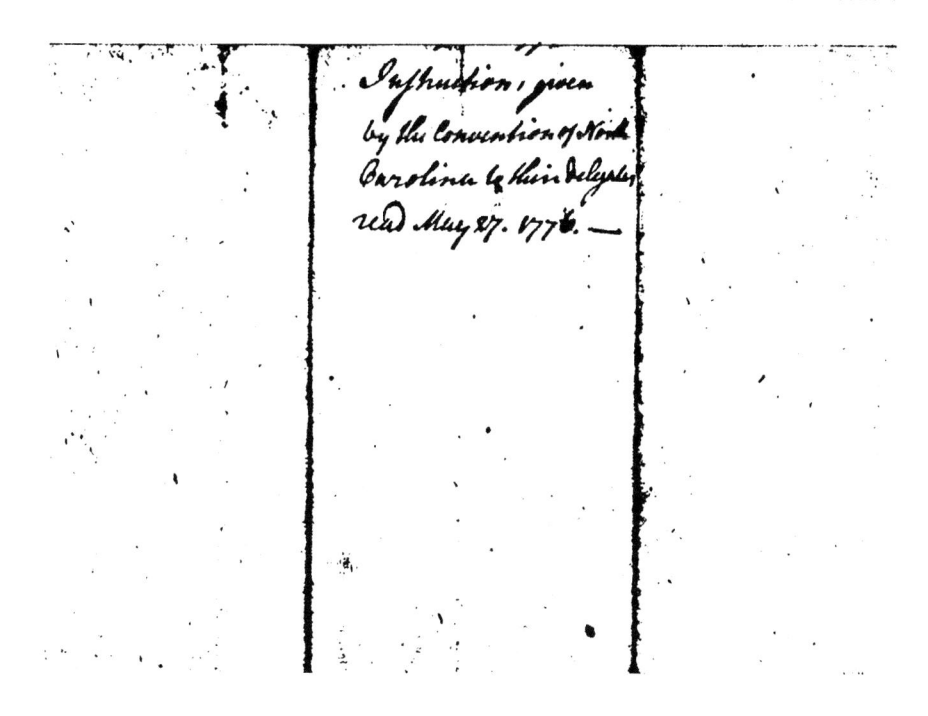

Reproduced from copy in State Archives, State Department of Archives and History, taken from original sent to Continental Congress and in National Archives, Washington, D.C.

HALIFAX RESOLVES, 1776

(Transcription)

North Carolina   In Congress 12th. April 1776

The Select Committee to take into Consideration the Usurpations and Violences attempted and Committed by the King and Parliament of Britain against America, and the further measures to be taken for frustrating the same, and for the better defence of this province, reported as follows, to wit

It appears to your Committee that pursuant to the plan concerted by the British Ministry for subjugating America, the King and Parliament of Great Britain have usurped a power over the persons and properties of the people unlimited and uncontrouled, and disregarding their humble petitions for peace, Liberty and Safety, have made divers Legislative Acts, denouncing War, Famine, and every Species of Calamity, against the Continent in General.

That British Fleets and Armies have been, and still are daily employed in destroying the people, and committing the most horid devastations on the country.

That Governors in different Colonies have declared Protection to slaves who should imbrue their hands in the blood of their masters.

That the Ships belonging to America are declared prizes of War, and many of them have been violently Seized and Confiscated.

In Consequence of all which multitudes of the people have been destroyed, or from easy Circumstances reduced to the most lamentable distress,

And Whereas the Moderation hitherto manifested by the United Colonies, and their sincere desire to be reconciled to the Mother Country on Constitutional principles, have procured no Mitigation of the aforesaid Wrongs and Usurpations, and no hopes remain of obtaining redress, by those means alone which have been hitherto tried, your Committee are of Opinion that the House should enter into the following Resolve.

Resolved, that the Delegates for this Colony in the Continental Congress be impowered to Concur with the Delegates of the other Colonies in declaring Independency and forming foreign alliances—reserving to this Colony, the Sole and Exclusive right of forming a Constitution and Laws for this Colony, and of appointing Delegates from time to time (under the direction of a General representation thereof) to meet the Delegates of the other Colonies for such purposes as shall be hereafter pointed out.

The Congress taking the Same into Consideration unanimously Concurred therewith. By order of

Jas. Green jun Secy.

[Transcription from copy in State Archives.]

CHAPTER TWELVE

Sam took 'Jericho' from inside the rail-fence corral where fifteen horses stood grazing in the shadows of early morning light. He lifted his saddle from the fence and threw it on his horse's back and was tightening the girth when he noticed that General Jones' horse was gone from the hitching post in front of the log cabin that served as headquarters.

The sun had been up for only an hour and about thirty militiamen were just beginning to stir from their small log huts that curved in a semi-circle around the open space in front of General Jones' headquarters. Several naked-to-the waist men stretched and yawned as they walked from their cabins. From where Sam stood, the mess hall was just to the right of headquarters and was the largest log structure at Camp Quanky.

Adjacent the mess cabin was a large brick oven with an iron grate on top for pan cooking. Here a stout, red-faced soldier with a white apron and a pale blue, frayed-sleeved shirt stood over sizzling side meat that filled the dry air with an awakening aroma. Directly behind the cook was a small circular pit lined with large ash-caked rocks centered beneath a five-gallon pot of grits that hung from an iron rod held steady by two sturdy forked limbs.

Sam tied 'Jericho' to the fence and moved along with other militiamen toward the mess cabin.

When he took his wooden plate from the brawny cook, he walked to the large black pot and scooped a cup of grits.

"Hey, 'Shadow', General Jones wants you at the courthouse by ten o'clock. He told me to remind you," said the cook, as he flipped the shrinking side meat on to Sam's wooden plate.

Sam looked to the cook and nodded, acknowledging that he understood. He then went and sat straddle a large log to eat his food.

The nickname 'Shadow' had become second nature to him since General Jones has assumed command of the militiamen. Nicholas Long now served as quartermaster and Sam served as General Jones' aide-in-camp.

Sam did not especially like what he was called by the other men, but the soldiers amused themselves with the name, which implied that the General and he were inseparable. There had been something special about his relationship with Allen Jones before the militia was called to Camp Quanky that became stronger now that the General depended on him.

Reading dispatches and keeping the General abreast of all the latest news caused Sam to feel an intimate part of the command at Camp Quanky.

He was required to be in attendance at important meetings and to take down whatever needed to be recorded. General Jones would signal with a nod whenever notes were to be made at the meetings. It was seldom that Sam was not at the side of his General. Even some of the soldiers at camp would seek advice from him and often times he was able to supply the necessary information without having to consult his commander.

Swinging his right leg across the log, Sam stood and walked back to the cook with his clean, wooden, plate. As he walked past several soldiers converged around the black pot dipping second helpings of grits, he overheard a young recruit say, "I had some grits in that last helpin' and I just wonder if there's any such thing as grits without any grits?"

Sam slapped the young soldier on the shoulder.

"You must have got the grits on top. They're the ones that's gritty. Next time don't be so all-fired fast. You new recruits have to learn everything the hard way."

There was a whisper among the soldiers and they all laughed as Sam walked to his horse. He knew he had just been made the target of the new recruit's wit. It did not matter---the men at Quanky made fun of anything or anybody. This sort of thing was what made life easier at camp. The soldiers always seemed to have some scheme or prank contrived for the new recruits. Those young men who first became acquainted with soldiering were objects of well-laid plans of the more seasoned militiamen. Some young men learned faster than others and Sam felt that he had just encountered one of the quicker recruits at Camp Quanky.

Mounting his horse, Sam turned away from the rail fence toward Quanky Road. He felt the intense heat beat down from the brilliant sun. Even though it was only eight o'clock, it was already too hot to hurry his horse. So, 'Jericho' moved at his own pace along a road laden with silty dust made fine by the wheels of wagons and the hooves of horses. Each clopping step stirred small clouds of dust that slowly settled back to the earth from the air that was too thin to hold it. It had been hot and dry for three weeks and Sam could remember only one good rain since the adjournment of the Congress back in mid-May, some nine weeks ago. Now on July, the twenty-second, the governing body of North Carolina had come again to Halifax.

As he turned off Quanky Road onto King Street, Sam considered how fortunate he was to have been present at the meetings of the Congress. After the official act for independence proclaimed in the Halifax Resolves, the Congress was faced with many problems. The colony had to be prepared for war, a standing army had to be raised and trained, a sound money system had to be established and money had to be borrowed in order to finance the war.

When the Congress neared its final days, it became evident that a temporary from of government had to be formed. So, a committee was appointed and later brought forth a resolution for the new government. The delegates promptly adopted the resolution and the new government was called the 'Council of Safety'. Sam recalled how pleased all the delegates had been when Cornelius Harnett accepted the Presidency of this new government.

Sam thought of the letter that General Jones had shown him the previous day. Cornelius Harnett had written much about the recent sessions of the Council. The meetings at Wilmington had been concerned with hostile Indians west of the colony, Tories throughout, Sir Henry Clinton on the coast with armed British troops, and general unrest among the people.

Looking to his right at the large white home of John Hamilton, reminded Sam of the disturbing part of Harnett's letter that told how the Council had directed all the county committees to require all suspected persons to give inventories of their estates. The commanding officer of each town was ordered to arrest all who refused to take the 'Oath of Loyalty' and to bring them before the Council for trial. John Hamilton had not taken any such oath---nor had any oath been presented him. Hamilton would soon have to take the oath---now that the Council of Safety was in Halifax.

Sam taxed his memory and tried to recall all the members of the Council who were elected at the last meeting of the Congress. There was Harnett, of course, who would be ably assisted by Samuel Ashe of Wilmington, -----Thomas Jones and Whitmel Hill of Edenton, James Coor and John Simpson of New Bern,--- Thomas Eaton and Joseph John Williams of Halifax, ---Thomas Person and John Rand of Hillborough, and there was Hezekiah Alexander and William Sharp of Salisbury. Sam thought back over the names and was not sure he had remembered all of them. After all, it had been over two months and names like Hezekiah and Whitmel weren't the easiest names to recall.

As Sam was tying his horse up at Martin's Livery, he looked down King Street toward the Roanoke and saw John Hamilton standing in front of his store. Upon seeing Sam, Hamilton turned quickly and went inside. All along King and Market, the stores were coming to life. Shutters were being tied back and bright sunlight penetrated the small windows and fell on the many articles and wares now available for purchasing.

Walking across King, Sam saw General Jones coming from Dudley's Tavern. He hurried his steps and caught up with the General in the courtyard.

"General Jones, I thought you said the meeting was at ten o'clock."

General Jones turned and said, "Oh, Sam I thought I'd go on over and unlock the doors. Some of the members will come early. I've never known Harnett to be late for a meeting. You come on with me. We need to raise the windows. The courthouse needs to be aired out before we begin."

"You want me to stand at the door the same as I did when the Congress was in session?"

"Just for today, Sam. I'll send someone else tomorrow."

Soon Sam and Allen Jones were moving about inside the courthouse. Sam raised the windows and General Jones moved the podium to the center of the President's platform. A brisk breeze swept through the courthouse when Sam raised the large window behind the platform. The musty air that had been accumulating for several weeks moved slowly out through the open windows.

When everything seemed to be in order, they walked to the entrance. General Jones instructed Sam how he was to greet each member and gave some well-chosen words of praise that were to be said to Cornelius Harnett. As Sam was acknowledging his instructions, Cornelius Harnett walked through the front entrance. General Jones met him before Sam had a chance to offer any welcome. Sam knew there was a sincere mutual admiration shared by these two gentlemen that was not common among the other leaders. There seemed a sense of knowing what thoughts ran through each other's mind---these two had dwelt for many long, long hours on matters that had caused them to wield such an understanding of each other.

General Jones turned to Sam.

"I've asked Sam Pickett to stand at the door today. I'll send you a guard tomorrow who'll stay here for the duration of your meetings. I'll be needing Sam at Camp Quanky. We're getting more recruits and the new men need to be prepared for the training program."

Harnett extended his hand.

"I remember you, Sam. I'm happy to see you again."

General Jones and Harnett walked toward the President's platform.

"Thank you, Sir." Sam was left talking to himself.

"Who is this John Hamilton? I had a letter from him about two weeks ago," Harnett said as they walked away.

Sam strained to hear what the General said but they were too far from him for the words to be audible.

Soon all the members arrived and Sam welcomed each one at the door. After some heavy backslapping and hearty greetings, Harnett moved to the chair, previously occupied by Samuel Johnston.

Sam watched as Harnett pounded the gavel, and thought of the great authority vested in these few men. They shared all those essential powers that had previously been embodied in the Congress. This Council of Safety was now the governing body of the independent colony of North Carolina. Harnett looked tired. These continuous meetings of the Council were beginning to sap the energy of its President.

Harnett put the gavel aside.

"Gentlemen, I have taken the liberty to ask General Allen Jones to come to our meeting today. Since he is now in charge of the militia in Halifax, I feel that we will be working closely with him during our stay here. There is also an item of business on the agenda today that the General will need to consider. Would you like to say anything to the Council before we begin, General Jones?"

General Jones stood and faced the group of men.

"I would to welcome all of you to Halifax. I'll be at Camp Quanky while the Council is in session and will be available any time you need me. If I can be of service, just leave word at Dudley's Tavern. I get my mail there each morning."

"We are happy to know that you'll by close by," said Harnett.

He then turned to the members of the Council.

"Gentlemen, I too, would like to welcome you here. I hope all of you had a pleasant trip to Halifax. I know these meetings are a hardship on all of you and I would personally like to commend you for your promptness and faithful service to this body.

On my way to Halifax, I had the opportunity to evaluate the effect that the RESOLVES OF COUNCIL AGAINST THE TORIES has had on the people. During my trip, I talked with people and I am convinced that we have struck a severe blow to the Tories since we have required that they pledge their property or their lives for the cause of America. It is a bitter dose for the Tories to have to take the 'Oath of Loyalty', but we must know where these people stand. I think it has been most effective."

"Especially since the word was being spread along with the news that Clinton has been defeated at Charles Town," added John Rand, enthusiastically.

"I just know we can justify what we have required of the Tories---but you know, it does not set too well with me that a man's property and possessions be taken in the name of liberty," said Joseph John Williams, who did not seem as convinced as Harnett and Rand.

Samuel Ashe turned quickly toward Williams.

"You must remember, John, that what we do is for the freedom and the rights of all mankind. These measures are indeed severe, but the times we are experiencing are troubled times and severe measures are necessary."

"I, too, admit that I have had misgivings about the 'Resolves in Council', but I stand with Mr. Ashe in the right to do it because of the state of emergency that now exists in this colony," added Harnett.

Just as Harnett finished his comment, a loud knock was heard at the door. Sam had just sat down but now jumped from his seat and opened the door.

A young Continental stood in the doorway. Sam could tell by the uniform that he was not a local soldier.

"I need to see the President of this body."

Sam pointed toward Harnett and the soldier moved quickly toward the platform. The young soldier walked past him as quickly as he had entered.

Sam and all the members of the Council watched as the young man spoke to Harnett in confidence and handed him a large scroll and a brown envelope.

Harnett began to open the large envelope. There was a strange expression on his face as he spoke.

"Gentlemen, I beg your indulgence---."

He silently read the contents of the envelope.

There was a hushed silence in the courthouse as Harnett's face registered deep emotion. He looked out at the group and then spoke so loud the other men were caught up in the excitement of his words.

"Gentlemen, the Continental Congress of the United Colonies has adopted a Declaration of Independence. As of July 4, these colonies have been free and independent States of America."

"We stand united now," shouted Thomas Person.

"And we were the first to propose it. Right here in this courthouse," added James Coor, in a voice loud enough to be heard across the street.

The members of the Council stood and walked to the President's platform. There was no order in the courthouse. All the members were eager to see what had been delivered to the President.

"It needs to be proclaimed throughout this province," said Thomas Eaton, as he approached the platform.

"In the most public way possible," added Whitmel Hill, closely following Eaton in words of support.

Sam watched with interest as Harnett untied the scroll and held it up for all to see. He then passed it to Hezekiah Alexander.

"All the committees throughout the colony, or in the state, should get a copy of this as soon as it can be printed," said Alexander, as he held the document high enough for all to see.

"How should it be proclaimed and where would be the most appropriate place," asked Harnett, as he watched the scroll being passed around.

"Since this is the first place it is to be revealed in this province, we must set the example for all the other towns in this province. Good notice should be sent out in advance to the people. They will need time to prepare for such an occasion," suggested Samuel Ashe.

"We'll erect a platform right here in front of the courthouse," said William Sharp.

"I have soldiers who are excellent carpenters. Leave the platform to me," demanded Allen Jones.

"We are being carried away from any kind of procedure," said Harnett, realizing that everybody was talking and nobody was listening. "Will one of you make a proposal to the chair? We need to be getting back to order. You'll have time to read the 'Declaration' after the meeting."

All the members returned to his seat and Samuel Ashe stood to make the proposal.

"Mr. President, I propose that since the Continental Congress of these thirteen colonies has on the Fourth of July declared that these states of America are free and independent---that we here resolve that the committees of the respective towns and counties of this state upon receiving said 'Declaration' ---do cause the same to be proclaimed in the most public manner----in order that the good people of this state may fully understand and be informed."

"We need to set the example here in Halifax," added Thomas Eaton.

"Mr. President, I propose that we set aside Thursday, the first day of August for proclaiming the 'Declaration' at the courthouse in the town of Halifax and that all free holders and inhabitants of this county be requested to give their attendance. The time for the proclamation should be midday- so that the people will have time to get here and the place should be in front of the courthouse," suggested Joseph John Williams.

"I am overwhelmed by this news. I completely forgot to ask for a vote on Mr. Ashe's proposal. However, I will ask you now if this is in agreement with all of you. Let me see the hands of those who favor both of these proposals," said Harnett.

Harnett counted the hands. The vote was unanimous.

"I would like to propose that the honor of making the proclamation be given to our President---Cornelius Harnett," offered John Simpson.

"I am thankful that I have been allowed to be a part of this great fight for independence. Let me see the hands of you who favor that I do it in the manner that has been suggested." Harnett counted the hands and the vote was again unanimous. "So shall it be done!"

There was a brief pause as Harnett looked at some papers on his desk. Selecting a letter from the papers Harnett continued.

"Gentlemen, if we are done with this business, there is a matter that needs the attention of this Council." Harnett opened the letter. "A Mr. John Hamilton has asked that he be allowed to come before the Council and is suppose to be waiting outside our door. I would like for the Council to give audience to this gentleman from Halifax. Sam, will you ask him to come in?"

Sam, pulled the door open and the prompt John Hamilton came inside, took off his cocked hat, cast a reticent look at Sam and then walked quickly to the President's platform. He looked as distinguished as any member of the Council.

Hamilton stood erect with his cocked hat under his right arm.

"Please be seated Mr. Hamilton," said Harnett, indicating a chair to his right. "I have told the Council that you wish to be heard and we are now prepared to listen."

John Hamilton sat facing the members of the Council. The chair he occupied was situated between Harnett and the other members of the Council. And he had only to turn his head when speaking to the President.

"Gentlemen, as some of you know, I recently made a trip to Charles Town to buy goods and merchandise for my company."

Joseph John Williams suddenly interrupted Hamilton.

"Mr. President, Mr. Hamilton lives in our town and is well regarded by the people here. We all have hopes that your company will thrive for we are in need of your merchandise now more than ever."

"Thank you, Sir," continued Hamilton. "When I left Charles Town, I ordered all my goods to be shipped to New Bern to my warehouse. I have planned to move my merchandise by wagon to Halifax. I have recently been informed that all my merchandise has arrived at New Bern. The sloop, WILLIAM, that brought my cargo was seized and condemned. I have come to this Council to ask that my property be released, so that I may bring it here."

"There was a committee appointed to consider this incident but I fail to remember a report. Can anyone answer the question as to the reason these goods were seized? Mr. Simpson, you represent the town of New Bern, what do you know of this matter," questioned Harnett.

"I have information that the cargo belonged to a Tory merchant of Halifax and the order was given that the goods be seized and held," replied Simpson.

"How do you regard yourself in this conflict, Mr. Hamilton?" Harnett seemed surprised by what Simpson had said.

"Sir, I am a loyal subject of King George III. I have no part in this conflict. I request the release of my cargo---as an individual citizen whose rights to his property have been violated."

"You do realize that this country is officially at war with England, do you not, Mr. Hamilton," continued Harnett.

"I am aware of no such action. I have heard no news of war. Where do you hear such fulminations," asked the indignant Hamilton.

"The news shall be publicly proclaimed before the courthouse on August first. We have just received the news this morning. This nation has officially moved for independence," added Joseph John Williams.

"I can be no part of any action against the King," said Hamilton, his head now lowered.

"We are all freedom-loving people. We were in hopes that you would join our cause," said Harnett.

John Hamilton stood.

"Gentlemen, I suggest that if it's freedom you love so dearly---then give me my freedom to choose the form of government to which I must be loyal. I support the King and feel that I have a right to make such a choice. You men here are offering yourselves as the governing body of this colony or nothing---I regard this as nothing less than tyranny."

The men were so shocked by this statement, they had to be quietened by the pounding of the gavel. Harnett then leaned across his desk and looked down at John Hamilton.

"Then, your position is clear to us. The Council will consider your request and you will be informed. However, if it is determined that you cannot support our cause, you will be considered an enemy of America and treated as such. Do you understand?"

"I do, Sir," said Hamilton, trying to remain calm.

"Then you are dismissed from this Council." Harnett stood as he spoke.

The other members stood and John Hamilton turned toward them.

"I did not know what to expect when I entered this room, gentlemen----and I still do not know what you shall determine about my goods. I do thank you for your time and for this audience."

Hamilton then walked quickly to the front of the Courthouse and did not, in any way, acknowledge Sam's presence as he walked out.

When Sam closed the door, Joseph John Williams stood to be heard.

"Mr. President, I would like to mention that Mr. Hamilton has been approached on several occasions at his home by men of influence here in Halifax and as of this time, he has not consented to join us. When I saw him enter a while ago. I thought perhaps he had changed his mind."

Thomas Eaton stood.

"Willie Jones and I have been to his home to try to sway him from his position. We continually met with failure to influence him. He is---without any doubt---a loyal subject to the King."

"He will now have to rechart his course. Let us hope he will join us," said Harnett.

"He will never come over to our way of thinking, I'm sure of that," assured Allen Jones.

"Then, you will send the 'Orders' forth to him and we'll see if he signs the 'Oath of Loyalty'. He will be treated as any other Tory. He needs to be carefully watched." Harnett spoke with resolute determination.

"It is a great loss when a man of his statue and influence is not with us," commented Thomas Eaton.

"A man of great influence needs to be handled in a special way. General Jones and I will consider what needs to be done with John Hamilton," added Harnett.

"I always like to know where these people stand. I feel a compassion for all who are honest in their beliefs---even though they may differ from mine," remarked Thomas Jones.

Thomas Person was quick to react to Jones' statement. "I have seen the time when I differed with you , Thomas----and I fail to recall ever noticing that particular trait in you."

The members of the Council laughed as Harnett pounded the gavel for the noon recess.

CHAPTER THIRTEEN

Sam had not been to the Hamilton home since his fight with Lawson but felt that maybe Josie and George would be at the common for the Proclamation of the 'Declaration of Independence'. John Hamilton had make it clear that Sam was no longer welcomed, so he had only seen Josie accidentally on occasions. He felt a strong need now to see her and her family and to try to convince them that there was virtually no time left for them to take the 'Oath of Loyalty'. John Hamilton's attitude toward him had grown increasingly bitter since the meeting of the 'Council of Safety'.

Sam and all the other soldiers were given orders by General Jones to take part in the parade that was to escort the 'Council of Safety' through the streets of Halifax. So two days before the big parade, the soldiers practiced marching and soon the militia looked as if they were well enough organized for their coming performance.

The day for proclaiming the 'Declaration of Independence' soon arrived. At noon, the militia paraded through the streets with the Council of Safety following close behind them. The soldiers were ill clad but it was very evident that they were proud to be serving under General Allen Jones. Drums were beating, flags were flying, and the people were cheering as the militia and the Council passed. From King Street, the parade turned left at the town common onto Market Street and was soon at the platform in front of the courthouse.

The sun was bright and it was a glorious day. A large crowd had congregated by the time the Council arrived at the courthouse. As the huge crowd from the town common began to overflow, the people moved closer to the platform.

There was a great cheer as the members ascended the platform. When all were seated, Cornelius Harnett stood and another great cheer came from the excited crowd. Harnett began to open the scroll and raised his hands. Calmness settled over the huge crowd. He was the smallest man on the platform, but Sam knew that there was more to greatness than statue; greatness involved character, and the small man who stood before them exemplified that radiant quality.

Harnett began his presentation. "Good people of this independent state of North Carolina---"

There was rejoicing again and Harnett again raised his hands. "I come before you today to read this unanimous DECLARATION OF THE THIRTEEN UNITED STATES OF AMERICA.

The crowd was totally silent.

"WHEN IN THE COURSE OF HUMAN EVENTS, IT BECOMES NECESSARY FOR ONE PEOPLE TO DISSOLVE THE POLITICAL BANDS WHICH CONNECT THEM WITH ANOTHER AND TO ASSUME AMONG THE POWERS OF THE EARTH, THE SEPARATE AND EQUAL STATION TO WHICH THE LAWS OF NATURE'S GOD ENTITLE THEM, A DECENT RESPECT TO THE OPINIONS OF MANKIND REQUIRES THAT THEY SHOULD DECLARE THE CAUSES WHICH IMPEL THEM TO THE SEPARATION.

WE HOLD THESE TRUTHS TO BE SELF-EVIDENT--THAT ALL MEN ARE CREATED EQUAL; THAT THEY ARE ENDOWED BY THEIR CREATOR WITH CERTAIN UNALIENABLE RIGHTS; THAT AMONG THESE ARE LIFE, LIBERTY, AND THE PURSUIT OF HAPPINESS."

Two soldiers in faded uniforms stood to the right side of the platform and Sam and another soldier similarly clad stood to the left. Sam listened to every word read by Cornelius Harnett as he looked at the hushed crowd. He looked among the many faces for Josie. She was nowhere to be seen. Women with broad hats and silk dresses----men with white stocking, knee britches, buckled shoes, and cocked hats---members of the gentry, by right, stood closer to the platform.

Behind and to the side of the gentry were the country folk dressed in rough smocks and homemade garments. Merchants, barristers, tradesmen, farmers, housewives, nurses, manservants and children filled the dusty streets. There were fathers and mothers who held their children's hands and young lovers who found an excuse to stand close. There were children without parents and parents without children. There was hope and faith in those faces---each had behind it----a conscience of its own. Each conscience had a desire for all that was good in life. Some looked as if they were confident enough to conquer the world, and others looked at Harnett as if they did not understand all the big words----and yet even these people seemed to accept the fact that these words held great meaning. Some children played at their parents' feet and were not aware that they were witnessing an event that would change their future and future of their children's children.

Sam looked from the crowd to the face of Cornelius Harnett. His voice boomed loud enough for the people on King Street to hear.

"AND, FOR THE SUPPORT OF THIS DECLARATION, WITH THE FIRM RELIANCE ON THE PROTECTION OF DIVINE PROVIDENCE, WE MUTUALLY PLEDGE TO EACH OTHER OUR LIVES, OUR

FORTUNES, AND OUR SACRED HONOR. The signers from this state were: William Hooper, Joseph Hewes, and John Penn."

As Harnett read the names of the signers, a great shout went up from the crowd. Cannons were heard in the distance from Fort Quanky and the Roanoke River.

Sam and the three other soldiers quickly moved from their places and rushed to the platform. They lifted Harnett from the platform, lifted him to their shoulders and paraded him down Market Street. From Market Street, the soldiers turned right onto King Street parading their champion as the crowd began to flow in the same direction. When the soldiers reached Pittsylvania Avenue, they turned back. Several soldiers made way for the paraders, and the crowd in the street separated. When they arrived at the courthouse, the soldiers let Harnett down. He walked onto the platform and waved to the enthusiastic crowd, as the other delegates stood in front of the platform and followed his example.

There had never been such a parade as this in Halifax. It was a day that would long be remembered. It was the day the colony became a state. It was the day that began the long, hard fight for freedom---now the states were united.

It was late afternoon when Sam and the militia returned to Camp Quanky. The people were still celebrating throughout the town---so the militia was quickly given orders to patrol the street to see that order was maintained.

The sun was setting as Sam and three soldiers walked toward Dudley's Tavern. The soldiers mingled with the people along Market Street, and Sam walked inside the tavern. He saw Zeb Joyner sitting at the bar strumming his guitar. One of the men yelled from the back of the room. "Come on wid the song, Zeb. You said you'd have something special for us tonight."

Sam stood at the door and watched. He knew he was about to witness one of Zeb's original songs.

Zeb looked at the crowd and when he had their attention he spoke about all that had happened at the courthouse. "You all know that some special things have happened here in this town today. Well, I've got most of if down on paper. So now I'm gonna tell y'all what it's all about. "

Zeb strummed softly on his guitar as he began his song:
WE HAVE THE RIGHT TO FIGHT FOR OUR FREEDOM
NOW WE MUST FIRMLY TAKE OUR STAND
AND HAVE FAITH AND HOPE IN OUR FUTURE
IN THIS FREEDOM LOVING LAND
WE SHALL BE FREE, WE SHALL BE FREE

IN THE FUTURE YOU WILL SEE--WE SHALL BE FREE
WE HAVE THE GOD -GIVEN RIGHT TO WORSHIP
HOWEVER, WE MAY SEE FIT
AND WE'LL FIGHT FOR THAT RIGHT, IF WE HAVE TO
AND, BY GEORGE, WE'LL MAKE THE MOST OF IT.
WE SHALL BE FREE, WE SHALL BE FREE
IN THE FUTURE YOU WILL SEE, WE SHALL BE FREE
WE SHALL NOT BE DISMAYED BY FAILURE
AND WE'LL WITHSTAND ALL THE PAIN
THEN WE'LL WIN THE COMING BATTLE
FOR WE SHALL RISE TO FIGHT AGAIN
WE SHALL BE FREE, WE SHALL BE FREE
IN THE FUTURE YOU WILL SEE, WE SHALL BE FREE
WE CANNOT ENDURE THIS OPPRESSION
FOR IN THIS LAND WE MUST BE FREE
TO SHAPE THE LIVES OF OUR LOVED ONES
AND CONTROL THEIR DESTINY
WE SHALL BE FREE, WE SHALL BE FREE
IN THE FUTURE YOU WILL SEE, WE SHALL BE FREE
WE SHALL NOT HATE THE LAND OF ENGLAND
FOR THE ACTS OF KING AND PARLIAMENT
BUT, WE SHALL PART FROM THE REALM
TO FORM OUR OWN GOVERNMENT
WE SHALL BE FREE, WE SHALL BE FREE
IN THE FUTURE YOU WILL SEE, WE SHALL BE FREE.

The tavern was quiet. Sam had not heard such silence since the Montfort funeral. Then, the silence was broken as the cronies lifted Zeb and sat him on the bar.

Sam backed out of the tavern. There was nothing left that he could say to Dudley----Zeb had said it all and much better. That Zeb Joyner could make up a song faster than most people could sing one. As Sam walked down Market Street, he thought how unfair it was for any one man to be so talented.

There were fires burning throughout the town. Sam and the other soldiers had been told that some of the people would use this time as an excuse to destroy property and otherwise take advantage of the total confusion. So they moved among the people and issued warnings to those who were too disorderly. It was a chaotic night filled with excitement and trouble.

Around midnight, Sam and the soldiers returned to Camp Quanky. There were many people throughout the colony who would now have to take sides. The Hamiltons would have to make a choice and Josie----what would happen to her?

This new feeling of freedom bothered Sam because he knew there would be no freedom until the war was won----and the struggle was just beginning.

CHAPTER FOURTEEN

Sam had been excited and concerned about all that had been happening in Halifax. With the passing of the HALIFAX RESOLVES and the acceptance of the DECLARATION OF INDEPENDENCE, he now felt the people would be united.

He had been at Camp Quanky for over a month and his training had caused him to develop many new skills as a soldier. He was especially proud to be regarded as one of the better swordsmen in camp. Because of his many skills, General Allen Jones had placed him in charge of the training program. Working with the new recruits took up most of his time and he saw less and less of Josie, but thought about her more and more. It was so seldom that he saw her----his longing for her caused him to think thoughts that were not rational. He had considered even going directly to the Hamiltons and confronting John Hamilton---to settle their differences and ask Joise to leave the family. She could stay at his home and leave the Hamiltons to their chosen fate. Why should she have to suffer for her father's stubbornness?

Sam was training five recruits to use the sword when he was told to report to General Jones' headquarters. The General felt that there would be much close fighting before the war was over and wanted all the soldiers to able to defend themselves. He often said that close fighting was what won the battle.

Walking from the edge of the camp, Sam wondered why he had been summoned. After passing several log huts, he saw General Jones seated at a small table in front of his cabin. His black, cocked hat and dark blue officer's coat made him look like a professional soldier. Most of the regulars in camp still wore the clothes they had brought from home----only the officers had clothes that vaguely resembled anything military. General Jones could afford better clothes than the soldiers and had used his own money to get his outfit made.

As Sam approached the General, he thought how dedicated Allen Jones had become to the war effort. Since he had assumed command of the militia in Halifax, he had to stay away from his plantation in Northampton and Sam knew how devoted Allen Jones was to Mount Gallant.

General Jones looked intensely at a paper he held in his hand and did not see Sam standing before him.

""You send for me, Sir?"

"Oh, Sam---I've been waiting for you." He held the paper up as he spoke.

First For Freedom

"I have here a list of all he families in our area who might still be loyal to England. We are about to check on all these people and take whatever might be of use to us. The Council of Safety feels that these people have had ample time to sign the 'Oath of Loyalty'. There are some living here in Halifax who have been reluctant to sign. I understand that the Miller gentleman has left town. I called you here to get some information about John Hamilton."

"Yes Sir." Sam spoke guardedly, feeling a quickening of his heartbeat as he realized why he had been called to headquarters.

"You and I both know what he told the Council of Safety---do you know if he's willing to sign the 'Oath'?"

"I doubt if John Hamilton will sign any such oath, Sir."

"Well, the whole family will be informed and they will have to answer to the Council of Safety. I hate to do this, Sam, but I have to carry out orders, just like the rest of you soldiers."

"That means that all their property will be taken," added Sam.

"They will be treated the same as all other Tories. They would have been allowed to take some of their possessions if they hadn't waited so long. Hamilton now knows that they are subject to be investigated. Harnett made that clear."

"Do you think he still hopes for a reconciliation with England," asked Sam.

"That's out of the question, now. They'll be made aware of this predicament in the morning."

"How much time will they be given to sign the 'Oath'?"

"They've had time enough, Sam."

"Does the order call for the arrest of the whole family?"

"It say here the John Hamilton Family." Allen Jones looked again at the paper in his hand.

"It also states that no interested person should be given the right to present orders to the suspected family."

"Well, that leaves me out. You know, I'm interested in this family's welfare."

"I am very aware of that fact, Sam. That's the reason I called you here. I want you to understand---that the family may be made aware that the 'Orders' are to be presented to them tomorrow."

"I understand, Sir," said Sam, almost too low for the General to hear.

"Sam, I wanted you to hear this from me. I know everybody in Halifax will know about it tomorrow---and sometimes the facts get lost when people start talking."

"I appreciate you telling me, Sir."

"You've done well here at Camp Quanky, Sam. Why don't you take some time from your duties and see what you can to do to encourage the Hamiltons to leave town before they are arrested. I'll send for you when I want you back in camp."

"I'll be ready whenever you need me, Sir. I know mama will be grateful. Uncle John has a way of getting around the work that needs to be done on the farm." Said Sam as he turned to walk away.

It was late that afternoon when Sam rode down King Street and crossed Quanky Creek. He walked his horse. He needed time to think.

He recalled the words that Cornelius Harnett had spoken to John Hamilton. Tories throughout the state were being arrested and Josie understood little of all that was happening. She too, would be arrested--- she too---would be treated as severely as the rest of the family. Thinking of these things, Sam suddenly realized that he and General Jones were the only two in Halifax who knew the Hamiltons would be arrested. What would happen if the family left town during the night---other Tories had moved away and little had been done to pursue them.

When he arrived at his home, Sam took his horse to the stable but did not take off the saddle. He had decided he would be riding to the Hamilton's later that night.

As he walked through the front doorway, Sam saw his mother and Aunt Jenny at the table eating supper. Sarah Pickett stood when Sam walked into the room.

"Sam, what are you doing home? Is anything wrong?"

"No, nothing's wrong. Where's Uncle John?" Sam looked toward the empty chair at the table.

"He's gone to town. Come on and git something to eat. " Sarah Pickett pushed a chair back from the table as she spoke.

During the meal, Aunt Jenny asked him many questions about Camp Quanky and General Jones. He told her enough to satisfy her curiosity and soon Aunt Jenny left the table to go outside. Sarah Pickett sensed that something was wrong and waited until Aunt Jenny was gone before she spoke.

"What's ailin' you, Sam?"

"Mama, everything is going wrong. The Hamiltons are going to be arrested in the morning and they don't even know it."

"I thought you were getting too close to that family."

"It just don't seem right. Not George and Josie. I can understand why they would want John Hamilton--but not--George and Josie."

"Well, it's not for you to decide, Sam. Why don't you go on out to the barn and 'feed-up'. Your work will take your mind off what's bothering you."

Sam got up from the table and walked to the barn. He fed the cow and two mules, then loosened the girth around 'Jericho's' belly and gave him six ears of corn and some hay.

When he had finished in the barn, he walked back to the house; realizing that the work had not help him forget---the Hamilton's predicament still weighted heavily on his mind.

Walking inside, Sam could hear Aunt Jenny outside the house calling her cats. He sat at the kitchen table and talked with his mother for a while about the great celebration that had taken place after the reading of the Declaration of Independence. During the conversation, he learned that the celebration was the excuse Uncle John had given to start drinking again.

As he left the table to go to his bunk, he thought of what the Declaration of Independence meant to him and how it could be twisted to mean something so completely different to his Uncle John.

Light from a candle on the kitchen table faded into darkness of the front part of the room where Sam climbed into his bunk bed. He did not bother to take off his clothes and after the house was quiet; he slipped out of bed and crept from the house.

It was about ten o'clock and Sam led his horse from the barn. When he reached the road to Halifax he heard a wagon coming. Quickly pulling 'Jericho' to the side of the road, Sam remained behind some tall bushes until the wagon passed.

Watching from the bushes, he could see his Uncle slumped forward on the wagon seat. The horses pulled the wagon to the barn and stopped. There was a light in the house and it was only a short while before he saw his mother come outside. Sarah Pickett struggled with her brother and Sam could hear John Thompson mouthing some words that were not clear. Then, as John's feet touched the ground, he seemed to be completely revived and ran wildly toward the house barking and howling like a wild dog. This was his way of tormenting Aunt Jenny for having so many cats around the house.

John Thompson hated cats and had religiously promised Aunt Jenny that he was coming back in the next life as a dog and chase all cats down to Quanky Creek. It was funny when Sam first heard his Uncle tell how he would get even with Aunt Jenny in the next life, but the threat turned to a sad joke, for Aunt Jenny soon began to believe that John Thompson just might do it.

Sarah Pickett ran to the house in pursuit of her 'mad dog' brother. Knowing that his uncle would be calmed as soon as Sarah Pickett reached him, Sam mounted his horse and continued toward Halifax.

Two miles was not far to travel when it referred to distance---but distance was not what separated the Hamiltons and the Picketts. It was a matter of relationships, it was a matter of social standing, it was a matter of wealth, and it was a matter of tradition. Suddenly these things didn't matter anymore. Values were changing. The Hamiltons were now the ones who were not acceptable in Halifax. How ironic, it all seemed to Sam, only a few months had passed, now he was on the inside and Josie was on the outside. It seemed that some fateful force was determined to keep them apart.

It was close to midnight when Sam dismounted and walked up the long walkway to the Hamilton house. The large, white house loomed foreboding, and Sam hesitated momentarily as his foot touched the front step. Was he doing the right thing---helping a Tory family? What if the news got back to the men at camp? What kind of Patriot would help a Tory? Sam wondered if he believed all that he had felt so deeply about freedom. Then, he realized that there was something he felt more deeply and---that was his love for Josie. This thought caused him to move quickly to the front door.

He pounded the large brass knocker. There was no response. He pounded the door with his fist, loud enough for the slaves out back to hear. Soon, he saw a candle lighting John Hamilton's way.

"What on earth is wrong, Sam? What do you want at this hour of the night?"

"Let me in, Mr. Hamilton. I've come to help you." Sam pushed the door open wider. "Get your family together as quickly as possible."

"Well, come on in. What's this all about, Sam?" John Hamilton stepped back.

Josie was coming down the stairs as Sam entered the front door.

"What is it, Sam?"

"I don't have time to explain to each of you, Josie. Get George and your mother," ordered Sam.

"Do as he says, Josie," said Hamilton, looking awkwardly embarrassed in his nightclothes.

Sam turned to Hamilton as Josie hurried upstairs.

"Didn't you think the orders the Council of Safety put out against all Tories applied to you?"

"I am aware of the 'orders', Sam. I have waited for a decision from the Council and I have heard no word since that meeting. My family knows nothing of that day I met with the council. I've tried to keep them from worrying."

Sam had only time to ask this question before George, Josie and Abigail Hamilton entered the parlor.

"The Council of Safety has passed orders to remove all persons considered dangerous to the cause of America. All suspected persons will be arrested," said Sam, looking at Josie as he spoke.

"But we have done nothing to be treated as enemies," said Abigail Hamilton.

"It was thought that you would join the fight for freedom, but now the order has been given for you to be arrested tomorrow morning," Sam explained.

"What will we have to do to be acceptable to the Council of Safety?" Josie was white with fear.

"I don't think there's anything you can do now, since it's publicly known that you are loyal to King George. What I can't understand is why y'all didn't see this thing coming," said Sam, as he looked from Josie to the other members of the family.

"We don't believe in your cause, Sam," reminded George.

"What can we do, Sam," asked Josie.

"If y'all are so set in your thinking, I think you'd better find somewhere to go before morning," advised Sam

"We're one of the first families to come to Halifax. Is this Cornelius Harnett the one who has the orders," asked Abigail Hamilton.

"General Jones has the orders, Mrs. Hamilton---but you'll have them tomorrow, if you're still here."

"We must get our things together. How much time do we have, Sam?" John Hamilton looked to the great grandfather clock to his left.

"You'd better pack what you can take by horse and carriage and leave as quickly as possible," said Sam.

"George, help your mother and Josie. Get what you can together. I'll go dress and then wake the servants and give them their freedom. They have been good and faithful. I must take the time to do this." John Hamilton was frantically trying to remain calm.

"If you can get to Enfield tonight, you can catch the stage from there tomorrow morning. They won't be looking for you there," suggested Sam.

Hamilton paced the floor. "I'll write Willie Jones and tell him all that has happened---maybe he'll see fit to save some of my property. If we can get a stage to New Bern, I'll find friends and relatives there who'll help us." Hamilton seemed to be going in several directions ---then he stopped in his quandary and suddenly rushed upstairs.

"I dare not take my silverware on such a risky journey. Yet, I have no one---no place to leave it. George, get the mahogany chest and fill it with the best silver."

"I'll get the chest just as soon as I get dressed," said George, going up the stairs.

Sam walked to the dining room where Josie and Abigail were hastily gathering different articles from the drawers and placing them on a large center table.

John Hamilton came into the room. He was holding a small candelabra and was dressed in his riding clothes.

"You must all get dressed quickly. Forget about everything else. ---Now---be quick---" Hamilton grabbed his wife and pushed her toward the stairs. Josie followed her mother.

"Sam, don't mention that meeting I had with the Council of Safety. I'm going to speak with the servants. You wait here," said Hamilton, as he left the room.

Sam sat down on a large Windsor chair and looked around at the fine furnishing now illuminated by soft candle light from the single candelabra on the center table. What a shame to have to give up so much and all for the wrong reasons thought Sam.

It took George only a short while to dress and he was ready to travel when he came down the stairs. He placed the mahogany chest on the table and turned to Sam.

"I suppose you knew more about this revolution than all of us put together."

"I'm sorry y'all have to leave this way. I didn't think it would be coming this fast." Sam wanted to be more consoling, but he just could not find the words.

Josie and her mother came downstairs. Changed now to traveling habits, they began again their search through the drawers and cabinets.

George took the different articles from the table and put what he could inside a small trunk.

"All the silver is in the mahogany chest," said George.

"We'll see that it's carefully watched until we get to New Bern." Abigail knew the value of her silver.

John Hamilton came in through the back door. Sam could tell by his expression that he had just witnessed a very sad farewell to his slaves.

"Old Josh is getting the horses ready. How are you all coming along?"

"We're almost ready," said Mrs. Hamilton. "George, you take the bags to the front door."

"Sam, I want to thank you for coming here tonight. I know you took a great risk. I won't forget what you've done. I'll repay you one day. I don't know that I have anything valuable enough to give you for what you've done," said John Hamilton.

Sam smiled slightly, thinking of the most valuable possession of John Hamilton. She was the reason he had come. He wondered what Hamilton would say if he should tell him what would be acceptable.

Abigail Hamilton finished collecting all she could get into the valise she had brought with her from upstairs. For a moment Sam felt that she was going to say something else but when she opened her mouth to speak, no word came. She then walked to the front door to join her husband.

Sam and Josie were alone.

"I want to stay, Sam."

"Your place is with your family, Josie. There's no safe place here for you."

"How will I know where you are, Sam?"

"When the fighting is over I pray to God I'll be somewhere around here. It's the only chance we've got. When it's all over, you'll know where to find me."

"I pray that it'll come soon."

"There has to be a time for us, Josie," said Sam as he suddenly and boldly took Josie in his arms and held her tightly.

As they were embracing, George came into the room. He hesitated briefly and then walked to the couple.

"We must be leaving, Josie," said George, as he placed his arm around her shoulder.

Josie broke away from Sam and ran from the room.

George looked at Sam and extended his hand.

"Don't let any 'pirates' take over our secret cave at Quanky."

Sam started to laugh but quickly realized that George was not joking.

"I'll be on guard."

"Don't forget us, Sam."

George held his head low as he spoke and hesitated as if he had forgotten something.

Sensing why George stood motionless, Sam ran to his best friend. When he was close enough to hug George, he knew that this could be the last time he would ever have the chance to embrace his friend. Tears swelled in Sam's eyes and trickled down his cheeks to meet the wetness left by George's brushing face. Sam extinguished all the candles and closed the front door.

Standing in the yard, Sam watched as the carriage turned left on King Street. Tears flowed more freely now and the vision of the carriage became blurred.

No matter what the future held or how the consequences of the visit might affect his life----he was glad he had come.

CHAPTER FIFTEEN

Sam rode leisurely along the road that led from his home to Camp Quanky. General Jones had asked him to bring along his finest clothes, since they would be visiting 'Grove House' later in the afternoon. So, Sam had neatly folded his frocked coat and a pair of dark breeches and tied them in a knapsack behind his saddle. Knowing that Willie Jones wanted him to take 'Midnight' to the track caused Sam to look forward to the visit. He now wore his faded blue army pants and an old brown coat that looked contradictory to his new black cocked hat that he did not dare pack for fear of damaging its shape.

General Jones had talked with him at great length the day before about the convening of the new Congress which was already being referred to as the 'Constitutional Convention'. Now, in the middle of November, the delegates were again in Halifax to continue their work in governing the new state of North Carolina. A constitution would be necessary to give strength to the decisions of the new government.

General Allen Jones had seemed especially concerned about the mood of the people throughout the state. When word of the 'Declaration of Independence' reach the towns and counties, there was rioting and chaos that had continued and actually grown worse by mid-October when the time for electing new delegates to the Congress drew near. The people did not seem to realize the meaning of the new found freedom. "The way the elections have been handled is a strong indication that we need a stronger more permanent government" were words now remembered from his conversation with the General.

There were many incidents of lawlessness and abuses that had taken place when the people came to vote for new delegates to the Congress. Sam recalled one voting place in Guilford where a candidate with a whip had driven all opposition away from the poll. Since drunkenness and violence had characterized the campaigns of so many candidates, General Jones felt that some of the 'Radicals' who were now members of the new Congress had no business being in Halifax. Many of Allen Jones' fellow Conservatives had been re-elected by only a very narrow margin and some of the members of long-standing influence would not be returning at all. Even Samuel Johnston had lost his seat as delegate from Chowan. Sam was better satisfied, when the General told him that Samuel Johnston was appointed as public treasurer and would be present at the meetings even though he would not have a vote.

This new freedom that had so suddenly been thrust upon the people was considered a freedom that demanded no restraint. Sam sensed a developing attitude among the people of Halifax---a very dangerous attitude--that --some people thought that they had to answer to no one--now that they were free and independent. He felt strongly that the New Congress would have to inform the people of their responsibilities. The primary concern of the Congress would be to shape a new government from the present government with a constitution to give it power and stability. This provisional government no longer had the strength and authority to govern the people.

It was close to mid-afternoon as Sam crossed over Quanky Bridge and took the road to Camp Quanky. He thought of all the recent talk of 'Radicals' and 'Conservatives' and secretly admitted to himself that he did not know all the far-reaching philosophies of government. It was hard to comprehend all the words and deeds that now influenced the thinking of the delegates.

When he arrived at camp, Sam was met at the hitching post in front of General Jones' headquarters. The General quickly straddled his large white mare.

"You didn't forget to bring your good clothes, did you, Sam?"

"No, Sir. I'll change after we take 'Midnight' to the track." Sam patted the knapsack behind his saddle.

As they rode toward 'The Grove', Sam couldn't help but admire the new uniform worn by his commander.

"I've never seen you dressed in your official uniform, Sir."

"I had a dispatch from the Continental Congress just last week and I was informed that all generals were expected to follow instructions and meet the new regulations. All soldiers will have to follow the new regulations as soon as we are furnished with uniforms. How do you think mine looks, Sam?"

Sam told the General how good he looked in his dark blue officer's coat with gold buttons, lining and facing of buff. What would distinguish the General from other officers were the golden epaulettes on each shoulder and the white plume that waved from his cocked hat. These parts of his uniform told his rank.

The two riders crossed to King Street and continued along the main avenue until they came to Quanky Creek. At the bridge, the two riders turned right and continued on the shaded lane to 'Grove House'.

"Willie has been pining to see 'Midnight' stretch his legs. With all the business of Congress, I think he's due some relaxation."

"It'll be good for all of us-----especially 'Midnight'," agreed Sam.

A short while later they were riding up the shaded lane to 'The Grove'. "You know I've been thinking about this plantation and my place at Mount Gallant. Willie and I both have our barns full of tobacco and there's hardly any demand now that we've stopped trading with England."

"Will you be able to sell any on the northern market?"

"We'll just have to keep what we don't sell. Next year we'll plant more corn and wheat. That's what the soldiers will need."

Up ahead of them, Sam could see a rider.

"Looks like somebody's in a hurry to get somewhere."

Sam nodded at the General's words as he pulled 'Jericho' to the side of the road to make way for the speeding rider.

Willie Jones

"Sick man-----sick slave--"--yelled the rider hurrying past them.

Coming to the back of the house, General Jones pointed down the road toward the stables where Sam saw Willie Jones and Uncle Louie; they continued in that direction.

"Looks like you've got a 'runaway'," said Allen Jones, pulling his horse up to the hitching post and dismounting on the mounting block. Sam waited until the general had tied his horse before he dismounted.

"That was Jo-Jo who just past you on the road. I sent him to fetch Dr. Joyner. There's some sickness among the slaves. I've seen the symptoms before. Three of the last five that I bought at Edenton have died of the same disease. I need to go see about the other ones who are sick. When Dr. Joyner comes, tell him to come on to the slave quarters."

While they spoke, Uncle Louie brought 'Midnight" to the track and Sam mounted the horse from the fence rail. Spinning the horse to his left, Sam loosened the reins and let 'Midnight" go on his own. This horse had nothing to prove. He had done that long ago. Today the running was for pleasure. Turning at the far end of the track, Sam could see the bustling activity of more than thirty slaves coming and going among the buildings and along the road that led to the open fields.

Willie Jones, now walking briskly toward the slave quarters, stopped momentarily and waved. The homestretch was behind him and he came to the starting post where Allen Jones stood watching the smooth, graceful rhythm of the fastest horse in Eastern North Carolina. The second time around was as much riding as Sam wanted. His nose was getting red and had started to drip while his eyes were blurred with tears caused by the chilled November air that whipped past him when he was at full speed.

When Sam pulled his horse to a halt at the rail, he could see the buggy of Dr. Joyner, coming up the lane leaving a small cloud of dust in its wake as it moved closer to the stables.

"Midnight looks faster than he did when he ran against 'Golden Boy'. That's what I hate so much about this war. It doesn't give anybody a chance to enjoy anything, anymore," said General Jones.

Uncle Louie grabbed the reins and Sam dismounted.

"Sam, you go on up to the house when you've finished here. Willie said we'll need to eat early. The committee will be here at seven."

"I'll be there just as soon as I get dressed," said Sam, following Uncle Louie to the stables.

Allen Jones turned to meet Dr. Joyner's buggy; climbed up to the seat and pointed toward the slave quarters.

While Uncle Louie was giving 'Midnight' his rubdown, Sam took his knapsack from the front of the stall where Uncle Louie had stabled

'Jericho'. He moved to the next vacant stall and emptied his sack; put on his dark trousers, took out his frocked coat and shook it free of its wrinkles.

"Hey, Uncle Louie, what kind of disease is it that's killing the slaves?"

"Don't know. Didn't have it to de last slaves were bought."

"Do you know that it's not smallpox?"

"Ain't no soes wid what's killin'em. Some high fever, though."

"What does Dr. Joyner say he thinks it is?"

"He jest says high fever---high fever."

Sam left Uncle Louie mumbling strange prophesies of death, and walked to the outside. Stopping at the fence rail, he stood and looked down the road toward the slave quarters. Only a few small black children were outside the huts but some larger, older children wrapped in brown homespun played along the road. Here and there in front of the slave huts were the old women dressed in heavy wraps keeping their vigil over the young.

Suddenly the playing along the road stopped and there was stillness among the children and the old women. All stared at a cabin about midway down the line where four big male slaves were moving a body from the cabin to a cart at the side of the road. The death cart had sides lined with black wool on the outside and soft white wool on the inside. After carefully placing the lifeless body inside the cart, two slaves moved between the shafts and were followed by slow deliberate steps of the other two slaves. Dr. Joyner stood, along with Willie and Allen Jones, in front of the cabin and the stillness remained until the cart turned right and curved around the track toward the cemetery.

A young slave woman stood in the doorway directly behind Dr. Joyner and continued to look even after the cart had faded in the distance. Sam wondered, as he watched the woman, what she saw in the distance beyond her vision. Was she looking to another time----to another place---to something that only she and her people understood?

During this time of year, the slaves became more specialize in their work. The men were carpenters, tanners, coopers, blacksmiths, bricklayers, while the women knew weaving, carding, soap making, candle making and winemaking. Even though he could not see all the activity beyond the curve, Sam knew the log barns were filled with corn, flax, wheat, tobacco and cotton. There was always much work demanded of the slave after the crops were housed. The flax had to be beaten into threads, corn had to be shucked and ground, cotton had to be carded and tobacco dried and packed into hogsheads. Since tobacco was the main money crop, close supervision of handling the dried leaf was demanded. But now, since the market was off, the tobacco would be stored until a market was found.

All this work would now be temporarily interrupted when the death cart passed along the road. There was always a statue-like stillness, a customary reverence showing respect for the dead---and always allowed by the overseers.

Near the gristmill, on the right side of the road and directly in front of the slave cemetery was a small black building that ran lengthwise the road---the death house. Here the cart would stop and the body of the slave would be placed inside the wooden box made by the slaves at the cooper's shed. The simple coffin would then be placed on a long, wooden table and the lid kept open until all the slaves had paid their respect.

Shadows from the servant's quarters across the road were now beginning to lengthen. Dr. Joyner led his horse as he walked along the road with Willie and Allen Jones. At the far end of the racetrack, a small army of slaves was rounding the curve being led by two overseers. There was a low mournful hum that had a primitive rhythm---not of this land. The sound that came from the slave was the sound of mourning---- unmistakable sorrow for a lost friend or loved one. The sound grew louder and clearer and now seemed more of a chant than a hum. As the slaves approached the cabins, they veered off---each to his separate hut and then there was silence.

Sam opened the gate to his left and walked to the road to meet General Jones who walked ahead, leaving Willie to talk further with Dr. Joyner.

As he walked toward 'Grove House' with the General, Sam wondered if it were true that Willie Jones had acquired most of this great plantation from the Indians. It was rumored that fast horses had brought him most of the land that now lay between Quanky Creek and the Roanoke River. When he considered the character of Willie Jones, Sam rationalized that there could be no underhanded dealings by this man---even with the Indians--- but then, he'd never know, for the Tuscaroras had long ago moved North to join with their Iroquoian family.

Sam quickly dismissed his thoughts about the Indians and now felt a certain pride to be a guest at 'Grove House'. It was an uncommon experience for him to be accepted on this level in Halifax. General Allen Jones was not ordinary man---Willie Jones was no ordinary Gentleman.

CHAPTER SIXTEEN

When they had finished the evening meal, Sam and the General walked with Willie and Mary Jones to the banquet room.

"I've never in my life seen such a feast as was placed on that table," said Sam, as they entered the most spacious room in the house.

"Well, we have to enjoy it while it lasts. One never knows how long we'll be able to prepare a good table," said Mary Jones.

"You know Dudley is always bragging about his good food. He'll never believe you Sam when you tell him about this meal."

Allen Jones was as impressed with the food as Sam.

When everyone was settled around the large fireplace at the west end of the room, Sam took a seat in a high-back, green, cushioned chair similar to the ones occupied by the others.

He listened with interest to all that General Jones had to say about the war and the conditions at Camp Quanky. Sarah Pickett had always told him to listen whenever he was among people who knew more than he---and Sam knew--without any doubt that now was a time for listening.

General Jones told Willie that he had asked the Halifax soldiers to return home until early spring, since the November weather was so unbearable and now only a few officers remained in camp. The conversation then turned to politics and settled with a brief discussion about the committee meeting that was soon to begin. Willie spoke of his special committee that had been appointed to frame a 'Bill of Rights and Constitution for the State.'

Mary was concerned about the number of guests and so Allen Jones named the Radicals: Willie Jones, Griffith Rutherford, and Thomas Person. Then, Willie quickly followed by naming the Conservatives: Allen Jones, Thomas Jones, Samuel Ashe, and Archibald MacLaine. Richard Caswell and Cornelius Harnett would also be coming and they were considered moderates. Willie mentioned that he had invited Samuel Johnston and Thomas Burke because these two would have to reach some compromise or the Convention would be deadlocked from its inception. Even though Samuel Johnston was not an official delegate both brothers agreed that his influence with the delegates would be great.

Mary totaled the number of guest. "I have ten plus Willie."

Realizing that they only had thirty minutes before the seven o'clock meeting, Willie and Mary excused themselves from the room and hurried to prepare for the meeting.

General Jones found a clay pipe one the mantel and stuffed it with tobacco that he took from a pouch inside his large flapped pocket. He then reached down with a pair of tongs and took a coal from the fireplace. As he returned to his chair, he made a gesture toward the metal framed painting of Willie Jones that hung over the mantel.

"See that painting, Sam?"

"It's the first thing I noticed when I entered the room."

"I'm sure Willie selected that spot with care. It was painted in England when he attended Eton. Willie was a good student and made more friends than I did. I think he would have been a better student if he hadn't had so many friends. Friends often times have a way of infringing on one's time."

Sam admired the painting of the dark, handsome, younger brother. Even though General Jones and Willie shared different political views, it was evident that the General had a high regard for his brother. Willie was now thirty-six and only one year younger than Allen, but Sam had thought of Willie as being much younger until just recently. It was well known that the marriage to Mary had brought important changes to Willie's life style. It had brought maturity to the owner of 'Grove Plantation'. Serious thoughts of government rather than happy thought of horse racing, cock fighting and gambling now demanded his time.

After his education at Eton, Willie had returned to Halifax a polished gentleman. He had accepted the responsibility of leadership and was very influential with the people---so influential, in fact, he had been elected to the Presidency of the Council of Safety in September. It seemed that most people thought of Willie Jones as their spokesman for a more democratic government and all who knew him, respected his suspicions of any strong national authority.

General Jones quickly shifted his conversation from his brother to the Constitutional Convention. He seemed to think the delegates would be better informed than they had ever been, Many members had access to the constitutions of other states and the writings of John Adams to guide them in their thinking---even though it was discouraging that there were fewer Conservatives elected to this new Congress.

"You know I think Willie might have some good purpose in mind by asking the committee to meet here tonight. Willie has always had a gift for diplomacy. There are so many differences that have to be reconciled before the Convention gets too far along. I think what he's doing might really hurry things along."

"Do you think I could sit here by the fire while the committee is meeting?"

First For Freedom

"I don't see why not. You're as involved in this war as much as anybody else. Willie has asked that we stay the night and the guestroom has already been prepared. If anyone should ask why you're here tell them you are here as my guest.

"I promise they'll never know I'm here."

"I'm sure no one will object. Willie knows of your devotion to this state and after all this is his home and you are his guest. You just sit by the fire---who knows you might just learn something."

The General got up from his seat and walked to the large bay window, puffing continuously, as is if the coal had died down.

"Come over here, Sam. I want you to see this."

Sam walked to the window and stood beside the General and looked out into the darkness that was illuminated with a winding streak of about fifteen flaming torches along the road. The families of the dead were returning to their cabins.

" Have you ever attended a slave funeral, Sam?"

"No, Sir. I've heard people tell about them."

"A sight to behold, Sam. A sight to behold. It's a ritual mixed with ancient tribal customs and what they know of Christianity. Something different from anything I've ever seen---but who knows what's in store for us beyond this life---maybe their way is as close to heaven as yours or mine."

"I don't doubt that what they worship is as real to them as God and Heaven is to you and me, Sir."

"I've often thoughts that man's own seeking leads him to his just reward. The path those slaves take may better prepare them for an afterlife. If man has all the comfort and love he can hope for in this life, then what is there to look forward to? I firmly believe that there is a better life beyond this time and place. It may well be that these people will be more deserving than any others. One thing is certain; life on this earth has caused them to be more hopeful for what lies beyond the grave. Slavery is such an ugly business---families separated and sold to bondage----never seeing each other after the auction---runaway slaves---seeking freedom or lost loved ones. You know, Sam, in many ways, these people are searching for the same freedom we are seeking ourselves."

"Most of the slaves seem satisfied. From all I hear, they fare well enough if they have kind masters."

"Times will change. We may not live to realize it but it's not so much the relationship that is evil as it is the thinking. It seems the more enlightened man becomes, the more he seeks out of life. When material things are within man's grasp, his mind dwells on other things. Tonight, you'll meet many who have never wanted for anything other than power and authority. But then, that's human nature. Why should anyone strive for something he already has in his possession? The things most wanted in this life are those that extend just beyond man's reach."

A loud knock was heard at the front door and General Jones walked half way across the room before he saw Mary Jones coming down the stairs.

Sam moved to stand with his commander at the large arched doorway that opened to the hall. Sam inhaled the captivating aroma of fresh roses now hanging softly on the air that had been stirred by Mary's brisk movement to the front door. He had often secretly thought that Mary Jones was the second most beautiful lady in Halifax and tonight she looked more beautiful than he had ever seen her. Thick black hair hung in loose curls about her proud shoulders. Large, dark, blue eyes with long lashes looked upon the delegates as she extended her slender, white hand to greet the delegates as they entered. Her gown was a light blue silk and fitted closely her voluptuous figure.

Sam noticed that several delegates commented on her beautiful gown, which gave them opportunity to look even longer, and with added pleasure. High born and perfectly as ease with the associates of her husband was this glorious young lady who must have been destined to occupy the special place at the side of Willie Jones. Even though she was twenty years younger than her husband, she was his equal in social graces. Her presence seemed to make the gentlemen more aware of the many accomplishments of Willie Jones.

After speaking with the hostess, the delegates came immediately to the banquet room where Allen Jones extended a second welcome and Sam shook hands with all the delegates. Upon entering the room, the large bay window seemed to fascinate them. The carved mantel and the high wainscoting along the paneled walls showed evidence of skilled workmanship. The room was illuminated with soft light from wax candles set in silver sconces along the walls. Silver candlesticks were placed here and there on the sideboards and the long table at the center held one large candelabrum at the center and two smaller ones at each end.

Sam moved unnoticed to the side of the fireplace. The fine clothes worn by the delegates made him feel conspicuously inadequate even though he wore his best coat and breeches. These gentlemen with their large handsome frocked coats, beautifully woven waistcoats, silk ruffled shirts, tightly fitted breeches, buckled shoes, and some with powdered wigs, displayed the latest styles and fashions.

Sam thought of the times that he had seen the men at the courthouse and how different they looked now that they were dressed in their evening clothes.

Willie Jones appeared on the stairway and momentarily surveyed his guest until attention was cast in his direction. Willie slowly walked down the stairs. He was dressed now in a long, dark coat of blue velvet and large pocket-folds and cuffs that came to the bend in his knees. His shirt was light blue with bosom and wrist ruffles. Tight breeches the color of his shirt had silver buckles two inches wide at the knees where darker blue stocking were tucked under. Shoes of black shiny leather with silver buckles the size of those at his knees completed his outfit. Willie moved about the banquet room showing different pieces of furniture and explaining how he had acquired each piece.

The harpsichord seemed to fascinate the visitors more than anything else. So, when Willie came to it, he sat down and threw his frocked coat tails out behind him and played the melody of 'Barbara Allen'. When he finished, the delegates applauded for more but Willie moved quickly from the stool.

"I'll have Mary to play for you later. That's the only melody I've mastered on this instrument since we've had it. I just wanted to put Cornelius Harnett in the right mood for this meeting. There's an interesting story about this harpsichord. It seems a young stowaway hid inside it when it was shipped from England. That's a story too long for telling. I'll save it until there is ample time for you to enjoy it."

Willie moved, followed by the delegates, to the large grandfather clock and then to the oval mirror on the wall above the sideboard. The mirror was brought from England and was placed in a carved oak frame after it arrived. The frame took longer to finish than it had taken for the mirror to reach the colony. There were several Windsor chairs set against the walls that were worthy of attention. These chairs were seldom used, unlike the sturdier chairs around the large center table. Willie ended his tour at the large bay window that took up entire back wall. Here the delegates looked out into the night at the moonlight that was shinning down on the racetrack and the road that led to the Roanoke River.

Soon it became evident that all the invited guests had arrived and Willie walked to take his place at the head of the long center table. When all the delegates were comfortable, Willie stood and Sam took a chair by the fireplace.

"Gentlemen, I think all of you know each other, so I shall not be so formal as to introduce you. You all know the purpose of this meeting and I am sure that you gentlemen, as members of this select committee, realize that we need to get some understanding before we go too far in any direction. I know that deep feelings and strong convictions are held by many of you----and that these beliefs are not all the same. We need to reconcile as many of our differences as possible before we go to the Convention with any plan to be presented for adoption. We'll have enough differences after our plan is presented. I have taken the liberty to invite Mr. Thomas Burke and Mr. Samuel Johnston to this meeting because I feel they have much to offer. Although they will not have a vote on what we determine here, I am sure we shall benefit from their advice and counsel."

Sam noticed that Thomas Burke had raised his hand; Willie Jones nodded as he said, "Mr. Burke------"

Burke stood at his place to the left of Willie. He was a small man with a narrow face. His black hair was tied neatly with a black silk ribbon in a queue at the back. His light brown, broadcloth coat had large, pearl buttons and around his neck was a cloth of very fine white, linen with the ends dangling loosely at his breast. He wore a waistcoat, as did most of the delegates, with a connecting link midway its length.

"I know my views on the legislature are not shared by some of you here. Yet, I have not heard of a better plan than the one I have proposed."

Burke sounded as if he were apologizing for something to which he had been previously committed.

The white-wigged Samuel Johnston's hand went up immediately.

"As many of you know, I cannot agree with Mr. Burke's plan unless there are qualifications set for the members of the legislature. There should also be more restrictions on the voters who elect the members of the Senate. I feel that a voter should own as much as fifty acres of land to be qualified to vote for a senator."

"That seems to be moving from the principle of democracy, " said Willie Jones.

"How do you propose to get a man of quality---by people who cannot read the names of the candidates. I feel that we should have learned something by the way the recent elections were conducted," said Johnston, reacting strongly.

"That's a good point," said Harnett, from the end of the table opposite Willie Jones.

"The great difficulty, as I see it, is how to establish a check on the representatives of the people, to prevent them assuming more power than would be consistent with the liberties of the people," continued Johnston.

"We would have them stand for election at the end of each year. This would give the people a chance to elect another if they were not satisfied with the representative then in office," suggested Burke.

"That would seem a reasonable course. What do you say to that?" Willie Jones looked to Harnett.

Cornelius Harnett was then recognized. He stood and leaned forward with both hands resting on the table.

"I stand with Mr. Johnston on what I have heard of this proposal. All candidates for elections to the House of Commons should own three hundred acres of free land."

Sam listened intently as different members expressed their views. From where he sat, it was evident that a powerful General Assembly was wanted. However, Richard Caswell seemed disappointed that the Governor would not have more power---especially in times of war.

One delegate suggested that all counties have the same number of representatives in the House of Commons and since the number of people in each county was not known and since there was no time left for counting---this issue was quickly resolved with all understanding that there would be equal representation from each county.

As the meeting progressed into its second hour, Sam became aware that there was more concern for the state of the government than there was for the state of the war. Then, as the meeting moved along, he began to realize that there were more pressing matters that had to be settled. For there could be no successful rendering of orders to the commanders in the field unless there was a respected authority that was fully supported by the Congress. This Constitution would be that authority and it was desperately needed----now.

Some of the delegates felt strongly that the 'Constitution' would be ratified by the people while others were quick to realize that there would be no government at all if they waited for the votes of the people. Then, from the consensus of opinions, it was determined that a democratic process would have to wait until the state was more mature and there was more time for the people to be heard.

The large grandfather clock bonged away the second hour and the meeting seemed to be winding down. Then, Cornelius Harnett stood, as he had done so many times during the meeting.

"I want to make sure we do not overlook the fact that all people will have freedom to exercise their own mode of worship and that we make no preference of any one religion over any other."

"I feel positive that all of you know the many ways this one issue may go before it takes any direction," added Willie Jones.

"The birth of this state is going to be a long time in labor, I can see that is a certainty," commented Caswell.

"There has never been a birth without pains of labor. We must accept this as a fact and dedicated ourselves to the arduous work that is before us. We must keep in mind that this infant state must grow up with other sister states and play her part in the great family that is to be our nation," said Harnett, offering the much needed catharsis.

Willie Jones Stood.

"I have heard much here tonight that will serve as a foundation for the Constitution. Many questions have been answered that confused me before this meeting. I hope the meeting has been as rewarding to all of you as it has been to me---I want to thank all of you for coming-------"

Before the delegates could move from the table, Richard Caswell spoke, "I have one final question that I'd like to ask that is not related to the making of the Constitution. The question is this---how do we hope to stand against the British Navy. I feel we will fare well enough on land but we have no ships--we have no naval captains---we have no navy."

"That much is true. However, Hewes has given John Paul his naval commission. I have great faith in this gentleman. I learned much about the sea from his visit here two years ago. His efforts will bear fruit. You will soon see a navy," assured Willie Jones.

"We'll need some brave sailors, if they hope to even put to sea in what we now call ships," continued Richard Caswell.

"You'll have a brave one in John Paul. He nearly died at my house while suffering from pneumonia. I can truly say that I know this man has no fear of death," added Allen Jones.

"Well, since he took the name of Jones while he visited here with you, Willie, I am sure his character will not be questioned," said Harnett, smiling at the other delegates.

As Harnett made his remark, Mary Jones entered the room and was followed by three maids. The maids placed three trays of wine filled glasses on the sideboard to Willie's left. Mary held up her hands as if she were asking permission to speak.

"I shall not allow any gentleman to leave my home before he is refreshed. Willie had wanted to test this wine he has so long stored in the cellar. I feel sure that is the purpose of this meeting."

The delegates walked to the sideboard and served themselves a vintage glass of wine. The conversation that ensued was mostly about the house and the fine wine. For a while, the delegates forgot the business of state.

Then, the delegates encouraged Mary to play the harpsichord. They listened with pleasure as Mary played their favorite melodies. Not one request was denied and the gentlemen were astonished that Mary was such an accomplished young musician.

CONSTITUTION HOUSE

Moved in 1920 from its original site, the Constitution House was restored by the Daughters of the American Revolution. Future plans call for the relocation of the house in the historic area of Halifax. The house, a small one and one-half story, multi-use, frame building, typical of the region, has a side hall and two rooms furnished in the period of 1776 and is traditionally known as the building in which the first State Constitution was drafted.

CHAPTER SEVENTEEN

For several months Sam had been concerned about the Hamiltons; the way they had to leave and the loss of hope for a future with Josie and the loss of his best friend, George. It was difficult to keep his mind on anything when these thoughts constantly occupied his mind.

The growing loyalty to his outfit and to the cause of freedom seemed as important as any thing in his life. The soldiers were without guns and the few who owned hunting rifles had no gunpowder. The conditions at Camp Quanky were critical. General Jones had started an intensive recruiting program in early spring and now there were about three hundred men involved in the training program. With this call to arms, came a great need for even more equipment, uniforms, horses, wagons, blankets and gunpowder. Nicholas Long had salvaged everything in and around Halifax. The equipment and material were shipped to furnish soldiers already in the field.

Since there was never enough food or clothing to supply all the new recruits, many left to join with other outfits that were better furnished; others returned home to wait until uniforms and supplies would be available.

Being aware that Dudley was in charge of collecting silver, cause Sam to get a leave from Camp Quanky for several days to help with the collecting. When all the collecting was completed, it was to be given to General Allen Jones.

Now it was almost nine o'clock and Sam looked to his right as he rode down King Street toward Halifax. The home of John Hamilton was dark and vacant and Sam thought of that last night he had seen Josie.

Riding past the house, he reached inside his coat and withdrew a slip of paper. He walked his horse and glanced at the note that he read again by moonlight. MEET ME AT DUDLEY'S --TEN O'CLOCK--GENERAL JONES.

Sam had noticed the unusual activity at Quanky during the day and wondered why the General had not left his cabin the entire afternoon---and why he had left word that he was not to be disturbed except in case of an emergency. Then, when the private had brought the note to his cabin, Sam became concerned that something was wrong---something was brewing.

Sam stopped and tied his horse to the hitching post in front of Martin's Livery and walked to Dudley's Tavern.

He could see a faint light through the window as he knocked at the door. Dudley came to the door immediately.

"I'm sorry but we're closed," kidded Dudley, as he opened the door wider.

"What's wrong, Dudley?"

"Come on in, General Jones is already here."

As he entered, Sam could see General Jones seated at a corner table. Dudley closed and locked the front door, picked up a candle from the bar and led Sam to the back table.

General Jones stood and glanced at the large grandfather clock near the door to the game room.

"Right on time, Sam. That's what I like---dependability. Come on and sit down."

"Are you all right, Sir," asked Sam, as he took his seat.

"I'm fine, Sam. I've just been a little busy today. Why do you ask?"

"Some of the men in camp thought you might be sick."

"The men have grown use to my being among them, I suppose."

"They were aware that something unusual was happening inside your cabin."

"Well, the men are not to be told anything about what we are doing here. Sam, we've collected enough silver from the people to take to Edenton to exchange for gunpowder."

General Jones took a letter from inside this coat.

"I have a letter here from Samuel Johnston in Edenton, and he set up a meeting at Horniblow's Tavern. Abner Nash has found a man in New Bern who has gunpowder to sell. This man will be in Edenton next week, and he's ready to do business. Nash has been corresponding with Johnston, and they have worked out all the details. I had a letter from Nash last week, and I am satisfied that proper preparations have been made. There's no doubt about the character of the gentleman who has the gunpowder. The man's name is Louis Lanier and should be easy to recognize. He will be a dark-bearded man with a black patch over his left eye. He will be wearing a black wig and will be dressed in a light brown, suit."

"General Jones, you know, Sam and I have had some experience with a man from New Bern who wanted to sell us gunpowder."

"I still have not settle my debt, Dudley."

"He took my money and left town next morning before sunrise. Maybe this Louis Lanier knows something about Jonathan Lawson. Since they are both in the same kind of trade and since they are both from New Bern. It wouldn't hurt to question him."

"Where are we to pick up the powder," asked Sam.

"I understand that the powder will be stored in the warehouse at the dock," said General Jones.

"I don't know of anything we need more than gunpowder right now, Sir." Sam looked at Dudley who nodded in agreement.

"The Council of Safety has authorized me to use all the silver we've collected to make this transaction----and since Dudley was in charge of collecting silver in this area, he will be in charge of this venture."

"Well, when do we start for Edenton," asked Dudley.

"Before sunrise tomorrow morning," said Allen Jones, as he turned. "Sam, I'm sending two soldiers to help you with the silver. You men are to protect Dudley from any interference during his passage to and from Edenton."

Jones looked to Dudley.

"You are not to divulge any information nor have any contacts until you reach Horniblow's Tavern. A room will be provided for you at the tavern for the meeting. Now, both of you know how desperately we need the powder, so I need not tell you the importance of this mission. You both must be on guard at all times."

Sam and Dudley acknowledged their responsibility and after a glass of Dudley's homemade wine, they left the tavern.

All preparations were made for the trip and as the sun was rising the next morning, the large trunk filled with silver was loaded on Allen Jones' boat. The soldiers stood guard as the oarsmen placed the trunk securely under the canopy. Dudley boarded the forty-foot boat and settle down under the canopy next to the trunk. The soldiers came on board and the six oarsmen moved the boat from the dock out into the Roanoke River.

The boat moved swiftly through the dark water. Going downstream required little more than keeping the boat in the main stream until they reached the brackish water near the coast. There the fresh water married the salt water and the current slowed. More effort would be needed on the return trip when they would be moving against the current.

As they moved along, stabs of sunlight filtered through the tall trees along the bank in showy splendor and created changing patterns of shadows on the surface of the Roanoke. The river was narrow, then wide, and then narrow again, as it curved and straightened its meandering way toward the coast.

Sam and the other soldiers sat at the bow and watched the green shoreline slide pass them. The soft willows and the gnarled cypress were punctuated with white blooming dogwoods. Early morning was Sam's favorite time of the day and spring was his favorite time of the year. This day was especially beautiful with the sunrays reflecting off the surface of the Roanoke.

Dudley lay under the canopy with his right arm stretched over the trunk, as if he were protecting it. He was sound asleep and had completely missed the most glorious sunrises Sam had ever seen.

Sam moved carefully from the bow of the boat and made his way toward the canopy where Dudley slept. He settled down opposite the large trunk from Dudley and watched the contented sleeper. He smiled as he listened to the grunts, snorts, moans, groans and other weird sounds that came from Dudley. Then, Dudley became quite calm and seemed to be in a deep sleep. The oars slapping against the water and the sound of water splashing against the boat were now the only sounds Sam could hear.

Sam took his sword from his belt and made himself comfortable; reached inside his faded army coat and withdrew a letter. The edges of the envelope were worn and soiled from having been handled so many times. He had only this letter from Josie since that night the Hamiltons left Halifax. He slipped the letter from the envelope and unfolded the two wrinkled, worn pages. Sam knew each word of the letter but the flourishing handwriting of Josie seemed almost as beautiful as her voice. The words became sounds as he softly read-------

Dear Sam,

We arrived safely in New Bern. Where we shall go from here is yet to be determined. We are well situated for now but the feeling for independence here is as strong as it is in Halifax, so I cannot be certain about the future.

Father talks constantly about forming a fighting unit and it seems likely that George will join the army soon. I do not understand all that has happened thus far in this conflict, and I have doubts that I shall ever fully comprehend it all. Perhaps it is just as well. I feel that I have been caught between two opposing forces which I cannot control, so I must bow to the circumstances of these troubled times.

I have permission from Father to write this short note and it will be the last word you'll hear from me until the conflict has run its course.

I hope with the ending, there will be a beginning, a beginning for you and me. I can only hope that throughout this conflict you will not forget me. I cannot bear the thought that your love for me will be altered by what fate has in store for us. I can assure you that I shall remain constant in my pledge to you. You never need to doubt my love. I loved you when we were playmates and I never had any doubts, even then. If there ever is any change, it will be because you no longer care. Even if this be the case, I shall have enough love to sustain us for all our days.

Let us both pray that the times will be better and we'll be together again.
Love,
Josie

Sam carefully folded the pages and put the envelope inside his coat; made himself comfortable and was soon sound asleep.

At the end of the day, the tall slave of Allen Jones, who was in charge of the boat, pointed toward the shore? The oarsmen guided the boat in that direction and brought it to rest in a secluded cove that could not be seen from the river.

Enough food had been packed to furnish the travelers, so no fire was made the first day. When the knapsacks were emptied, Sam and the others soldiers made camp on shore about one hundred feet from the boat.

Dudley and two soldiers slept on board the boat. Sam did not have guard duty the first night so he stayed on shore with the slaves. The other soldier stood guard and would be relieved by the soldier on board the boat.

There was no breeze during the night and the gnats and mosquitoes were numerous. Sam got little sleep until early morning. When sleep finally came, it was abruptly interrupted by the sound of the slaves breaking camp.

When all the work was done and the boat was loaded, Dudley roused from his sleep and gave orders to move out; then went to sleep again.

CHAPTER EIGHTEEN

By mid-morning of the fourth day of traveling, the crew arrived at the Edenton dock. The boat was secured, and two slaves were left at the wharf to tend the boat. The other four slaves moved the trunk of silver from the boat onto the dock and placed two twelve-foot poles under two ropes that were tied around the trunk, then moved to take their positions at the ends of the poles. Two soldiers walked ahead. Sam and Dudley followed.

The party soon arrived at Horniblow's Tavern. The slaves were told to return to the boat. The soldiers, lifting the trunk, went to the back of the tavern.

Dudley lightly rapped on the back door and stood back to wait. Horniblow opened the door and immediately recognized Sam. The soldiers brought the silver inside while Horniblow spoke briefly with Sam and Dudley. Horniblow was dressed in purple silk. He was an elegant innkeeper, without equal in Edenton. His stout frame and jolly disposition were comparable to Dudley. However, this is where the similarities ended. Perhaps the most obvious differences were the demeanor and sophistication of Horniblow, whose business depended on a thorough understanding of the social graces and the behavior of the members of his select clientele.

The stairway to the second floor was at the back of the tavern where an open door led to the lobby. Sam walked to the door and motioned to the soldiers who quickly followed Horniblow and Dudley. The stairs were only wide enough for two soldiers to lug the trunk to the second floor.

Horniblow directed them to the room that had been reserved by Samuel Johnston. "This is Mr. Lanier's room. I'll go find Mr. Johnston and tell him that you are here."

After the trunk was placed on the floor at the center of the room, Horniblow excused himself. He would fetch Mr. Johnston from the game room.

The soldiers were stationed outside the door while Sam and Dudley stayed inside the room.

They were there for only a short while when a knock was heard at the door. Sam took a brisk step back and opened the door wider when he saw Samuel Johnston and a bearded man with a patch over his left eye, standing before him. As the gentlemen entered the room, Samuel Johnston walked immediately to Dudley.

"Christopher Dudley, I'd like you to meet Mr. Louis Lanier."

Dudley extended his hand.

"I'm mighty glad to know you, Sir."

"This is Sam Pickett who is in the service of General Allen Jones. Sam, Mr. Lanier wants to speak in private with the owner of the silver."

Sam nodded as he looked intently at the bearded man.

"I'll be outside if you need me, Dudley."

It was half an hour before the door opened again. Samuel Johnston and Dudley walked out and closed the door. The other gentleman remained inside.

"I think you have struck a good bargain," said Johnston, as he slapped Dudley on the shoulder.

"These letters of credit will be enough to supply our soldiers with powder for a good while," said Dudley. He patted the left side of his chest.

"I suggest that you get to the dock early so you can get the gunpowder loaded. You need to get underway quickly. This sort of business needs not to cause attention. There are Tory sympathizers in this town who will do anything to prevent that powder from reaching our soldiers in the field. I feel an obligation to General Jones to see that it is safely loaded and on the way to Halifax. I cannot guarantee anything after you leave the dock," said Johnston.

"We'll get a room and stay here tonight," said Dudley.

"This place is no place like Dudley's but we'll manage somehow," said Sam sarcastically.

"I'll be in the game room if you need me for anything." Johnston walked toward the back of the tavern.

"Did you ever see such a place? If I had this tavern in Halifax, I'd have to open a school to teach my crowd how to act," said Dudley, as they entered the dining hall.

"You men ready for some food?" Sam turned to the two soldiers who nodded at the suggestion.

"Well, let's get to the dining hall. Lead the way, Sam. You know the way around here," said Dudley, motioning to Sam with an outstretched arm.

The men walked to the dining hall and ordered the meal. When they were served, Dudley ordered a glass of wine for the men and told them to get some food for the slaves.

The men relaxed after the dinner and sipped the delicate wine as if they did not want to be finished with the delicious grape. Dudley leaned back and admired the many fascinating features of the tavern. The polished silverware on the table indicated that Horniblow's was a place for the gentry. Dudley, not being a member of the gentry, felt a little uncomfortable----but very impressed.

First For Freedom

As they talked among themselves, Sam saw the bearded man from New Bern walk past the door and enter the game room. Sam looked across the table at Dudley.

"You know, there's something about that gentleman from New Bern that bothers me."

"That gunpowder is what's bothering me. I won't rest easy until it's in Allen Jones' hands," said Dudley.

"I know I've seen him somewhere. His name is not familiar but that face behind that beard-----." Sam was trying to remember.

"Sam, we've got to git our minds on the trip back to Halifax. We've done what we come here to do," reminded Dudley.

"That man's supposed to be a stranger," continued Sam, "yet, there is something strangely familiar about him."

"The only thing I noticed about him that was strange was when we shook hands. There's a finger missing on his right hand," said Dudley.

"The middle finger is missing," added Sam, quickly.

"You noticed it, too," came Dudley's response.

"Not today---I didn't. I noticed it last year when he came to Halifax to visit the Hamiltons," said Sam, as he jumped up from the chair and hurried toward the game room.

"Jonathan Lawson-----," said Dudley, as he followed Sam.

Sam walked past the bar and entered the game room. There were several gentlemen sitting at the game tables who looked disdainfully at him. Sam's uniform was faded and worn, not fit to be called a uniform, and certainly not proper attire for Horniblow's game room. He immediately noticed the bearded man seated near the window with Samuel Johnston.

Sam walked up behind the gentleman and spoke as he turned to face Louis Lanier. "Well, I came to Edenton on business but I did not expect to have the pleasure of this meeting, Mr. Jonathan Lawson."

Johnston stood. "What do you mean? This man's name is Louis Lanier from New Bern."

"I'm afraid you have been misinformed, Sir. This is Mr. Jonathan Lawson, a Tory associate of Mr. John Hamilton," assured Sam.

"You're the one who's mistaken. Abner Nash wrote me about this gentleman. The description in his letter cannot be mistaken. This man has ammunition for the Patriots." Johnston was almost indignant.

"The only way a Patriot will get any ammunition from this man is from the end of a rifle," said Sam, as he drew his sword.

"I'm not accustomed to this kind of conduct. You, Sir, have insulted me in public and have questioned my integrity. Perhaps we can discuss this outside," said Lawson, as he stood and looked about the room at the other gentlemen who were becoming alarmed.

"That would be my suggestion," said Sam, now nudging Lawson with the tip of his sword.

They walked from the game room through the dining hall to the back door. Dudley and the two soldiers followed Sam and Lawson. Sam let Lawson walk several feet ahead as they left the tavern.

"Mr. Lawson, you had your choice of weapons the last time we met. As I recall, I had no choice at all. This meeting will be different. I'll make the choice of weapons----and my choice is the sword." Sam held his sword upward.

"I think that is an excellent choice. I would have made the same choice." Lawson turned to face Sam.

Dudley and the two soldiers stood at the back of the tavern to make sure there would be no spectators. Dudley did not try to intervene---he knew it would be useless.

Lawson quickly drew his sword. He swished it through the air and looked skillful in his handling of the weapon. Sam stood poised and waited as Lawson moved toward him. Suddenly it was steel against steel---maneuver and counter maneuver. Side steps and feigning movements. The skill of each swordsman caused the fighters to regard each other with greater respect as the fight continued. The steel clanged and it seemed that two equals had met--- yet each refused to accept the other as an equal. Lawson thrust his sword as Sam parried. Sam thrust his sword and Lawson parried---thrusting and parrying back and forth and neither fighter gained the advantage.

Sam stepped back and looked at Lawson.

"I see you're as skilled with the sword as you were with the blunderbuss."

"I have only shown you some fundamentals. Now I'll begin the lesson," said Lawson as he lunged forward.

Sam sensed the move and quickly stepped aside. Lawson's blade nicked Sam's right arm. Sam's thrust was more telling----for the blade entered Lawson's right side. Lawson fell to the ground as Sam withdrew his crimson sword.

"You learned well---I must say---you learned well." Lawson lay on the ground clutching his bleeding side.

The fight was over and Dudley opened the back door. Several men came to help Lawson back inside the tavern.

Dudley came to Sam's side and looked at his arm.

"Just a nick---you were lucky, Sam."

First For Freedom

"I know. I know. I'm glad it's finished. You don't know how glad I am that it's finished," said Sam, gasping for breath.

"The silver---the silver. Lawson's got the silver." Dudley turned quickly to the two soldiers

"Tell Horniblow to give you the key to Lanier's room. We need to get that silver."

Sam went along with Dudley and the two soldiers to Louis Lanier's room. When they went inside, Dudley discovered a small valise and forced the hinges from the lid and found thirty shillings inside the lining of the small suitcase. After he had counted the money, he looked at Sam and said,

"The ten extra shillings should be enough to pay for our trip up here to Edenton."

Sam nodded and Dudley felt better about the transaction. Sam rented a room across the hall from Lawson's room. Soon the silver was brought there. Two soldiers were placed on guard outside the door while Sam examined the silver.

Soon Dudley came to the room. And told them that Lawson had been moved two doors from the tavern to the office of Dr. Edwards. His wound was severe but the doctor assured Dudley that he would live.

Suddenly the door was flung open and Samuel Johnston stood before them. "Your name IS Sam Pickett---is that right?"

It was evident that Johnston was upset by all that had happened.

"Yes, Sir," said Sam, not knowing how to react.

"Well, Sam. I realize that you may have had trouble with Mr. Lanier or Mr. Lawson in the past---but the present is what concerns me. If this man is not the Tory that you claim that he is---I shall personally see that Allen Jones is notified of your conduct."

"Sir, I know this man is an imposter. General Jones sent us here to meet with Mr. Louis Lanier and this man is Jonathan Lawson," said Sam, defending himself.

"Names are not important. The gunpowder is what you came for and what is needed so desperately. The man you wounded had gunpowder, whoever he may be. You, young man, will be held accountable," said Johnston, as he slammed the door behind him.

"Well--- we have the silver and letters of credit to get the gunpowder---I think we're in good shape. We'll know more when we go to the warehouse tomorrow, Sam." Dudley did not seem too concerned.

The two soldiers were posted outside the door. Dudley told them to take turns sleeping. He promised that they could sleep all the way back to Halifax.

Sam smiled at the soldiers when Dudley gave the order. No one would sleep until the silver and gunpowder were safely stored on the boat and they were underway. Then, if anyone slept it was be Dudley.

Sam walked to the window and sat down in a large soft cushioned chair. He knew he would not sleep even if Dudley had allowed him. Sam thought back to the night when he had first met Lawson. Was he really a Tory? Did Lawson own the gunpowder? Then doubts of his own judgment began to affect his thinking. Had he acted too hastily? Was he thinking more of his own grudge against Lawson above the welfare of the soldiers when he had challenged Lawson?

Sam knew these questions would have to be answered before he left Edenton. There was no way he could make General Jones understand something that he, himself, did not fully comprehend.

Later that morning, Sam learned that Lawson's had moved from Dr. Edward's office during the night and that Lawson had walked to a waiting carriage. Sam felt relieved that the wound had not been fatal. Perhaps Samuel Johnston would understand now.

Dudley had bandaged Sam's arm and placed it in a sling the night before and would not allow him to help with the loading of the gunpowder, so Sam was in no hurry to get to the dock.

When he reached the wharf, the soldiers were sitting on the pier and Dudley was talking with a large burly man.

"I have been given orders not to let the powder be moved," said the man.

"Then these letters of credit are no good," said Dudley as he turned toward Sam.

"Mr. Louis Lanier, the owner, came by earlier and gave me my orders. You'll have to deal with him," said the man, as he looked toward the tavern. "Here he comes now with Mr. Johnston."

Sam and Dudley quickly turned toward Horniblow's Tavern. They could see a bearded man with a patch over his left eye. When they came closer, Sam was relieved to see that the man was not Jonathan Lawson.

"I have a gentleman here I'd like you to meet, Sam," began Johnston. "This is Mr. Louis Lanier from New Bern"

Sam extended his hand. "I'm Sam Pickett and this is Christopher Dudley."

"You fellows get up early. I meant to catch you before you left Horniblow's," said Lanier, as he shook hands with Sam and Dudley.

"You don't know how glad I am to see you, Sir," said Dudley.

"I understand we are suppose to make a transaction," began Lanier.

"We were suppose to make it yesterday," said Dudley.

First For Freedom

"I know I'm a little late but I feel I am lucky to be here at all," said Lanier.

"What happened to you, Sir," asked Sam.

"I was about ten miles from here----riding through a wooded area---making good time---when a masked man on horseback held me up. He gagged me and tied me to a tree ---then took all my letters of credit. I don't understand but he seemed to know I was carrying those letters of credit. That's the only thing he asked for. Did any of you ever look down the barrel of a blunderbuss? That gun he had looked like a cannon."

"And it's about as heavy," said Sam, looking quickly at Dudley, who smiled back at him.

"Where was the powder stored before it was shipped to Edenton," asked Dudley.

"It was shipped from New Bern last week by Mr. Jonathan Lawson. He's the only one who knew anything about the shipment," informed Lanier.

"Well, this is one scheme that Lawson won't profit from," said Sam.

"You mean it was Lawson who held me up?"

"He would've gotten away with it if Sam hadn't recognized him." Dudley looked intently at Samuel Johnston.

"Well, I'm glad I got here in time. Let's have a look at the silver," said Lanier.

Sam and the soldiers stayed on the dock with Samuel Johnston and waited as Dudley and Lanier boarded Allen Jones' boat.

Samuel Johnston turned to Sam.

"You know, Sam, I've always considered myself a good judge of other men---but it seems that I underestimated you. I certainly overestimated the imposter. I don't recall the last time I've had to apologize to a man for being wrong but I hope you will consider this poor effort as a sincere apology. I intend to write to Allen Jones and tell him about all that has happened here. I hope---in that way---to make up for the way I misjudged you."

"I appreciate that, sir. I know you are as happy as I am about the way things have turned out."

When Dudley and Lanier returned to the dock, they ordered the powder to be loaded and the silver to be moved from the boat. The transaction had been made and both parties were satisfied.

Sam went with the soldiers to take the silver back to Horniblow's Tavern while Dudley stayed at the dock and supervised the loading of the powder.

When they returned to the dock, the powder was loaded so they quickly boarded the boat. The oarsmen shoved the boat away from the dock and they were underway. The business in Edenton was finished.

Sam stood on the bow of the boat and turned to look back at the warehouses that now became smaller. He was glad to be on his way home. He was glad he had finished his business with Jonathan Lawson.

BOOK TWO

CHAPTER NINETEEN

In mid-September of 1780, Sam, along with all the other soldiers at Camp Quanky received orders that he was to be sent to join with Colonel Williams R. Davie in the southwestern part of the state. Providence was thought to be no more than six days away.

He had said his good-byes to his mother and Aunt Jenny at his home and learned that Sarah Pickett had not heard from his Uncle John since he had joined with General Lincoln at Charles Town.

Earlier that month, William R. Davie had been appointed Colonel Commandant of the cavalry, by Governor Nash, and had been given instructions to raise a regiment in the Charlotte area. Word reach Halifax that Davie had had little success in raising the troops and Cornwallis had moved his entire army into the Waxhax, about fifty miles from Charlotte. Governor Nash had immediately met with General Jones to consider the number of troops that could be sent from Halifax to aid the Patriots. It was quickly decided that all able-bodied men would be sent to join with the Continentals. Two hundred soldiers, four wagons loaded with blankets, gunpowder shoes and other supplies were to be taken along with fifty horses. Sam was to command the troops until they reached Davie.

Soon after returning to camp, Sam went to his cabin, packed his gear and was bringing it to the outside when he saw General Allen Jones coming across the open area.

"Sam, I have a favor to ask of you," said the General, as he sat on the bench outside Sam's cabin. "Sit down with me for a while. It'll be some time before you'll be leavin'."

"Yes, Sir." Sam sat beside the general and noticed a deep concern that Allen Jones seemed almost reluctant to admit.

General Jones took a packet of letters from inside his coat.

"I've been asked by my girl, Sarah, to entrust you with these. They were written to Colonel Davie. Sarah has not heard from him since he was wounded at Stono. He moves about so much--no one knows from one day to the next where to locate him. She's written him every week for the past month and her letters have been returned unopened. I thought she would become discouraged and forget him--at least until after the war. However, time has seemed to make her even more faithful in her devotion."

"Time has a way of making one's love grow stronger--if it's the right kind of love," said Sam, thinking of Josie.

"Well, I promised Sarah I'd get her letters to him. When you deliver these, ask Davie to write a word to her. She has become so despondent, her mother and I are becoming concerned. This sort of thing can cause her to become ill. She's had little use for food lately and seeks always to be to herself. Tell Davie these things and maybe he'll find the time to scribble a note. I know how dangerous it must be to write anything--there are so many ways his letters could fall into the wrong hands. Tell him--if he does not consider the risk too great, we would appreciate a letter to Sarah."

Sam took the packet of letters and put it inside his knapsack.

"You can assure Sarah that her letters will reach Colonel Davie. I know how much they mean to her," said Sam, as he stood and threw the sack over his shoulder.

General Jones took a map from inside his coat and handed it to Sam.

"Stay to the route I've marked and you'll find Davie, if he hasn't moved since he last wrote Nash."

Soon --Sam was moving among the soldiers checking the wagons and supplies..

No more than fifty of the two hundred soldiers carried long hunting rifles that had been in their families for generations and had been handed to them by their fathers. There were only twenty swords among the men. These few weapons had been pounded and shaped by the hands of the blacksmiths from left over pieces of metal that would have been farm implements and tools in more peaceful times.

Each enlisted man who was fortunate enough to own a rifle was to provide a ramrod, priming wire brush, and a pouch containing a cartridge box with thirty leaden balls. A quart canteen, a blanket, and a knapsack were issued to the footsoldiers. Colonel Nicholas Long seemed to have more men than he had supplies.

The men were clothed in their usual attire. Some wore homespun shirts, some wore leather with breeches of the same material. Long stockings of different colors came to their knees. Most of the soldiers wore cowhide shoes and there were no more than a dozen pairs of boots in the entire company. Their coats and waistcoats were of many dimensions and color as various as the shades of autumn. Powder horns dangled loosely from the shoulders of those who owned rifles. On their heads were, round, broad-brimmed hats and scattered thinly among the soldiers were black cocked hats owned by those who were fortunate enough to have boots. This company of unseasoned soldiers was of no particular uniform but their appearance was not what captured Sam's attention. He felt there was

First For Freedom

a spirit among these men that could not have been higher---even if General George Washington were commanding them.

Sam mounted 'Jericho' and turned to the soldiers.

"Mount up---move out."

He felt he was more fortunate than the other soldiers were since Sarah Pickett made his clothes. She had labored for many days on the brown, leather, hunting shirt with the fringe around the neck, on the shoulder and about the shirttail. His breeches matched his shirt and were the color of brown leaves. His cocked hat was black and held snugly his thick brown hair that was tied in a queue with a black ribbon.

It was close to noon when the parade of soldiers left Halifax. Sam looked back over his shoulder after they had crossed Quanky Bridge and wondered if they would be recognized as a fighting unit or if perhaps their appearance would be an advantage if they should encounter the enemy along the way. If they split up no one would know them from any other hunter or farmer.

Thinking of the training of these men caused Sam to wonder what they had to offer other than manpower. They were all inexperienced and too poorly equipped to offer anything more. Those flintlocks were only effective at close range and it would take an average of three minutes for them to reload. Sam thought of all he had heard of the heavy artillery of Cornwallis' army and how devastating the cannons would be against these simple weapons.

During the long ride, Sam and the soldiers camped at those selected spots marked on the map. Each day he studied the map and considered how many miles they had made; then calculated how much farther they would have to travel before they reached Providence.

Many times, along the way, Sam thought of the war. It seemed that a massive storm had brought death and destruction to the country since the lightning first struck at Breed's Hill in Boston. The claps of thunder had grown louder and louder until the sounds were heard throughout the land. There had been a brief lull in 1778 when England was ready to give the colonies virtually everything they wanted---except independence. By that time too much had happened and nothing short of independence would be accepted for the French had finally agreed to two treaties to support the American effort. The diplomacy of that grand old man, Benjamin Franklin, coupled with the overwhelming victory at Saratoga were enough to sway the French to join the colonies in the fight for freedom.

Sam fancied how the huge black clouds of war had then moved South by sea and by-passed all the colonies that lay between the northern Colonies and Georgia. The British, under General Clinton, had moved into Georgia and the rage and fury of clashing armies lay waste the land. When the fighting subsided, the British held Atlanta and Savannah.

Names of Generals and commanding officers who took part in the violent campaigns in Georgia were not familiar to Sam. There was news of one Halifax soldier whose name was more than familiar than any other. It had been reported at Camp Quanky that the British front line at Atlanta and Savannah was made up of North Carolina and South Carolina Loyalists who were led by the notorious John Hamilton.

The storm to the South had affected the climate in Halifax as well as the entire state. General Jones had sent all trained soldiers to General Benjamin Lincoln's command at that time; then new recruits were drafted and the training cycle had continued at a hectic pace. Soldiers were sent out who were not mature enough to leave home.

Soon the storm swept across South Carolina and was felt most severely at places like Charles Town and Camden. With the conquest of South Carolina, General Clinton left command of the British Army in the south to his most capable officer---General Cornwallis.

For some reason, not known to Sam, Cornwallis delayed his invasion of North Carolina and for a while there was nothing left of the American Army in the South to resist any movement the British might make. Guerrilla action replaced the fighting of large armies and the delaying tactics of Cornwallis gave the Patriots of North Carolina time to organize their forces.

These scattered forces were now moving to the southwestern part of the state. Manpower just might prove a deciding factor for it was certain the colonials could not match the British in weapons.

After six days of hard riding and marching, the Halifax soldiers arrived at Providence, where Davie had taken post. Sam was satisfied they had made good time, for they were half a day ahead of schedule.

When he had turned the horses and supplies over to the quartermaster, Sam was asked to report to Colonel Davie's tent. There---he spoke at some length with his new commanding officer and when Davie finally asked about Sarah Jones, Sam withdrew the packet of letters from his knapsack. Colonel Davie talked with keen interest about the opportunities for a lawyer in Halifax. From the gist of the conversation, Sam was brought to full realization of Davie's hope for a future with Sarah Jones. He was, without a doubt, as devoted to her as she was to him.

Sam quickly became impressed with his commander. Colonel Davie was tall and handsomely dressed in his uniform of dark blue. The buttonholes of his coat were edged with narrow white lace where large white buttons held it snugly to his body. He had a superior authority about him that Sam knew was indispensable to any officer who commanded as many men. Sam knew Davie's record as a soldier and admired him all the more when Davie did not speak of his many accomplishments. He seemed more concerned about all the fighting that was yet to come.

His eyes had an intelligent look and his dark hair swept over his ears. He had a perfect nose that enhanced his oval face. His lips were perhaps a little thin for his more prominent chin. What impressed Sam, more than anything else, was Davie's personality. Davie was sensitive, intelligent, and dedicated to the cause of freedom. Here was a man who was willing to sacrifice everything, including his life, for independence from England.

Early in the morning of the second day, General Sumner rode into camp with about two hundred soldiers. After consulting with Davie for an hour, the two officers emerged from Davie's tent. Colonel Davie immediately selected a company of twenty seasoned, Calvary soldiers and gave orders for the rest to move to Salisbury to wait for General Sumner. Colonel Davie asked Sam to accompany him to Charlotte while the rest of the Halifax soldiers were to move to Salisbury to await further orders. Sam did not know why they were going to Charlotte but as he prepared to evacuate camp, he learned that General Sumner had ordered Davie to attack Cornwallis' foraging parties and to skirmish with the advancing light troops.

Obeying General Sumner's orders, the troops entered the town of Charlotte in the late afternoon of the twenty-fifth of September. As they rode down the main street, a young Continental rode quickly up to Colonel Davie.

"Cornwallis is coming about five miles down the road!"

"That's why we're here," informed Davie.

"You'd better not be here long," warned the soldier, as he turned his horse and rode away.

Disregarding the warning, the troops continued into town and Sam noticed they were coming to rising ground. The entire town was situated on top of a hill. Two main streets intersected a right angles with a court house neatly nestled at the center. Sam counted forty house, all empty for the news of Cornwallis' army had already reached the townspeople.

When they came to the courthouse, Colonel Davie dismounted his company and told Sam to stay close to him. He ordered the soldiers to take post behind the garden fences on each side of the street. Davie then led the way to the courthouse. Looking around as he entered the courthouse with Davie and six more soldiers, Sam could tell that the first floor had been used as a market place. Evidently the second floor was where court was held. Since the courthouse was not occupied, Davie ordered the men to go out the back door and stand at the side of the courthouse. There were ten Calvary men with Davie and ten across the street behind the fence. All the men had their rifles loaded and had their horses close by so they would be ready to leave in a hurry.

All the soldiers were well situated and quietly waited. If the British were to pass through town, they would have to use the main street.

Soon the rumbling sound of marching soldiers was heard and the dragoons could be seen coming down the street. The legion of Tarleton led the advance, the main body following close behind. When they were within thirty yards of the courthouse, Davie ordered the soldiers to open fire. The advancing British seemed startled by the unexpected attack and quickly fell back. The whole British Army was abruptly stopped in its advance.

The Continentals reloaded and stayed in their places. Suddenly the appearance of Tarleton checked the retreat of the Red Coats. Sam could see the Colonel in the midst of the confused Dragoons. The Continentals could hear his voice.

"Legions! Remember you have everything to lose and nothing to gain."

The retreating soldiers stopped ----regrouped and returned to the charge.

While the Continentals were reloading for the third time, Colonel Davie shouted from the side of the courthouse.

"Move out quickly--- move out! ----NOW!"

Davie's company hurried from the town with the British in hot pursuit that lasted for several miles. Local support from the riflemen along the road made it possible for Davie's men to escape.

Two days later Davie and the company joined with the rest of the army at Salisbury, where men and officers to raise new recruits had assembled. Here Colonel Taylor's regiment from Granville was united to Davie's command.

While Cornwallis lingered at Charlotte, news reached camp in early October that the British had been completely defeated at Kings Mountain. The victory brought new life to the soldiers and was a severe blow to Cornwallis who hastily abandoned Charlotte and retired to Winnsboro, South Carolina.

The exodus of the British was celebrated with as much rejoicing as the victory at Kings Mountain. North Carolina was again free of any major British army.

CHAPTER TWENTY

In December, General Nathanael Greene's army absorbed all the troops that had operated under Colonel Davie's command. Sam was concerned and felt a sadness now that he was being taken from Davie's command.

Shortly after his arrival, General Greene met with all the officers and urged Colonel Davie to accept the important position of officer of the Commissary Department. This work involved great labor and little honor. Sam heard that Davie was reluctant to accept anything that would take him from the fighting. Greene soon convinced Davie that there could be no army without provisions. This was the weakest part of the army. There were shortages everywhere----not enough of anything----yet the demands on the soldiers were greater than they had ever been. Davie's love of fame was great but his love for his country was greater, so he accepted the office.

Major General Nathanael Greene of Rhode Island succeeded General Gates in command of the Continental army in the South, December, 1780.

General Greene began immediately to organize, train and equip the two thousand men under his command. Most of the men were untrained and not fit for fighting. Over three hundred were without arms and more than half were too naked to even face the bitter December weather. As Sam moved among the soldiers, he could only estimate that about eight hundred were properly equipped and armed well enough to meet the enemy. What he saw in this great multitude of men was very repetitious of the two hundred who marched with him from Halifax.

While the Continentals were being shaped into a fighting force, word reached camp that General Daniel Morgan had defeated Colonel Tarleton at Cowpens. Earlier in the month, General Morgan had been dispatched from Greene's army to move into South Carolina and join forces with Sumter and then press toward Augusta. Evidently General Cornwallis had learned of Morgan's movement and had sent Colonel Tarleton to stop the Continentals.

Upon hearing the news, there was wild rejoicing throughout the camp. The Continentals were now beginning to rally from the disasters of South Carolina. Hopes were spurred to new heights and it was told that Colonel Tarleton had barely escaped with this life.

One of the most talked about incidents of the Battle of Cowpens was the hand to hand fight that ensued between Colonel Tarleton and Colonel William Washington. It seemed that Tarleton had emerged from the fight with a slight hand wound and Colonel Washington had run him from the field. Sam heard many accounts of the fight and each time new details were added. The soldiers always placed more emphasis on the victories and as little as possible was said about the defeats.

Soon after Daniel Morgan's brilliant victory over the British, General Greene directed all the troops to move with his army to Sherill's Ford on the Catawba River to meet with the victorious commander, who was being pressed by Cornwallis.

After about one month of marching, the two generals met and completed the detail for their campaign against Cornwallis. All the Continentals were informed of the plan and were told what was expected of them. The idea was to draw Cornwallis as far from his base of supplies as possible. It quickly became evident that the plan was working for Cornwallis was following close behind as the Continentals moved toward Guilford.

First For Freedom

Sam began to realize that General Greene was a master of retreat. From maps of the area, he had accurate knowledge of the streams, roads, fords and the countryside.

General Greene was more familiar with the area than most officers who had grown up in North Carolina. Even with all this knowledge and ingenuity, Greene could do little to insure comfort for his men.

The retreat from Catawba to Guilford was the worse time Sam had ever experienced. The bitter January weather was cold and wet. The half-naked soldiers marched down roads ankle deep in mud made soft and sloppy by the hooves of horses and the turning wheels of wagons that moved ahead. They were drenched by torrents of rain and sleet; made to wade through freezing water but always moving---never staying at one place more than eight to ten hours. All were weak from hunger, without blankets, without rest, without sleep and had to leave the dead by the side of the road for want of time to give them a proper burial.

After twenty-two days of marching, the army joined forces with other troops at Guilford Court House. The British had reached Salem only twenty miles away.

Cornwallis had followed closely behind and had been drawn two hundred and thirty miles from his base into enemy country. It was thought that he had lost as many men as Greene during the march and when Cornwallis tried to recruit Loyalists in the area, the thought was confirmed.

Word was received in camp that three hundred Tories attempted to reach Cornwallis but were surprised by 'Light Horse' Harry Lee's battalion and cut to pieces. Nearly one hundred were reported killed and most of the others were wounded.

For several days men from the surrounding countryside filtered into camp and from estimates Sam had heard, the army now total close to four thousand. It was believed that Cornwallis' Army of seasoned veterans did not number three thousand.

General Greene was careful in selecting the battlefield. After much consideration he chose a field near the Great State Road, which was on the brow of a hill. There was a slope for about half a mile that led to a valley crossed by a small steam. This road ran through a large open area and to the right of the highway was an open field, which still had stubbles of cornstalks from the previous summer.

Greene stationed his army along the hill and Sam was posted with the North Carolina troops behind a rail fence about mid-way the slope. This first line of defense was under the command of Butler and Eaton, assisted by Colonel William R. Davie, who refused to be left behind. The second line was about one fifty yards behind the North Carolina soldiers. Here the Virginia troops were posted in the woods. Just behind the Virginia line were the Continentals who made up the third line of defense. All of these men were seasoned soldiers who had proven themselves in previous battles. On Sam's right were Colonel William Washington and his cavalry; to his left were Colonel Lee and his legion of Virginia riflemen. Captain Singleton was posted in the center of the road with two six-pounders.

When the soldiers were in place, General Greene rode among his men and checked each line of defense. All the North Carolina soldiers had long rifles resting along the fence rail when General Greene came to the front line.

"Fire your rifles and retire behind the second line. Wait until they're close enough for your bullets to reach them."

Sam turned and watched the General ride to the crest of the hill where he waited.

It was cold but fair and the sun was shining brilliantly when the British came across the small stream at the base of the hill. It was a little after noon and Sam heard the thunder from Singleton's cannons behind him. The deafening noise caused him to forget how scared he was but he was quickly reminded of his fear when Cornwallis answered with his own artillery. The Red Coats marched forward in precision and the bayonets glittered with a blinding effect on all the soldiers who waited quietly for the British to come within firing range.

Colonel Tarleton's Calvary led the advance. Fire from Colonel Lee and the Virginia riflemen slowed the Red Coats momentarily. Lee and his men held their ground until another British regiment advanced. Now the British line became more extended and Lee fell back with his men and took a position in the second line of defense.

The British came on in full force led by General Leslie. The red wave moved steadily toward them. Now they were within range and Colonel Eaton ordered them to fire. Blazing fire came from the fence rail but caused only a slight hesitation in the British advance. All the soldiers along the fence began to scramble toward the second line of defense. Passing behind the second line of defense, Sam turned and could see General Leslie waving his sword over his head and shouting from his horse.

"Charge! Charge! ---"

These orders were so loud they were heard above the battle noise. The British came on with bayonets charging beyond the first line. Sam along with the other North Carolina soldiers, scattered behind the second line to the edge of the woods. Finding refuge behind a tree, Sam reached for his powder horn to reload. He grasped the ends of a loosely dangling

First For Freedom

rawhide---his powder horn was gone. Now he was helpless to do anything but watch for he had no other weapon.

The British advanced to the second line. The Virginia soldiers stood firm until the British came closer, but when charged, they too, fell back. The British were moving to the third line of defense where General Greene passed among them shouting words of encouragement. Here, veteran soldiers received the enemy and the fighting was close and fierce. The battle raged with great violence---each side striving for victory. Sam could hear shrieking screams of pain, thunder of cannons, firing muskets and shouting commands. The battle noise was deafening even from the edge of the woods.

Suddenly Colonel Washington pressed forward with his Calvary and the British line swayed. Howard and his men with fixed bayonets immediately followed Washington. The tide was beginning to turn and British fell back under the onslaught of Washington's men. Then Cornwallis brought up the heavy artillery and stopped the advance of the Continentals. The Red Coats turned and retained their position as Cornwallis brought up fresh troops.

Then the British line became more extended and there was immediate danger that the Continentals would be completely encircled. Seeing this precarious development, General Greene ordered retreat. The Continentals moved from their positions in good order, then there was a scattering of troops as they veered off in several directions.

Sam ran quickly to join the retreating soldiers. As he looked back at the battlefield, he could see that the enemy was too crippled to pursue the straggling Continentals. On the field were left two ammunition wagons, artillery, and several of Greene's horses. From what he could see of the battlefield, there were as many Red Coats left lying along the road and in the opening as there were Continentals. Both sides had suffered great losses.

General Greene halted the army about three miles from the field of battle to collect what he could of the scattered army; then fell back to the Iron Works to take post.

Two days after the battle, Greene's headquarters received news of a proclamation from Cornwallis' camp. He urged "all loyal subjects to stand forth and take an active part in restoring good order and government" and offered pardon and restoration to all rebels who would surrender themselves to royal authorities. This news was regarded as an admission of defeat, for it was evident that Cornwallis was, in his own way, asking for help.

Sleet and rain swept by sharp fierce, March wind all but brought to a halt any activity in camp the second day. When Sam arose the next morning, he was as tired as he had been the day before. He, along with twenty other soldiers, was told to report to Colonel Davie, who was waiting in the north end of the camp.

While walking through the camp, Sam noticed the wind was blowing even harder than it had the previous night and in the wake of the dissipated storm had blown hundreds of bedraggled soldiers to Iron Works.

When Sam arrived at the edge of the camp, he was handed a shovel from Colonel Davie.

"We've had little time to see to our dead. There are at least twenty men who need to be buried".

Colonel Davie proceeded to instruct the soldiers about the width, depth and length of the pit that was to be dug.

The drenching rain the night before had made the earth soft beneath a thin frozen crust. Water seeped into the five-foot wide trench and completely covered the bottom that stretched out twenty feet in length and about four feet in depth. The shallow pit was little more than a sloppy mud hole by the time it was finished.

Davie rubbed his hands briskly to generate heat as he looked to a stout, red bearded officer.

"Get the dead and bring them here. There's no need to cover the pit until all the dead are counted."

Sam did not know the officer in charge but quickly followed the detail back to camp. Davie walked a short way with the soldiers and then turned off toward headquarters. The tents for the wounded were located about mid-way the camp.

The burial detail walked among the many ragged, hungry, half-dead soldiers who staggered about the camp as if they had no destination. Perhaps by moving they could assure themselves that they still had life. There were soldiers on forked crutches, soldiers with arms in slings, soldiers with bandages about their heads---even the wounded could count themselves fortunate compared to the ones they were now tending, thought Sam.

As Sam walked inside the first tent, with three other soldiers, he could smell the sickening stench of death. Two wounded soldiers raised up on their elbows to watch the dead being wrapped in worn, tattered, blankets to be dragged from the tent. While Sam and the other three soldiers were removing the dead from the first tent, the other soldiers moved along the row of tents to seek out the dead.

Twelve soldiers were removed from the midst of the moaning and groaning wounded. Of the dead, there were three who had no wound but had fallen to another deadly foe---pneumonia.

First For Freedom

When all the dead had been removed, the red-bearded officer held up a worn blanket and folded the corner.

"This will give you a better grip. Use the blankets for stetchers and haul them to the pit."

Sam grabbed one corner of a blanket and moved with three other soldiers to join the procession now headed for the large grave. Walking among the soldiers, Sam could not tell the officers from the enlisted men. The uniforms and rough clothes were so tattered and muddy that any distinguishing characteristics they might have had were gone. Weary, half-naked soldiers huddled around small fires to keep warm but looked up from the fire long enough to notice the moving train slowly making its way to the death pit.

After two hours of work, all the dead had been brought to the edge of the long pit. The bodies were wrapped in the blankets and given to two soldiers who were in the pit. These two placed the bodies in a row and covered them with the blankets. Sam looked down at the hulking mass of death and felt an aching pain in the pit of his stomach. There was a steeping odor coming from the pit. He had to turn away from the grave.

"Cover the hole," ordered the officer, who stood with folded arms and hands tucked under his armpits.

Sam and the other soldiers grabbed the standing shovels and hurled the sloppy earth over the dead bodies. There was little feeling in his feet and his hand became numb with cold long before the hole was filled.

When the work was completed, Sam walked back to his tent. He noticed that some of the soldiers had found salted pork and were munching away like half-starved dogs. He was hungry before the burial but now he only felt a sickening pain in his stomach.

About mid-afternoon, Sam was called to stand guard over ten prisoners captured at Guilford. The prisoners were held under guard at the south end of the camp.

After taking a long-rifle from a thin Continental, Sam walked to the backside of the camp where the prisoners were huddled under a large oak tree. The wind was fierce and the prisoners were scantily clad. Sam had been fortunate enough to find some burlap to wrap around his feet after the burial detail but his clothes were as ragged and worn as the prisoners. As he looked toward the huddled mass, he realized that they were more unfortunate than he. Several men had severe wounds for which there was no treatment. All the prisoners had beards and Sam thought they all looked alike.

Most of the Continentals had grown beards, too--not because they wanted the growth--there was just no time to shave. Sam had mentioned to one of the soldiers that his face was the only warm place on his body during long march from Catawba to Guilford.

There were many young, fuzzy-faced soldiers who were not mature enough to grow beards but were old enough to fight for their country. --- and old enough to die. Some of these young soldiers had been left on the battlefield at Guilford.

As Sam moved back and forth, he could hear mumbles he thought were comforting words to those few who were in pain. Some of the prisoners watched him and one of the men spoke.

"We've got a couple of men here who need help--I fear that one is dying."

Sam turned to the voice.

"I can't leave my post to help you. We, too, have lost many men, as you well know."

Another man spoke,

"Will you see about a blanket?"

"I'll see what I can do when I'm relieved," promised Sam.

The prisoners did not speak again until Sam's replacement arrived. After speaking quietly with the new guard, Sam handed him the flintlock rifle.

As he approached the prisoners, two of the men stepped back for Sam to see the wounded. He looked at the face of one young soldier whose right arm was resting across his chest. His left arm was severed at the elbow and wrapped with dark blue cloth that had turned crimson with blood from the wound. The boy was breathing heavily and his eyes looked tired and dilated. He couldn't have been over twenty two years old thought Sam as he moved to the next soldier.

Sam looked down at the prostrate soldier. His right hand clutched a bleeding wound just below his heart. Blood still issued from the wound and the prisoner's hand was streaked with red lines. Looking from the wound to the soldier's face, Sam realized that there was something familiar behind the dark, black beard. As he leaned down for closer look, his knees buckled and he dropped to the side of George Hamilton.

"George----oh----George----George Hamilton----"

George opened his eyes and looked at Sam. "Sam Pickett---Sam you mean you're here, too."

"I'm here, George."

"Well, I'm not ----sure who won the battle---but I feel---I'm losing this fight."

Each word seemed to drain the little strength that remained in his weakened body.

"Don't talk, George. You need rest."

"I'll soon rest, Sam. Take my uniform and sword---and whatever I have left to Josie. I think----she---might want something of mine.---I'm cold, Sam."

Sam took George's hand and it was cold.

"He's lost so much blood," said one of the prisoners behind Sam.

"Take care of Josie, Sam. She'll ---be needing you when this ----fight is finished. Oh, Sam, I'm so cold."

Sam released the cold hand.

"You just rest, George. I'll see about getting you a blanket."

Sam ran from the prisoners to the commissary and told the supply sergeant he needed a blanket for a wounded soldier. There was no blanket available for anyone, so Sam ran quickly to the tent where the wounded Continentals were quartered. Finding one of the soldiers dead, Sam took the blanket from the body. With it folded under his arm, he hurried back to the south end of the camp.

Sam nodded to the guard and walked toward the prisoners. They all looked up as Sam came near. No one spoke. The blank stare in George's dark blue eyes told Sam that he was too late to bring any comfort.

He walked to where George lay, sat down, and looked at the pale face behind the dark beard. With two fingers of his right hand, Sam pulled the lids over George's lifeless eyes. His hand rested momentarily on the cold cheeks of his boyhood companion. He tucked the blanket around the body and moved quickly away from the prisoners

As he walked back to his quarters, Sam thought of that times in his youth when he and George had been so close, good times---times spent making letters into words, making words into sentences---making sentences into thoughts--that had meaning---learning to read. Then---those days of happiness, laughter, and fun at Quanky Creek. Those glorious days playing 'Pirates'----making the raft they called the 'Golden Hind'--and digging out that cave on the bank of the creek that was concealed behind the thick growth of bushes---known only to them.

Sam thought how death was like a thief. Death had robbed him of the happiness of his youth. It had taken a part of his past that had meaning.

Sam thought of all those angry faces he had seen charging the Continental lines at Guilford and the soldiers who were left lying on the battlefield. How glorious had been the feeling of death when it came to the enemy. Now--this self-same death had taken a friend. In the heat of the battle, life was not real and death had no meaning. No time could be taken to think---but now the battle was over and now he had time to consider how precious was the life of his friend. George's life was real for he had shared it and death had meaning---new meaning. For the first time, Sam understood that death did not always come with a sudden blow; it could come in part to the living when close friends are taken. Now George was dead and Sam felt that a part of his life had been lost at the Battle of Guilford

As he approached his quarters, his pace slowed and a strange tender feeling possessed him. He could only think of that day when George had been tied to the pine tree down by the Roanoke River and left naked. He began to laugh---tears swelled in his eyes and blurred his vision and his laughter turned to sobs.

Sam met with Colonel William R. Davie early the next morning and asked for all the personal effects of George Hamilton. Davie understood Sam's request and had the effects sent to Sam's tent about mid-morning.

Sam accepted the bundle, covered with a ragged, blue blanket and tied with hemp cord.

"Here's a list of all the dead and wounded from your outfit," said the aide, as he handed Sam an envelope.

Sam sat on the ground and untied the bundle as the aide walked away. He placed the neatly folded British uniform on the ground and read the official papers. George Hamilton---Twenty First Foot---Second Regiment----enlisted April 4, 1779---New Bern, North Carolina.

He put the papers on the uniform and picked up a pocketknife that George had carried since his fourteenth birthday. The only other item in the bundle was a very thin pocket watch with 'George' inscribed on the back plate. Not much, thought Sam, to account for one's life, especially one who knew life so well.

At noon an assembly was called and orders were read to all troops who had been in the army for one year. These soldiers were to return to their hometowns and report to the officer in command. It was reported that Cornwallis was moving toward Wilmington and General Greene would move the Continentals South. Even though he had held the field at the end of the battle at Guilford, Cornwallis had not chosen to follow. He had been stopped in his advance----General Greene was satisfied with that victory.

CHAPTER TWENTY-ONE

Sam and fifty North Carolina troops returned to Halifax in late March. After they had crossed Quanky Creek, women and children walked along with the soldiers. Some of the women asked questions about loved ones and followed the troops all the way to Camp Quanky. The war had been hard for the women. Sewing and weaving cloth for the soldiers and having to do the work that had been left by the men was something they had readily accepted. What was so unbearable to some of the women was accepting the fact that their husbands and sons would not be returning. Now more women would have to be told that their loved ones had not survived the Battle of Guilford. Halifax had lost ten men in that battle. When he reached Camp Quanky, he would turn the casualty list over to General Jones. Sam was glad that he would not have to tell the women.

He reported to General Jones and gave his personal account of the Battle of Guilford Court House. After answering many questions, Sam turned over the casualty list and was given three days leave to visit his family.

Riding from Camp Quanky, he turned right at Quanky Bridge onto the road that led to 'Grove House'. He thought about the bundle that contained George's personal effects and had determined that he would leave it inside their cave at Quanky Creek. He would give it to Josie, if he ever had the opportunity. Somehow, Sam felt that these things should be left at a place that had meant so much to his friend, and there was no place in Halifax that had meant more to George than their secret cave.

Thinking of what he was about to do, Sam turned off the main road onto a wooded path. Some people would not understand and he would have no explanation if he were ever asked why he was performing such an act. It would be better not to mention it to anyone---except Josie.

He tied 'Jericho' to a small bush and then untied the bundle from behind his saddle. With the bundle tucked under his left arm, he pushed his way through a reed thicket and tramped along a now hidden path. Tangled briars and thick undergrowth were unyielding ---so he made his way around the growth to walk among small pines and holly. Large pines grew in abundance throughout the area between the main road and Quanky Creek, but as he neared the creek slim birch and willows rose up around him and the pine trees became less numerous.

His best memories were connected in so many ways with Quanky Creek. Here, his boyhood had been spent, hunting coon, possum, and squirrel. He remembered that he had six rabbit boxes that he and George would check whenever they were fishing in the creek. He would take rabbits home and his Aunt Jenny would skin them and cook them for the family. His Uncle John thought rabbit was as good as chicken. Sam had fished for catfish and perch, had swum on hot summer days when the Roanoke was overflowing to make Quanky deeper. He had once known the creek as well as he now knew the road from his house to Halifax. The huge cypress, fallen moss-covered logs, and the meandering creek fifty feet below were all familiar to him once again.

Slipping over the edge of the cliff, Sam carefully edged his way down the steep incline. When he came to the base of the cliff where Quanky rippled gently at his feet, he became aware that his surrounding had changed from what he had seen from the top of the cliff. But then, only his position had changed. He thought of the war and how human positions could be altered to see entirely different views.

The cave was not over three hundred yards from 'the Grove' and was located on the same side of Quanky Creek. It had been ten years since he had last visited the cave and now new growth had caused great changes in the appearance of all that was once so familiar. For some unknown reason Sam had expected to find this special spot unchanged. Now, like himself, it had matured to something different---yet it had retained some of those characteristics that were still recognizable.

As he looked downstream, he noticed a large boulder protruding from the bank on his side of the creek. That's one thing that hasn't changed, thought Sam. Now he knew his bearings. The cave was upstream about thirty yards. Clutching his bundle under his arm, he walked among the bramble and growth toward the boulder. The bushes that had once concealed the cave so well had grown and the cave was hidden even better now.

Sam hesitated for a moment at the base of the cave and looked at the large fallen cypress that stretched the width of the creek. He and George had played 'Robin Hood and Little John' on that log bridge. He smiled, remembering how he had let George knock him off the log into the shallow water. There was nothing that had pleased George more than to defeat Sam in some game that demanded physical strength. Near the fallen tree and just a few yards from Sam's feet were the remains of a raft. Some of the notched logs were still held together but no one else would have recognized them as a part of the 'Golden Hind' that had once dominated these waters. He and George had worked on that raft for a month and had ridden it down Quanky to the Roanoke on its maiden voyage.

Sam turned away from the creek and started up the bank. Making his way through the thick brush, he came to the entrance of the cave. He looked inside and could tell that there had been little weathering. The walls were as solid as ever and the beams were all intact.

He untied the sword from the bundle and then opened the blanket. He removed the knife, gold watch and George's official papers and put them on the floor of the cave. He took the wrinkled, red officer's coat and unfolded it; held it up and shook it. Then, he laid it flat on the floor and straightened the sleeves as he pressed out the wrinkles.

Sam started to button the coat when he noticed the corner of an envelope protruding from the inside pocket. He withdrew the letter and immediately recognized the familiar script. There was no doubt----there was no other hand like Josie's. He held the letter up to see the date of postage and read aloud---'March 1, 1781'. About two weeks before the Battle at Guilford, thought Sam as he opened the letter.

New Bern, N.C.
March 1. 1781

Dear George,

I welcomed your last letter and was relieved to know that you were safe and well. I fear for you and Father. My nights are sleepless and there is no way I shall rest until this war is over.

I failed to tell you in my last letter that I am staying with Aunt Maggie. She is as staunch for the Patriots as Father is for the Loyalists. I am convinced that no one would dare question her loyalties, so I feel safe and secure. She is one of Mother's sisters who has always been kind to me. Since Mother's death last Christmas, she has taken me for her own.

I wish there was a way I could write to Sam but Father has written that I cannot communicate with anyone in Halifax. He says the letter would never reach the one to whom it might be intended and that there are many Patriots who would like to know the whereabouts of any member of the Hamilton family---especially now that he has become so well known.

I was happy to read in your letter that you agreed with me about returning to Halifax when the war is over. I know that you and I still share a deep devotion to Sam.

With all the changes this war has brought, my love for him has not wavered.

I know you and Sam shared a rare companionship in our youth and I was always envious of both of you, knowing that I was never a part of that relationship. I am thankful for all those good times we spent together when Father made you two tolerate my presence. I shall look forward to even better times in the future.

Please let me hear from you more often. Whenever I hear news of the war, I become so restive for another letter. Pray that this conflict soon ends and we shall be reunited.

Keep your hopes alive

Love,
Josie

Sam folded the letter and placed it back inside the red coat and thought about the sad twist of fate by which he had received word from Josie. He then laid out the knee breeches with the top tucked neatly under the coat. He put the pocketknife and watch inside the pants pocket; put George's official papers inside the coat and moved out.

Leaving the cave, Sam walked with careful steps along the path and had turned to climb the steep incline when he noticed a moving bush about twenty yards up the path. He stopped to determine what was causing the phenomenon. There was stillness all around except that singular moving bush. Turning back to the footpath, Sam walked cautiously toward the bush. When he was about thirty feet away from it, the bush ceased to move. Not knowing what lay behind the growth, Sam stopped to get a closer look.

Suddenly Looney Oney bounded onto the footpath. She stood there as if she dared him to come closer. She had not changed in appearance from the first time he had seen her. She was wearing the same old felt hat and dark ragged coat. Across her shoulder was a twisted blue denim strap that held her brown burlap bag at her side. Oney looked downstream toward the cave as though she expected to see someone else coming along the footpath. Sam watched her cloudy eyes but could not see beyond them. What scattered thoughts dwelt behind those eyes were known only to Looney Oney.

"What-cha-doin' heah, young Man?"

"I've got my reasons for being here, Oney."

"So, you know Oney."

"I've known you since I was a young boy." Sam looked closer at the small woman. There was no noticeable change that he could see. How could she remain so much the same?

"You de Pickett boy. Ah knows your Ma. You got a good Ma. Give me stuff when I come to her back door. Knows Aunt Jenny, too. You home from the wah?"

"Just got back today. I haven't even been home yet."

"Dees bad times, young man. Gwan turn to worse times before dey git better. Ah seen de wind makin' circles in the tops of de trees, in de deep swamp. Wind don't come from nowhere and don't go nowhere. Wind dat makes circles---bad sign. Been bad times fuh Oney ever since Ah had to leave 'De Grove.' Mister Willie say he don't need no medicine woman tendin' his people."

"Mr. Willie believes in Dr. Joyner. The doctor has his way of curin' people, too, Oney."

"Slaves dead now dat would be live if Ah could doctor dem."

"Some diseases don't know any cure."

"De doctor don't know de cause. Ah knows de ways spirits comes and goes. Dere's ways to keep'em from coming and dere's ways to make'em leave when dey heah."

Sam nodded as Oney spoke. He then turned to the bush at his right.

"Why did you hide behind that bush when you saw me coming?"

"Some people don't mean Oney no good. When Ah seen you coming, Ah thought you were dat Hamilton boy dat used to play heah."

"George Hamilton is dead, Oney. He died fighting for the British."

Looney Oney shook her head.

"De boy daid. De boy daid. His time wah cut short. Some people hurrys to de death. Ah tried to tell him--Ah can see the future and Ah can see the past---Ah can see the first--Ah can see the last"

"Are you saying that George didn't have any choice?"

"Bad people can't be helped when de times is good. But good people can be helped when de time is bad. Bad times comin'. You needs one of Oney's charms to git you through dese bad times. You got money?"

"What do you have in that old bag that'll help me, Oney?"

"You listen to me and you take heed.
Oney's going to do you a good deed
Oney's going to keep away all harm
Just as long as you've got dis charm
Oney's gonna give you what you need
Oney's gonna give you what you need."

She took the strap from her shoulder and placed the burlap bag on the ground and began fumbling among her possessions. She withdrew a small leather pouch and took out a shiny pebble.

"Dis charm to be kept in yo right pocket. Long as you has it----ain't nothin' to harm you."

Sam took the speckled stone and held it up to the sun. It looked much like one of the pebbles he had collected in the shallow waters of Quanky when he was younger. He felt the smooth texture of the stone and wondered what significance it held for Oney.

"You got de money---it's youse."

Sam reached in his pocket and handed Oney a shiny coin.

"Are you sure this charm will bring me luck?"

"De charm is as good as you thank it. Got to believe. Dat's what de matter wid people. People scaid to believe dat good is as easy to call up as bad. Most time good mo' willin' to come dan bad."

Oney held the coin tightly in her hand and quickly picked up her burlap bag. She flung the strap over her shoulder and seemed eager to leave now that she had made her transaction.

"Tell yo Ma you seen Oney. Ah wants her to know Ah'm still alive. Ah be by to help wid de choppin' when de time comes. Tell her---I be by."

Looney Oney had a habit of rhyming her words and chanting. The chant that Sam heard had a lively beat----. "Some say Ah'm Looney -- Some say Ah'm mad --Some say Ah'm good and some say Ah'm bad-- People would be surprised if they only knew what Ah see when I make my brew-----

With these words, Oney disappeared behind the thick undergrowth and was gone almost as quickly as she had appeared.

Sam walked back downstream and climbed to the top of the steep incline and turned back to see moving brush along the footpath that led to Oney's cabin.

He felt better knowing that he now possessed one of Oney's charms. He had always felt that he could have what he wanted most in life if he believed strongly enough. Now, it was comforting to know there was, at least, one other human who shared his belief. Maybe the stone was not just another water-washed pebble----- there was no reason why it couldn't bring as much luck as a four-leaf clover or the foot of a rabbit---if he thought it could. Looney Oney thought it was lucky---and she had his farthing---so it had proven its worth as far as she was concerned. Thinking how Oney had hurried off after the transaction made Sam wonder who was really 'looney'. Somehow the word 'Looney' did not fit Oney anymore. But, fate, luck or whatever the future held for him would not be any more disastrous just because of a simple pebble---and if it did bring luck---it would be worth much more than a shiny farthing.

As he struggled through the thick brush toward his horse, Sam speculated about the time George had burned down the Hamilton smokehouse. Whatever strange forces moved among the lives that Looney Oney touched would never be known to him. He knew that. Perhaps what had happened to George was the work of a more powerful being. When there was no way to know, maybe it was wise to do good to those who claimed a higher power. ---"Good could be called up as easy as bad"-- and if worse times were coming---he would need all the luck he could find and he would welcome it from any source---even Looney Oney.

Sam spent the next three days at home and told his mother and Aunt Jenny all he knew about the war. He did not mention George Hamilton. There would be a better time for that, he thought. A time, perhaps, in the future when he would have a better understanding of all that had happened at Guilford. A time when he could find some kind of justification for George's death. A time when all was settled and life had meaning and purpose again.

While at home, he learned that his Uncle John had been missing since the Battle of Charles Town and sensed that his mother had accepted the fact that this time Uncle John would not be coming home.

Sam worked hard at Camp Quanky. He had been give the rank of Lieutenant by Colonel William R. Davie and General Jones placed him in charge of the drilling and marching. The two hundred troops had all seen battle and were based at Quanky awaiting further orders. Still the training was required of these seasoned soldiers who would soon be sent out as a fighting unit. There were no new recruits. The counties and towns had long ago given up all their young men.

Sam visited Dudley's Tavern as often as possible. There were still some of the old cronies but most of Dudley's customers were soldiers from camp. The soldiers talked about the war and different acts of bravery but listened intently to travelers who brought news from other parts of the state. The atmosphere at Dudley's Tavern was different from what Sam had enjoyed before the war. There was a stiffness shared by the soldiers who chose to drink alone. The cronies huddled at a back table and talked quietly among themselves. The light-hearted Dudley had lost his enthusiasm for his job and now only seemed eager to get his days work done. Zeb Joyner seldom came to the tavern to sing. Even though no fighting had taken place in Halifax there was a prevailing mood of apathy that came with the uncertain times. Dudley told Sam that Zeb had said there was just nothing to sing about anymore.

Sam had been in camp two weeks when General Jones received word that Cornwallis had moved from Wilmington and was headed toward Halifax. Governor Nash had come to Camp Quanky and there was much speculation about his presence in Halifax. General Jones and Governor Nash were inseparable as they studied and speculated about the movement of Cornwallis.

The tranquility at Halifax was suddenly changed to chaos when the news about Cornwallis' movement caused the people to quickly react. The women gathered their silver and other valuables and found places to hide them. Governor Nash and General Jones were quick to realize that the occupation of the town by the British was imminent.

Soldiers were dispatched from Camp Quanky bearing orders for the townspeople. Since there was no safe hiding place in Halifax, the women and children were told to take what they could gather and go to the swamps. There were some women who refused to leave their home. Mary Jones and her sister Elizabeth were two who were not willing to leave Halifax.

At camp, the soldiers were gathering their equipment and gear in preparation for evacuation when Sam was told to report to headquarters.

Abner Nash

Governor of North Carolina 1780-1781

General Jones and Governor Nash were standing in front of the General's cabin studying a map when Sam arrived.

First For Freedom

"Sam, we want you to go immediately to Enfield and proceed south along the Old Huckleberry Swamp Road. Cornwallis is now coming through Edgecombe County and according to the last report was quartered about fifteen miles south of Fishing Creek. When you determine his exact location, get back here as quickly as possible," ordered Jones.

"I should be back by noon tomorrow, if I can get a fast horse."

"I have sent for the fastest horse I know about. He is being brought here. Don't get too close to Cornwallis. I don't need to tell you about the scouts that he sends out well ahead of his main force," cautioned General Jones.

"Sir, are you going to let me ride 'Midnight'?"

"Do you know of a faster horse? If you do, I'll send for him."

"With that horse, I can make it to Enfield by dark," said Sam, looking at the sun.

"Well, you must be on your way. Remember, Sam, your duty is to report the position of Cornwallis--nothing more. Be careful and get the word to us. We'll wait here until we hear from you," added Nash.

Sam went to his cabin and quickly gathered some of his gear and walked back to headquarters to wait for his horse.

His wait was not long for he soon saw a soldier riding down the road from the 'Grove'. He was leading the frisky, black stallion, 'Midnight'. As he watched, Sam thought of the time the horse had raced for Allen Jones. Now, he must race for all the people in Halifax.

He mounted the stallion and rode across Quanky Creek; then moved along at a good speed but chose not to hurry his horse for he had many miles to travel and he did not want to tire his horse too quickly.

The road to Enfield was well traveled. Stages, wagons and carriages, and horses had worn two parallel paths that stretched out before him. He looked to his left and right as he rode along. The crops and open fields needed their tenders. The corn was beginning to grow along with the grass and it was hard to tell one from the other. Some fields needed plowing but the men were not present so the crops suffered from the strangling grass that the women and children could not control. There were large fields where armies of slaves had chopped. These were clean and even though their masters were away the work had not stopped.

The gentlewomen of the aristocracy had taken over the job previously held by their husbands and the work had continued. Then, there were fields that were fallow and no crops were planted. These were the small fields owned by the farmers who could not afford slave labor and had no children to carry on the work while they were away at war. There would be no plowing of this land until the men returned, if they returned at all. Sam thought of the names and faces of those who had left Camp Quanky to fight and knew some of the land would have new tenders after the war. He thought of the march from the Catawba to Guilford---the battle at Guilford---George---the letter from Josie----Josie.

Sam was about five miles from Halifax and had not seen anything for the last two miles. His thoughts had made him completely oblivious to the countryside.

The road ahead merged through a thick wooded area. Now, there were trees growing thickly on each side of the road and the open fields were behind him. He rode about two miles before he came to a clearing. He was thirsty and decided he would stop at Sadie Jackson's Ordinary for a drink. 'Midnight' would need water and a short rest before he continued to Enfield.

Sadie's Ordinary was located about mid-way between Halifax and Enfield and served as an oasis for travelers. Sadie ran a good house known for its fine food and hospitality.

As he approached the red house, Sam thought how the travelers who came to Dudley's Tavern had nothing but praise for Sadie and how at times it seemed to bother Dudley when they harped on the fine food served at Sadie's Ordinary.

Sam pulled reins and stopped in front of the cabin. He saw the stout, blonde Sadie, standing on the porch sweeping. She was talking to her daughter, Jessica, who was working among the flowers that grew under the window at Sadie's right. As he walked up the well-worn path, he noticed a broad smile on Sadie's chubby face that made him feel welcome. Her large, blue eyes sparkled as she spoke

"Well, if it isn't Sam Pickett. Where're you off to, Sam?"

"Hello, Miss Sadie. I'm on orders to see if I can locate the whereabouts of Cornwallis' army," said Sam, as he slapped the dust from his breeches.

"Is he coming this way," asked Jessica.

Sam turned to the pretty young blonde who sat among the flowers. She was dressed in a worn, faded brown dress but her clothes did not hide her radiant beauty. As Sam looked at her, the thought that Sadie must have looked much like her daughter when she was eighteen years old.

"Seems they'll be passing the road right in front of your Ordinary. Y'all need to get to Halifax," said Sam.

"Sam, this place is all that me and Jessica owns in the world. We've been up against bad time ever since Henry passed away. When the British taste my good food, they'll not harm us," said Sadie.

Sam looked quickly toward Jessica. "I'll be coming back this way tomorrow and y'all can ride to Halifax with me, if you change your minds."

"They'll likely just pass our place, Sam. We'd still have to face them when they get to Halifax," said Jessica.

"They'll probably stay a while when they get to Halifax," said Sadie. "I think we'll be just as well off if we stay here,"

"You might be right, Sadie. I need some water for my horse."

"There's a bucket at the well. Help yourself," said Sadie, pointing to the well at the side of the house

Jessica came to the well where Sam was drawing the water.

"I heard yesterday that the river was high. How will the army pass over the water, Sam?"

"I'm sure they'll find a way. It may slow them down but they'll make it across."

When he had finished watering 'Midnight', Sam took the bucket and filled his canteen. He was aware that Sadie and Jessica were determined to stay and was not convince that they would be safe even if they did go to Halifax.

Sam returned to the front of the house and mounted his horse. Sadie and Jessica waved from the front yard at he rode away. Sam looked back and waved and thought that the British soldiers would be treated with hospitality but wondered how the British soldiers would treat such a beautiful woman as Jessica Jackson.

After riding for about three miles, he came to the swamps just north of Enfield. The road was built up on each side and there were bridges ahead that spanned the creeks. He soon passed over the bridges and entered the town

He rode to the livery stable and paid a short, squat man named Clayton Russell for a stall and feed and told him of his mission. Sam decided he would sleep near the stall. He was not taking any chances that his horse would be stolen. Too much depended on 'Midnight'.

While taking the saddle off 'Midnight', Sam talked with Russell and learned that all the town's people had left and Cornwallis was about fifteen miles to the South. Russell told Sam that he would be leaving town early the next morning. Since there was enough feed in the barn to satisfy all of Cornwallis' horses, Russell decided he would set fire to the barn before he left town.

After placing his saddle against the front stall and folding his saddle blanket, Sam stretched out on the loose hay, placed the blanket under his head and was soon asleep.

He arose about four o'clock, saddled his horse and was soon out of town on the Huckleberry Swamp Road. He had not seen Russell when he left the barn but knew he was still there.

A thick fog made it impossible for Sam to see more than a few yards ahead. After walking his horse for two miles or more, the sun began to disperse the fog and Sam could see better so he kicked his horse to a gallop. He crossed over Fishing Creek and was riding along and making good time. The road ahead was curved and Sam wanted to check it before he continued on his way, so he pulled his horse to a halt and tied 'Midnight' securely to a bush at the side of the road.

He climbed a tall sweet gum tree and looked south along Huckleberry Swamp Road but could see nothing. He made himself more comfortable on the limb and glanced down the road once more. Something was moving---Sam quickly looked around to make sure he was alone. Realizing that he was safe---he looked again. There was something moving ---and it was coming toward him. The small moving object became more visible and he could see a rider coming along the road. Then ---there were two riders----and then, for as far as he could see there was a continuous streak of red. The whole army of Cornwallis was moving along the road toward Enfield. Looking quickly at the sun, Sam figured he was about three hours away from Halifax. He could make it back by noon. As these thoughts flashed through his mind, he slithered down the tree and quickly mounted 'Midnight'.

The horse was at top speed when he reached Enfield. He looked to his left and right as he passed through the town. There was no sign of life. Up ahead was a raging fire. As he rode by the livery stable, Sam knew there would be nothing but ashes left by the time Cornwallis entered the town. He rode as fast as 'Midnight' could carry him for the next four miles and then slowed his horse to a walking rest.

He was coming to the red house at the side of the road. As he pulled his horse up to the hitching post, he saw Sadie and Jessica standing in the doorway.

"Y'all better get your horse hitched up and ride with me to Halifax," yelled Sam.

"Like I told you yesterday---we're stayin'," came Sadie's reply.

"I need to freshen my horse," said Sam as he hurried to the well.

After drawing the water from the well, Sam took a large bucket to the hitching post and put it down for 'Midnight' to drink.

"Don't worry about us, Sam," said Sadie, as she and Jessica came to the hitching post.

"I can't make you two come, you might be just as safe here," said Sam

"Sam, that's the finest horse I've ever seen, but you're going to kill him if you give him too much water," said Jessica.

Sam quickly snatched the bucket from 'Midnight' and took it back to the well. While he was talking to Jessica he was not aware that 'Midnight" was drinking too much.

"Don't y'all take any chances with those Red Coats. They can be as mean as they come," warned Sam, as he mounted 'Midnight'.

"You git on to Halifax and warn the people in town. We'll fare well enough," yelled Sadie, while she watched Sam ride away.

The wooded area was soon behind him---then the open fields flashed by as Sam gathered speed. He had no time to look in any direction except straight ahead to the road that led to Halifax. He kept his head low and covered the ground from Sadie's Ordinary to Halifax in less than two hours.

CHAPTER TWENTY-TWO

It was around noon when Sam rode into Camp Quanky. As he approached General Jones' cabin, he could see the soldiers were preparing to move out. General Jones and Governor Nash were standing where he had left them the previous day. Sam was breathing hard as he hurried from the hitching post.

"Sir-----the-----British-----army is by this time---in Enfield. They'll surely be here by tomorrow." Sam gasped for breath as he spoke.

"Good work, Sam," said Allen Jones, slapping Sam on the shoulder. "I knew we could depend on you. We need to put aside everything that looks like the military and make Cornwallis think this is just another village."

"What men, women and children we leave can find refuge in the swamp. They will be as safe there, as they will be anywhere else," said Nash.

"We'll want all the ladies to know that they'll be having unwelcome guests if they stay in their homes," said Jones. "Let it be known that the homes with the finest furnishing will be occupied by the high-ranking officers."

"Well, in that case, I suppose Mrs. Willie Jones will have some very distinguished guests, since 'Grove House' is the finest home around here," added Sam.

General Jones looked at Sam as if it were the first time he fully realized the seriousness of the situation.

"Sam, you go to 'Grove House' at once and prepare Mary for her forthcoming visitors. Tell her to be careful what she says. She has a way of letting her emotions overrule her tongue at times. I'm glad Willie is not here. He'd probably want to stand guard and protect 'Grove house' from the whole British Army".

"I'm on the way, Sir," said Sam, as he hurried to his horse.

******

Sam returned to camp Quanky about two o'clock and went to General Jones' headquarters. All was ready for the evacuation. Jones and Nash sat at the small table watching several soldiers load the last wagon.

"Sir, I told Mrs. Jones to be prepared for the British. I feel confident that she'll be ready when they arrive," said Sam, noticing the soldiers.

"Get yourself a chair and sit down, Sam," said General Jones.

First For Freedom

Governor Nash took a map from inside his coat and pressed it down on the table. "You know, I've been studying this map and I can't determine where Cornwallis is headed."

General Jones leaned over and looked at the map.

"Looks like Petersburg to me---if he continues the way he's going."

"We could be of great assistance to the Continental Army in the North if we knew his plans," added Nash.

Sam quickly thought of George's uniform and how he could make use of it.

"Sir, I have a British uniform I brought back from Guilford. I could walk among the Red Coats and never be recognized. There are nearly three thousand soldiers in that army with Loyalists joining them every day. One more face will be nothing new to the soldiers."

"Sam, you know that's too risky. I couldn't allow you to get that close," said the General.

"When the Red Coats are foraging and setting up camp, there is no order. I wouldn't be taking any great risk."

"I think he might be able to gain some information, Allen."

"I have George Hamilton's papers and I've lost about thirty pounds since that march we make from Catawba to Guilford. I'm sure George's uniform will fit me." insisted Sam.

"I think we need to take the chance," said Nash, in support.

"I don't like it, Sam. You've done your share," said Allen Jones.

"But there's still so much left to be done. I'll be careful and stay in the background. I won't take any chances."

"Sam, you know you'll be shot if you're detected," said Jones, emphatically.

"I'm willing to take the chance if you're willing to give me your permission."

Governor Nash turned quickly toward General Jones and spoke with resolute authority.

"I know what happens here in Halifax is your responsibility and I know how you feel about Sam. But think of what will happen to the people in Virginia when Cornwallis moves north. Think how important it will be for General Washington to know Cornwallis' moves before he makes them."

"Where will you stay when the army has settled and camp check is made," asked General Jones, beginning to concede.

"General Jones, I have a cave at Quanky Creek that is so well hidden, that I, myself, could hardly find it the other day. There is no living person who knows where it's located. I could spend the night there and move among the soldiers during the day."

"Allen, if you don't give this young man your permission, I just might pull rank on you and do it myself."

"Well, I've always said it takes a good general to know when he's been defeated." General Jones turned to Nash, "and it takes a better one to know when he's outranked."

"I know my way around Quanky Creek in the dark. They'll never find me there."

"If you should gain any information about Cornwallis' plans, come to Warrenton and let me know immediately." General Jones stood as he spoke.

"Then it's settled," said Nash, smiling at the General.

Soon Sam led his horse past thirty soldiers on horseback; five wagons loaded with hay, corn and supplies; then the two hundred and seventy foot soldiers, who waited for the signal to move out. When he came to the head of the train, he mounted 'Jericho' to ride along beside General Jones and the Governor.

When they reached King Street, women and children followed them as far as Quanky Bridge.

Just as they arrived at the creek, a young boy rode wildly across the bridge to where General Jones had halted the soldiers. The boy recognized General Jones at once and shouted as he crossed,

"Tarleton is on his way here. He's east of town about four miles."

General Jones looked quickly to Governor Nash.

"Colonel Tarleton is not moving with the main body. He's east approaching Halifax from a different direction."

Nash turned to the boy.

"How many men does he have, son?"

"I didn't count'em. I was in the woods hunting when I seen'em. Pa just told me to git here fast. There was maybe two hundred." The boy looked as though he hoped the number he gave would satisfy the governor.

General Jones wheeled his horse and sat up straight in his saddle.

"Take the hay wagon and block the bridge from the other side. Move the other wagons to this side of the bridge and turn them over. Set fire to the hay when they come to the bridge---that should slow them down."

Sam and the Governor moved to the side as the wagons were being brought forward. General Jones selected his best riflemen and stationed them behind the overturned wagons.

"We'll leave about thirty soldiers here at Quanky while the rest of us move across the Roanoke."

Turning from the Governor to the men, who would be left behind, Jones continued, "you men just slow them down for a while. Keep them from crossing for the next hour and then come to the Roanoke. We'll leave horses here for you."

Even as the General waved his arm toward the Roanoke the men were off and running. When they arrived at the river, there was immediate pandemonium. The Roanoke had been flooding for several days and the ferry that was available most all year round floated about forty feet from the submerged loading ramp. Soldiers in flustered panic hurried to gather the scattered boats floating here and there along the edge of the river. When the boats were gathered, the soldiers loaded them with their hunting rifles and powder horns and knapsacks..

Sam took 'Jericho' about fifty yards upstream dismounted and slapped his horse on the hindquarter. Knowing that Willie Jones' stables would be the place his horse would stop, Sam hurried back to the river.

Four soldiers had secured a barge and made it available for General Jones and Governor Nash. Sam moved to be close to his commander and jumped on the barge behind the general. There was a hectic struggled among the soldiers to gain places on the barge.

"Shove off---shove off," ordered General Jones. "This barge can't carry all of us across."

Soldiers clung to the side of the barge that now was only inches above the water. Directly behind the barge were several boats loaded to capacity with men dangling over the sides. Some of the soldiers held to the sides of the boats and with only their heads and shoulders above water. Men who were good swimmers moved out ahead of the rest.

The most amazing thing about the crossing was that two hundred and seventy men were accounted for when they reached the north bank of the Roanoke.

After about thirty minutes of waiting, the riflemen from Quanky came riding along the road to the river. Seeing the soldiers on the opposite bank, General Jones stood up and yelled.

"You men move up the river to the rapids and wait there for us."

The riders waved, acknowledging the orders, then hurried upstream along the river road.

All was quiet and the soldiers were well concealed by the time the British came to the river's edge. Sam could see the Red coats crowded along the south bank and it looked as though they were trying to determine how they would cross the river. Then General Jones stood and let down his hand. Shots from hunting rifles fell about the feet of the Red Coats as they quickly dispersed to get out of range. Colonel Tarleton stood firmly in his tracks defying any shot to move him. Shouting commands brought the dragoons to order and Tarleton moved them along the river road downstream.

General Jones, who was watching the movement, stood up from behind a fallen tree where he had taken post.

"They're moving downstream to find a place to cross. We'll go upstream and cross over at the rapids. We can do little more here."

Sam walked along the north bank with the soldiers; crossed over at the rapids where the other soldiers waited. Sam parted company and started back toward 'Grove House'

It was dark when he arrived at the servant's quarters.

Uncle Louie was disturbed when Sam aroused him from his sleep but hurried to the stables to help saddle the horse. Sam did not explain anything to Uncle Louie but thanked him for taking care of 'Jericho'.

Sam stood at the door of the stable and watched the road while Uncle Louie saddled the horse.

"Dis hoss always comes hera when he's hungry. Dey always come back to whar dey was raised when dey git loose and hungry. Dey jist lack people."

Sam smiled at his philosophical old friend as he mounted his horse.

"He knows where to find good feed. You've got a special way with horses, Uncle Louie."

He rode quietly from the barn and then along the lane from 'Grove House'. Only three people were to know his reasons for staying in Halifax. Governor Nash had made that clear at Camp Quanky.

The moon was shinning brightly along the road that led to the wooded tunnel but as the road merged into this wooded area the light faded to cast shadows along his darkened way.

Soon Sam turned off the road to the path that led to his secret cave. He knew Halifax would be quiet now that darkness had fallen but he had doubts if any women and children would sleep.

CHAPTER TWENTY-THREE

About mid-afternoon the next day, Sam sat outside the cave and could hear the sound of drums in the distance. He quickly entered his cave and got dressed in the British uniform, which was a little tight at the waist.

Soon he was watching through the bushes at the front of the cave and could see the British soldiers making camp along the opposite bank of Quanky Creek. He could also hear soldiers setting up camp downstream about one hundred yards from the cave on his side of Quanky Creek.

As he watched the soldiers, he thought of the night when the Hamiltons had to leave Halifax. George's parting words now echoed in his mind. 'Don't let any pirates take over our cave at Quanky'. Well, the 'Pirates' had arrived, and they were taking over. In his youth, the 'Pirates' were imagined and he and George had little trouble dealing with them. They had never imagined more than ten invaders at the time----but these men were real and there were nearly three thousand.

Sam crept quietly from the bushes and made his way to his horse. As he led 'Jericho' along the wooded path to the main road, he could hear the thunder of hoofbeats. The foragers are on their way to 'Grove House', thought Sam. He waited in the woods until the soldiers passed, then he saw a lone rider coming down the road. This would give him a chance to test his uniform. He mounted 'Jericho' and moved quickly onto the road.

Sam held up his hand as the British soldier came near.

"I seem to be detached from my company. Where's headquarters," asked Sam boldly, as if he demanded an answer.

"Just the other side of the bridge, Sir," said the soldier, pointing down the road toward Halifax.

He felt it would be safe for him to continue into camp for the soldier had not recognized anything unusual. Pleased that he had passed this test, Sam realized the British soldier had shown respect for George's uniform, and hoped that his rank as captain would not cause too much attention.

Coming to Quanky Bridge, Sam joined the British soldiers who were crossing the creek. To his right and off the road was the charred frame of the hay wagon that had been used to block Tarelton's way the previous day. The other wagons were nowhere to be seen---evidently the British had confiscated them for their own use.

As he moved along with the soldiers, Sam began to realize that headquarters for the British were being set up at the same location where General Jones had vacated. The British now occupied Camp Quanky.

While the British were getting settled, foraging parties would continue to gather all the supplies they could muster. No place would be safe from these Red Coats. The countryside would soon be stripped of all that was useful to the soldiers and the horses would trample the crops. The shops, stores, and warehouses would offer little to the invaders since most of the owners had moved their goods to places of safety. Outside the town there would be plundering and looting of property and wanton killing of livestock. The soldiers would take whatever they wanted; Sam felt helpless knowing that there was no way to stop them.

When Sam entered Camp Quanky, he quickly noticed many soldiers resting in the shade of the tall trees that surrounded the camp. The small log cabins were occupied by the soldiers who reached camp first. Sam thought of the hard labor that had come from the Patriots to construct these huts---now being used by the British soldiers as sleeping quarters.

He had just tied his horse to the hitching post when a band of about thirty foragers rode wildly into camp. Sam casually moved to the shade of a tall maple about ten yards to the left of headquarters; sat down and removed his cocked hat.

He wiped the dust from his hat as he watched the soldiers gather around the looters to inspect various articles. Then, they became loud and boisterous as they began to trade and bargain among themselves.

Colonel Tarleton walked from Headquarters and the soldiers quietened down. Tarleton stood erect in his bright red officer's uniform. His sword dangled at his side and his plumed hat gave him a distinction not common among the other soldiers.

Tarleton seemed amused while he watched the soldiers who were about twenty yards from his cabin. One of the soldiers held up a pair of red underwear and began a mock auction. The colonel was caught up in the excitement and did not notice a young, slender girl who had slipped past the officer of the guard and now stood behind him. The young girl looked toward the guard and spoke quickly as Tarleton turned in surprise toward the feminine voice.

"Sir, I came here to get my pony. Your soldiers took him from my father's yard. I have followed closely behind your men and see my pony is tied to that tree," said the girl, pointing toward the small sycamore.

First For Freedom

Lieutenant Colonel Banastre Tarleton, commanding British cavalry troops, called "Bloody" Tarleton for his outrages against civilians and soldiers in the Revolution. This picture is from a portrait by Sir Joshua Reynolds, painted for Tarleton's mother in 1782.

"You are a brave child to be so bold," said Tarleton, as he regarded the young girl.

"Your men have not harmed me. I hope you will be kind enough to see that my pony is returned. I'll take him and hope you'll see that I am not stopped by your soldiers."

Sam watched with interest as the young girl walked to her pony. Tarleton seemed astounded and spoke quietly to the guard. The girl untied her pony and led it from camp without being questioned.

A young aide came from inside headquarters and stood beside Tarleton. He held a paper in his right hand as he spoke.

"Sir, I have information that the home of Mr. Willie Jones will be suitable quarters for the general."

Tarleton turned to his aide.

"I'll need to visit the home as soon as we're settled here. Get word to the men that they'll have thirty minutes to rest before we start preparing camp. General Cornwallis will want to inspect this camp as well as his own headquarters. He'll be here by noon tomorrow and we have much to do before he arrives."

Tarleton's orders were abruptly interrupted when several soldiers, led by General Leslie, marched into camp. Immediately behind the General were two British prisoners bound with ropes and followed by four armed Red Coats.

Sam recognized General Leslie from the Battle of Guilford and knew he was Colonel Tarleton's commanding officer. This was the first time he had seen the General at such close range. General Leslie tied his horse and walked with quick, short steps to where Tarleton stood. He looked to be about twenty years older than Tarleton and he had an air of authority about him. He was not as tall as Tarleton and had to look up as he spoke to the Colonel.

"We have two men who have been arrested for grossly mistreating two women at the red house between here and Enfield."

Oh----Sadie----Jessica---Jackson-----thought Sam, straining to hear more.

"What are we to do with them?" Tarleton looked toward the prisoners as he spoke.

"What can we do? One of the hardest lessons a soldier must learn is that he is bound to follow orders. And, as you know, we have been given orders by General Cornwallis to execute any soldier found guilty of murder or any other high to crime, " said Leslie, his brown eyes show an intensity that gave extra meaning to his words.

When Sam heard the word 'murder' he took a deep breath to control his emotions.

"Was there any threat to the soldiers from the women," Tarleton asked

"One of the soldiers reported that there were no weapons found in the house, so, there couldn't have been any threat to harm the prisoners.

First For Freedom

When we have this many men to control we can only be firm in executing our orders. I will prepare the orders to be read. It will be your duty to see that they are properly enforced. Sound the bugle for assembly," General Leslie walked inside the cabin as Tarleton spoke with the officer of the guard.

"I'll wait with the prisoners until you're ready for me."

The bugle sounded and Sam moved quickly to take a place among the soldiers. When all the soldiers in camp were gathered, General Leslie walked from headquarters and handed Colonel Tarleton the order. Tarleton read it silently and the general took his place at a small table that had been brought from inside headquarters.

The two prisoners were moved directly before the assembly of soldiers and centered in front of General Leslie's table.

The bugle sounded again and Colonel Tarleton stepped forward.

"Your attention----these two men have been caught and charged with mistreating two women outside this town. I understand that the older woman died as a result of the injuries. When this army passed the red house, the two women gave no evidence of hostility. What prompted these two soldiers to commit such a dastardly crime is not for me to decide. I have been given strict orders to execute any soldier who uses this war as justification to commit any felonious act.

If we do not control the men in our ranks, we stand little chance of defeating the enemy. What I do here is to impress all of you that any act such as the one these two men committed cannot---and will not be tolerated. The foul acts of these two will be paid for with their lives. Signed---General Leslie," said Tarleton, reading from the order. He then turned to the officer standing to his left. "Proceed---with your duty."

"Get the prisoners ready," shouted the officer.

Two soldiers stepped forward and moved the prisoners to the side of headquarters. They were placed in a kneeling position and the soldiers tied a black cloth over their eyes; then moved quickly out of range of the four riflemen, who had assumed a position about seventy feet away.

The officer shouted----"READY-----" The four riflemen dropped to their knees.

The commanding officer looked to the riflemen and back toward the blinded soldiers and gave the order---AIM-------FIRE!"

The silence at Quanky was shattered by the loud reports from the four rifles and the two prisoners slumped forward on their faces.

There was murmuring of disapproval from the soldiers as Tarelton walked to the officer in command.

"Move the bodies outside the town and bury them. Place no marker on their grave." He turned to the soldiers. "You are dismissed!"

Eight soldiers picked up the bodies and moved them to a nearby wagon.

Tarleton quickly walked to join General Leslie and the two officers went inside headquarters.

Sam moved from the soldiers to his horse. While he was untying 'Jericho', a tall, thin private walked up to him. He smiled as the soldier spoke.

"How do you like this town, Sir?"

"I just got here, soldier," said Sam, not wanting to get involved in a long conversation.

"I understand the river is overflowing and we'll be here several days," said the soldier.

"I don't think a river is likely to stop General Cornwallis," Sam mounted his horse as he spoke.

"I heard there are some lovely ladies in this town, but I'd be afraid to speak to one of them after what just happened," continued the soldier.

"I feel the same way," agreed Sam.

"What regiment you with, Captain?"

"The Second, and I've got to get back to my men," said Sam, turning his horse away from the soldier.

"Don't be talking to no pretty ladies----HEY---CAPTAIN-----The second is quartered here at headquarters. HEY-----CAPTAIN----HEY--"

Sam heard the private but did not turn back. He rode to the right side of the road and nodded to the foot soldiers who were arriving. There were hundreds of troops already at Camp Quanky and they were still coming. Wagons loaded with supplies, horse-drawn cannons, and more foot soldiers moved along Quanky Road in what seemed a never ending convergence.

After passing Quanky Bridge, Sam continued on the road to 'Grove House'. He could not see the troops quartered on this side of Quanky Creek but knew they were just across the patch of woods that separated the road from the small stream. There were no soldiers along the road and it was getting dark as he entered the shaded tunnel.

CHAPTER TWENTY-FOUR

When Sam came to the path that led to his secret cave, he did not turn off. He decided to go to 'Grove House' to let Mary Jones know that Colonel Tarleton would soon be at her home. That quick mind of Mary's might just be keen enough to gain some information from Colonel Tarleton. It was important that he speak to her before she spoke to Tarleton. He was concerned about what had happened at 'Grove House' earlier that afternoon. Those foragers had little or no regard for anybody.

Soon he rode past 'Grove House' to the stables. Sam wanted 'Jericho' out of sight in case soldiers came while he was there.

After taking his horse to the stall, Sam loosened the girth and was closing the door when he felt a sharp pain just below his left shoulder.

"Don't cha-move ---or Ah'll put dis pitch fork through you."

Sam did not move but spoke quickly. "Uncle Louie---it's me---Sam Pickett."

Pressure from the end of the fork was released and Sam turned to Uncle Louie.

"Sam Pickett---you could git yoself kilt. What-cha-doin'- in dat uniform?"

I'm trying to get to 'Grove House' to see Mrs. Jones. There are British soldiers who'll be here soon. I need to speak with her before they come."

"Dem soldiers dat comed here took off all de chickens and hogs and sed dey'd be back fuh mo de morrow."

"Uncle Louie, don't you try to be brave with these soldiers. There are over three thousand of them. Just let them do what they come to do. Don't you try to stop'em."

"Ah ain't bout to try to stop all of'em but when Ah seen you Ah thought Ah could git one fuh Mr. Willie---beings he ain't to home."

"I'm going up to the house. Look after my horse. I'll be back in a little while," said Sam, as he left the barn.

Sam walked briskly past the servant's quarters to the corner of the big house. Then, he stopped and listened. There were hoofbeats in the distance. Looking from the edge of the house, he could see what appeared to be four riders coming up the lane toward 'Grove House'. Sam hurried to the back door and tried to open it. Finding the door locked, he began to pound as hard as he could. He was still pounding when he saw a light through the window. The door was slightly opened. "Who is it," came a voice from inside.

Sam pushed the door open and rushed inside.

"What do you a want? You soldiers took all our food this afternoon!"

Sam knew that Mary had not recognized him.

"Mrs. Jones---I'm Sam Pickett."

"Sam Pickett---but the uniform!"

"Listen, there'll be soldiers at your front door in just a minute."

"Is that why you're here, Sam?"

"I'm sure one of those soldiers is Colonel Tarleton. He'll want to check your house to make sure it's safe and comfortable enough for General Cornwallis."

"Well, I'm sure I can't stop him."

"You're not expected to try to stop him. He'll be here for a while and we would like mighty well to get some information from him," said Sam, as they walked from the room.

"What can WE hope to learn from the British, Sam?"

Mary Jones led Sam into the banquet room, holding the candle to light the way.

"General Jones would welcome any information we might gain about General Cornwallis' movements. We know that Halifax is just another town on his route. We need to know his destination. Where he plans to set up his next headquarters."

There was a loud knock at the front door just as they entered the room. Sam quickly looked around for a place to hide.

"Hurry! Come get to the cellar."

"They'll look there first," said Sam, hesitating.

"Get behind the drapes!"

"There's not enough room, there," said Sam, looking for a better place.

"I know---the harpsichord.------there's enough space behind the harpsichord. It's been used before. There's an opening at the back."

"That's it. They'll never think to look there," said Sam quickly pulling the large instrument from the wall.

When he was concealed, Mary pushed the harpsichord back against the wall and hurried to the front door.

Sam made himself as comfortable as possible. He had to lie flat on his back with his knees tucked under his chin. There was some latticework at the base of the instrument and Sam could see through the holes where the strips of wood crossed to form small squares.

"I'm surprised to see you so soon. I was told that you arrived only this afternoon." Sam could hear Mary as she entered the banquet room.

"I was most anxious to see your home. I have heard so much about it since my arrival,'" said Tarleton, who stood with his plumed hat tucked under his arm.

The colonel's character seemed to change as he turned to the three soldiers standing at the arch doorway.

"Search the house. Let no room go unchecked."

The soldiers scattered, each in a different direction, one to the cellar, one to the upstairs, and the other to check the rooms on the first floor.

Tarleton looked around as if he were taking inventory of the room.

Mary Jones stood before him in a dark blue gown that hung neatly about her white shoulders revealing her perfectly formed neck. At her waist, the gown opened and white silk with golden embroidered patterns of flowers made up the lower front half of her gown.

Soon one of the soldiers rushed into the room tugging a young lady behind him. Sam recognized Elizabeth Ashe. Her features were sharper than Mary's but the resemblance was very noticeable. Her pale green gown had dark green lattice strips from the waists to the top of her dress where it clung snugly over a tightly fitting bodice, which made her figure more attractive. A white collar opened at her neck. Her hair was curled, as was Mary's, and was a shade lighter than her sister's. Both had the same dark eyes. That trait was strong in the daughters of Joseph Montfort. Not only were their physical features similar; there was sophistication, wisdom, wit, culture and a far-reaching background of high-breeding-- that was unequaled by any other ladies that Sam knew but was shared only by these two ladies.

Elizabeth jerked away from the soldier.

"I've heard you British were civilized but this GENTLEMAN has not mastered the art of knocking before he enters a LADY'S bedroom."

"Colonel Tarleton, this is Mrs. Elizabeth Ashe. She is my sister and an INVITED guest," said Mary.

"I had not expected to have the company of two such lovely ladies," said Tarelton, as he looked with interested eyes from one lady to the other.

"My home is available to you and your officers. However, I do not promise you the hospitality you would receive under different circumstances," came the quick reply of Mary.

"I assure you, we shall get along well during our stay here," promised Tarleton.

"I'll do all that's in my power to help you and your men get along---if nor well---at least as quickly as possible," retorted Mary, looking at the other two soldiers who entered the room.

"You men wait outside," ordered Tarleton.

When the soldiers were gone, Tarleton returned his attention to Mary.

"I did not expect such wit from the ladies in Halifax. I have met some of your men and it would be flattery to say that they even speak the King's English."

Elizabeth stepped toward Tarelton.

"I understand you met one of our men at the Battle of Cowpens. A Colonel William Washington. How do you regard that gentleman, Colonel Tarleton?"

"Oh! Colonel Washington. I understand he is an illiterate, ignorant simpleton who is barely able to write his own name," informed Tarleton.

"Ah! Colonel Tarleton, you should know better than that-----for you bear on your person proof that he knows very well how to make his mark," said Mary.

Colonel Tarleton quickly reacted by unconsciously rubbing the top of his scarred left hand. The sword of William had left a telling mark obviously noticeable.

"Oh, you ladies can be very proud of your men. By the way, where are all your brave men? Did they leave you ladies to do the fighting for them? I should like to meet some of your men," said Tarleton, who was being dreadfully outwitted.

"Even Colonel Washington?" Elizabeth's words were as daggers to Tarleton's ego.

There was a wounded look in Tarleton's eyes but he immediately responded.

"I would be happy to meet Colonel Washington----face ----to---face."

"Why Colonel Tarleton, if you had looked behind you at the Battle of Cowpens, you would have enjoyed that great pleasure," quipped Elizabeth, twisting the dagger until it became too painful for Tarleton to bear.

"You ladies don't seem to realize who is in command here." Tarleton grasped the hilt of his sword.

At that moment, General Leslie came into the room. Tarleton turned as the General spoke.

"Colonel Tarleton, there does seem to be some question about who IS in command here."

Leslie looked to Mary and Elizabeth.

"Forgive me for letting myself in. One of the soldiers told me that Colonel Tarleton was here so I saw no need of knocking. I'm General Leslie. I hope my men have not inconvenienced you."

"Ah--General, General Leslie, this is Elizabeth Ashe, my sister. Colonel Tarleton has already had the pleasure ----ah-----privilege of meeting her."

General Leslie nodded as Elizabeth Ashe acknowledged the introduction with a quick smile.

"General Leslie, my husband, Willie, has some vintage wine in the cellar that can only be enjoyed by a gentleman with fine taste," said Mary.

She briefly glanced toward Tarleton, then continued her conversation with Leslie. "Would you like a glass. I know you could appreciate it as only a ---gentleman can."

"That would be most refreshing----but only if you ladies will drink with me," cautioned Leslie.

"Come with me to the cellar Elizabeth and hold the candle."

Elizabeth took a candelabra from the table and led the way

When the door to the cellar was closed, Colonel Tarleton turned to his commander.

"If you had not entered, Sir, I'm afraid I would have lost my patience with those two."

"A gentleman of your rank would not harm a lady," assured Leslie.

"I am proned to act too quickly at times, I suppose," apologized Tarleton.

Elizabeth Montfort Ashe

"Just because you are a ranking officer does not mean that you will not be held accountable for your conduct, Colonel."

"I shall guard myself against impudence during my stay here. I don't expect we'll have to contend with this kind of behavior when we get to Virginia. The ladies there are said to be polished, gentle, and well-bred."

Sam could see the two officers coming toward the harpsichord as they talked. "You know, Colonel Tarleton, when you think about it----you might have just added some luster to your character here tonight."

"What do you mean, Sir."

"The rubbing---Colonel---the rubbing. You were getting the rubbing when I entered."

"Oh, I see what you getting at."

"What was the conversation all about," asked Leslie, as he sat down at the harpsichord.

"Mostly the Battle of Cowpens, Sir."

"Did they try to get any information from you?"

"What kind of information?"

"Did they ask anything about where we're going or how long we plan to stay here?"

"Nothing, Sir."

"You know I talked with you about Yorktown and what General Cornwallis and I discussed. You're sure you didn't mention Yorktown."

"I'm sure. I wouldn't be so foolish to mention any of our plans."

"Well, it's not our plans. It's just an idea that the General has been considering since we left Wilmington."

Leslie hit one of the keys that sounded a high shrill note just above Sam's head.

"However, that is not my reason for coming here tonight," continued Leslie. "Colonel Tarleton, there seems to be a spy among the soldiers."

"A spy---in out ranks?"

"A private in the second regiment reported that he talked with a captain at camp this afternoon and the captain did not know where the second regiment was located---even when he was standing in their midst."

"Where was the Captain seen?"

"He was last seen riding from camp. He's not among the soldiers on the other side of the bridge. I suggest you look for him on this side of the creek."

"I'll send some men out the first thing in the morning."

"I strongly suggest you do it tonight. I think tomorrow will be too late. You just might be able to locate him, if you act quickly," ordered Leslie.

"I'll start immediately then, Sir." Tarleton put on his hat and walked straightway to the front door.

General Leslie picked some deafening notes above Sam's head as he amused himself while waiting for the wine.

Soon Mary and Elizabeth came up from the cellar and Leslie stood as they entered the room.

"I want to offer my apologies for Colonel Tarleton's conduct. He felt tired and decided he would retire early. He is a very capable officer but hot-tempered at times. He seldom gets so emotional." General Leslie looked as if he did not understand all that had transpired before he entered the room and now seemed to be asking for some explanation.

"I can't imagine what made him so upset," said Mary, placing the bottle on the side table.

"He must be getting weary of this war," added Elizabeth. She handed Mary three glasses.

"Oh, I'm sure he is and I am sure that I am, too," responded Leslie.

"We hope you will make your quarters in our home, General. It is so difficult to make conversation with men who do not recognize their superiors," said Mary, handing the General a glass of wine.

"I am sure such fine quarters will be reserved for General Cornwallis. I shall be quartered nearby. I somehow feel that my rank would be challenged if I were to stay here," said Leslie, jokingly.

General Leslie made some comments about the house and the fine furnishing and was especially interested in the harpsichord. Mary then proceeded to tell him about the instrument.

"It is the work of the English. Willie had it shipped here when he was last in your country. I can truly say, at this time, it is the most valuable piece in my home. I have found it to be most useful when we have guest."

Sam cringed in his hiding place that now seemed to be getting smaller with each word that came from Mary's lips. He remembered the way Mary had played the harpsichord when he came to the meeting with Allen Jones. He remembered how long some of the songs were that she had played.

Mary walked with General Leslie to the front door and spoke of different furniture and objects until she closed the door behind him.

When they heard hoofbeats along the lane, the sisters pulled the harpsichord from the wall and Sam came out from behind it.

He stood and shook his legs to stimulate the circulation. Soon, he had feeling and was ready to travel.

Sam told the sisters he had heard some interesting conversation while they were in the cellar and learned that Mary had taken her time in locating that special bottle of wine for General Leslie.

Sam started for the back door but stopped as if he had forgotten something.

"Before I go, could I trouble you for some clothes? I'd hate to ride into General Jones' camp and be shot for a Red Coat. My other clothes are down at Quanky Creek and I'm not about to go back there tonight."

Mary hurried upstairs and soon returned with a suit of Willie Jones' finest clothes.

"I want you to take these before the British come again. I'm sure they'll ransack the house when they return and take what's left."

Sam quickly accepted the clothes.

"This just may be the finest suit I'll ever wear. When I meet with the General, I'm going to immediately ask for a promotion in rank."

"You deserve a promotion after all you've been through tonight," agreed Mary.

"I'll change in the stable and get Uncle Louie to hide this uniform. I don't want the British to find it."

After bidding the sisters farewell, Sam crept cautiously from the house to the stables. He told Uncle Louie about the uniform and then rode across Willie Jones' plantation toward Warrenton. It was a long way to where his general waited but he knew it well and now it was the only safe way to go.

CHAPTER TWENTY-FIVE

Five months later

When Sam had finished his last meal of the day, he walked slowly from the mess cabin to the late afternoon shade of the maple tree next to General Jones' headquarters. Sitting there, he watched the soldiers hurrying to eat while others emerged from the cabin at a slower pace now that they had finished eating. The leaves on the various trees were casting their last colors, as the late October nights grew too cold for them to continue their fight for life. This sylvan spot seemed almost to glow in one last tremendous effort to show its splendor. Now, at the height of their beauty, the leaves were falling to blanket the ground. Sam wondered what it would be like if these colors could but endure for all time. Then, thinking that would be demanding too much of nature, he realized there could be no appreciation of anything so beautiful if it were not loved for its time and place in the scheme of things.

Sam looked about the camp and considered how he had not been conscious of anything beautiful when he had last sat under the same maple and looked upon the British soldiers. Five months had passed since Camp Quanky had been occupied by Tarleton and the Red Coats. Things looked different then. The British had made this spot a haven for the enemy and for that brief time it had lost all its beauty. For even though the beauty was present and not seen----then it held no meaning---no significance---no relativeness to anything that he held dear.

Many things had happened since that day in May. When he had located General Jones at Warrenton, he related in detail the words spoken inside 'Grove House'. Not fully understanding the significance of the word 'Yorktown' --Sam was astounded when the General dispatched a rider to the North bearing a scribbled note. This reaction was enough to assure him that his lingering at 'The Grove' had been worth the risk.

Upon hearing that Cornwallis had withdrawn from Halifax, General Jones ordered the soldiers to pack their gear and move back to Camp Quanky.

When they arrived, immediate orders were issued for the soldiers to mend the broken fences, repair the equipment--and in general to re-establish the routine that had been so abruptly interrupted by the British. Soon the camp was again humming with activity.

General Jones no longer sent out soldiers from camp since there were no new recruits. The training program was discontinued. There was no time left for training and no young men left to train. The only soldiers who left camp were the one who were sent out by Colonel Long with supplies for the soldiers in the field.

Good news had come to Halifax in early October when Sam and the soldiers were told that General Nathanael Greene had recaptured most of the lost territory in the South.

From talk among the soldiers and the people at Dudley's Tavern, Sam had sensed a prevailing spirit of hope; enhanced by enthusiasm of all the men in camp, including General Jones. Now all the news was good and there was an air of confidence among the people that the war was beginning to end. Everybody knew more than anybody, but this great expectation shared by all fell short of any final victory of any actual surrender of the entire British Army. Sam felt the people should keep their thoughts a secret if victory was ever to become a reality. Expecting too much too soon could cause the Continentals to lose support just when it was needed most.

Suddenly these thoughts were interrupted and Sam leaned forward to see Governor Nash speeding along Quanky Road and then up to the hitching post. After tying his horse, the governor hurried toward headquarters, stopping only long enough to speak with a soldier who past his way.

"Get the bugler----Get the men together!"

After General Jones had spoken briefly with the Governor, he held up his hands.

"Attention! Attention! Listen up, all of you. Governor Nash has brought some good news. It seems that a General by the name of Cornwallis has surrendered at a place called Yorktown!"

No words were heard beyond these; the soldiers began to jump up and down and hug one another. The yelling men were without control and General Jones let out a whoop that was equal to anything heard from the soldiers.

"MEN---MEN----SOLDIERS," shouted General Jones.

The noise died down and General Jones continued.

"News has already reached the townspeople and all of you will remain soldiers until you are properly discharged. You'll be on duty during the night until the people have settle down. I don't know what to expect from the people, so you soldiers will have to patrol the streets to see that no one is hurt. Don't let things get too far out of hand, but let the people have their way as long as they do not become violent and destructive.

These words fell like dead leaves that had only a moment before been a part of something radiant, for the men would now have to dampen their enthusiasm and see that order was maintained.

It was dark by the time the soldiers marched down King Street. They veered off in groups of ten to the streets that ran perpendicular. All along King Street were small fires that lighted the way. Children ran tempestuously along the way yelling and screaming. The older children seemed to know what they were yelling about but the younger ones followed in support of something important that they did not fully comprehend. Wagons and carriages passed them as they came to the town common; horses were tied to every hitching post as people from the surrounding countryside converged in town.

"Let's do what we can to see that no one is injured. Don't let anyone destroy any property or set fire to anything. When all is calm, we'll meet back here at the common," said Sam, as the soldiers separated to move among the people.

At the common, a huge fire was being fed logs from a wagon. It was the largest fire in town and other fires radiated from this hub. Men, women and children joined hands to form a large circle around the fire and moved to the left and then to the right being directed by a fat man clapping his hands and telling the people what they were to do next.

Sam nudged his way through the people who seemed to be coming from everywhere---not bound for any place. At the corner of Martin's Livery was a wagon loaded with hay that had drawn a crowd of men. As he came closer to the wagon, Sam could see one man pouring corn liquor from a jug that he had taken from beneath the hay. He only had one mug but it was free to those who extended a grasping hand.

Behind the stables was another fire where younger people dance wildly to the music of a fast- playing fiddler who stood in their midst and danced even as he played. Some of the older men who had too much to drink joined in with the younger crowd. ---not caring where they celebrated--- and the young people not caring to have them there.

Satisfied that little harm could come from the crowd, Sam fought his way back to Market Street. In the distance, dinner bells were ringing now being echoed by the louder bells from Reverend Ford's church only one block away.

All along Market Street, men, women and children were pushing and shoving to make their way only to be pushed and shoved by others going in a different direction. Booming sounds from the cannons on the Roanoke and Camp Quanky joined with the sounding bells as the music of freedom reverberated throughout the town and the surrounding countryside.

When Sam came to Dudley's Tavern, there was a thickening of the crowd and new faces outnumbered the regular cronies who now congregated at the side of the tavern where five kegs of ale were placed on a long bench---free for all who could turn the tap. Evidently, Dudley was feeling a part of the joy and excitement. Ordinarily-- Dudley would not be giving his ale to the cronies. But then---this was not an ordinary time.

The furor and chaos continued and Sam walked back and forth from Martin's Livery to Dudley's Tavern helpless to do anything but share in the great excitement.

Around midnight, most of the younger people and women had found places other than the streets. The huge fire at the common was dying down; the wagons at the corner of Martin's Livery were empty of everything but hay, and all the kegs were drained at Dudley's Tavern.

Sam walked from the Tavern along a now quietened street to meet with soldiers at the common. Here and there along Market Street were men who sat at the side of the buildings---now sleeping away their spirits----seemingly tranquil and at peace---- not only with England---but also with the world.

CHAPTER TWENTY-SIX

October 29, 1781, was an important day for Sam. He, along with the other soldiers, was given his discharge. Now, only a small town militia remained under the command of General Jones. There was still some fighting in the South. They, too, would soon get word from the North the storm had subsided ---the war was over.

Sam lay on his bunk bed reading Josie's letter. Dudley had made a special trip to Camp Quanky to bring the letter on the day of Sam's departure from the army. He had read it to his mother and Aunt Jenny and both agreed that he should bring Josie home when she returned to Halifax. Sam's lips moved silently as he read the letter again.

New Bern
October 16, 1781

Dear Sam,

I have learned just today that the conflict is at an end. I have not heard from Father directly, but I am sure you are fully aware of his efforts in the South. He has been so involved in this war that I fear what will happen to him, now that it's over.

Mother died last Christmas and I had a bad time. I was slowly beginning to accept her death when word came to me in May that George was killed at Guilford. I was again sick with grief for several weeks. However, I have regained my health and now feel strong enough to travel to Halifax.

Mother provided for my future and my inheritance is such that neither of us shall ever have to want for anything.

I hope you will be at Dudley's to meet me. Now that I am without family, I hope to soon have one of my own.

I pray that your feelings for me have not changed. War changes so many things, I hope it has not changed your love for me.

Thoughts of you have constantly sustained me throughout these five bitter years and I want to be with you for all our years to come.

Look for me. I shall be in Halifax as soon as I can get passage on the stage.

Love,
Josie.

Sam looked up from the letter at his mother who was sewing at the kitchen table. Sarah Pickett had managed to survive the war better than most women in Halifax. She had been use to hard times before the war. So, when the war came, she had been quick to adjust.

When the British came to Halifax, Sarah packed food and blankets and took Aunt Jenny to the swamps and had stayed with Looney Oney. There, they remained for four nights, while the British ransacked all the houses. Sarah and Aunt Jenny had returned to the house after the British left, only to find Aunt Jenny's cats patiently waiting. There were no chickens, no hogs, no horses, no cows and no feed. Sarah told Sam that Aunt Jenny was baffled by all that had happened but was relieved to find all her cats at home.

By the time Sam had returned home from Warrenton, Sarah and Aunt Jenny had made the house fit to live in again.

During the morning, Sam had talked with his mother at great length about the official letter she had received from General Lincoln. It was highly complimentary but ended with a detailed explanation about his Uncle John's death at the Battle of Charles Town. Sarah Pickett had many times feared for her brother's safety, but now accepted the fact that he had died in the service of his country. John Thompson's life had served a good purpose. Sarah would always remember him that way.

Aunt Jenny, too, accepted the fact that John Thompson was dead and subsequently noticed numerous stray dogs coming to the house to harass her cats. It was as if some alien spirit had stirred the dogs to haunt her cats.

John Thompson had promised he'd return to chase her cats to Quanky Creek and there was no way to convince Aunt Jenny that he had not returned to fulfill his vow. When Aunt Jenny could not rid the place of the stray dogs, she had summoned Looney Oney to come and study the situation.

Looney Oney had prepared a bluish, green foul smelling liquid that she spread around the barn. The pungent odor emitted by the foul concoction smelled like rotting eggs and had caused all the cats to scurry from the barn as if a pack of wild dogs was pursuing them. Feeling depressed about all that had happened, Aunt Jenny came to realize that Looney Oney had made the concoction too strong.

"Oney may know about spirits, but she don't know nothing about cats," was Aunt Jenny's reaction.

When the wind was from the East, the odor drifted as far as the house. The smell was so repugnant, Sarah Pickett had asked Sam to take a shovel and cover the places where Looney Oney had poured the liquid. The fresh

First For Freedom

earth smothered the scent and Oney's smelly spell was terminated. One by one the hesitant cats sniffed the air as they slowly returned to their habitat. It was a week before all the cats found enough courage to challenge the odoriferous spell.

He felt in his right pocket and took out the shiny, speckled pebble that he had purchased from Looney Oney. He lay back on his bunk and looked at it; then quickly bounded from his bed, he walked across the room and deposited the speckled stone in a pewter mug which held his other collected pebbles that he had found in the clear waters of Quanky. It belonged among the things of his youth.

During the morning Sam had shaved closer than usual and dressed in his finest clothes. He had been ready since morning to make his trip to Halifax. He did not know what to expect in town, but if Josie was on the stage---well he wanted to look his best. Just as he was leaving the house, he stopped by his pewter mug. He looked down at the pebbles and all his pebbles were in a circle around the one that he had gotten from Looney Oney. There must be something magical about that stone, thought Sam. He picked up the speckled stone and put in his right front pocket. Then, he said to himself --'maybe good things can come to those who think good things'. Now, was not the time to take any chances.

About mid-afternoon, Sam left his home. It would be after five o'clock before the stage arrived but he was eager to get to town. People were still excited about independence and he wanted to get to Dudley's to hear the latest news.

As he rode into town, he thought how fortunate the town and the people had been during the war. All the stores and homes were standing and there had been little damage. Perhaps, the most trying time experienced by the people was when Cornwallis and the Red Coats occupied the town.

As he pulled reins in front of Martin's Livery, he was thinking that Halifax was a perfect place to raise a family --or as George would say 'rear' a family---somehow George kept coming back at the most unexpected moments.

He dismounted and walked toward Dudley's Tavern.

When he entered, he walked to the counter where Dudley stood and was greeted by the men at the tables. The men were in a jovial mood, but Sam could not immediately become acclimated.

Dudley leaned across the counter.

"Sam you'll never believe what I've had to listen to here today." Dudley raised his hands and shouted.

"Hey, you fellows, hold it down. Sam and me want to hear some of these war stories. Not that I'm gonna believe what I hear, but some of what y'all are sayin' just might be worth listening to."

Sam had just taken his seat at the counter when Zeb Joyner came up to him. Zeb had not served in the army since his work at the gristmill had been so important. It seemed the army needed the meal more than it needed Zeb. When he got to the counter, he turned his back to Dudley and faced the men in the tavern. He held up his hands and the tavern became quiet.

"Let me tell y'all about the fight I had at Quanky Bridge, when we were occupied by the Red Coats of Cornwallis."

"That won't Cornwallis that occupied you, Zeb. That was your old lady. I heard she throwed you in Quanky Creek to sober you up." Came a voice from the back of the room.

The men laughed but Zeb continued.

"You fellows don't want to hear nothing worth listen' to. I tell it was one of the most unbelievable fights of the entire war."

"And your old lady won. We all know the war is still going on for you, Zeb," said another cronie.

"You fellows don't know what I went through."

"If I know you---Zeb--more went through you than you went through. Since you spent most of your time in this tavern while we soldiers were away fighting," said a man standing next to Sam.

Dudley raised his hands.

"Hey, y'all give Zeb a chance." Dudley turned to Zeb.

"Zeb, I never knew you joined the army."

"You don't haft to join the army to fight your old lady," said a fat man, seated directly in front of Zeb.

Zeb looked down at the man contemptuously.

"To tell the truth, I'd rather fight a Red Coat --any day--like I was saying, about that time at Quanky Bridge. The Red Coats were behind me when I came up to the bridge at Quanky Creek. I was 'bout half way across the bridge, when I saw these other Red Coats coming across from the other side. So, I stopped my horse, made him rear up and then I made him jump off the bridge. We must have fallen fifty feet to the water below."

"Was the horse hurt," continued the quick-witted, fat man.

It was impossible for Zeb to continue. The laughter was so loud that Zeb had to wait patiently until it subsided.

"Was the horse hurt," repeated Zeb mockingly. "Let me tell you that horse was buried so deep in the mud at Quanky, he never came up. That's the only reason I came here today----and that's to see if any of you know of a horse for sell--cheap. But, since I'm here on business--I might as well have another mug of ale."

Dudley drew a mug of ale and handed it to Zeb. Zeb turned to pick up the mug and did not see his wife, Jezebel Joyner, enter the tavern. Zeb put the mug to his lips,

He suddenly became aware of the silence. He then turned and saw his robust, two hundred pound wife, standing in the doorway.

Jezebel stood there momentarily and then walked up to Zeb.

"Zeb Joyner, you're about as low-down a man I ever lived wid. I knew you won't on your way to see about buyin' no horse---and--and this sure ain't no livery stable. I thought I'd find you here."

Zeb placed his mug on the counter and backed up two steps.

"Hold on Jezebel----just hold on---. Dudley here is the one who's got the horse for sale."

Dudley immediately came to Zeb's rescue.

"Oh yeah! She's some fine horse. Y'all will be mighty proud to own a horse like the one I've got. Zeb and me was just about to bargain over her."

"I know where you can find a horse, Zeb. The onliest thing wrong is the horse has got four broke legs and stuck at the bottom of Quanky Creek," came a voice from one the cronies directly in front of Jezebel.

The crowd roared with laughter but Jezebel did not join them.

"Dudley, you ain't got no horse for sale and Zeb ain't got no money. So, how do y'all speck to do business," asked Jezebel.

"We trusts one another, Jezebel," said Zeb, as he looked to Dudley for support

"Speak for yourself, Zeb," said Dudley.

"That's more'en I can say for myself. I don't trust neither one of you. You ought not lost that horse you had. You'd thank you owned as many horses as Willie Jones the way you're all time bettin' and losin' horses," said Jezebel

"Hush! Jezebel. I was just tellin' the fellows about how I lost that last horse at Quanky Creek, during the war. You know, I told you how I made him jump over the bridge and all, " explained Zeb, trying to make Jezebel understand.

"That horse you owned wouldn't cross that bridge at Quanky Creek if the whole British army was behind him. Zeb, you told me that many-a time. That's the reason I didn't mind you losing him. That horse wouldn't never git on that bridge---much less jump off'en it," said Jezebel.

"Now why did you have to say that, Jezebel? It's got to place you can't trust nobody." He took Jezebel by the arm.

"Come on, you ain't got no business in this here tavern."

"I'm going by the butcher shop and you'd better be home before dark," said Jezebel as she left the tavern

The men watched and before a word was spoken Zeb was back in the tavern.

"I come in this establishment to get away from her. Now she's coming here. What kind of business you runnin' here, Dudley? Lettin' a woman walk right in just like she's a paying customer."

"She's your wife, Zeb," said Dudley.

"Don't remind me. Don't remind me. Hey, Dudley, I've got this here song I've been working on for about two weeks. I think it's the best thing I've ever done. I'll be wanting you to hear it."

Jesse Turner had not spoken but now wanted to understand what had happened to the Hamiltons.

"Tell us how you save the Hamiltons from being arrested, Sam!"

Sam had never mentioned that he had been to the Hamiltons house to warn them about the 'Order for their arrest' to anyone except Dudley and now Sam looked at Dudley and was in a state of bewilderment.

"General Jones told me all about that night you slipped out to the Hamilton's house to warn them before you ever came to me with the story," said Dudley.

"How did General Jones know what I did for the Hamiltons, Dudley?" Sam still did not understand.

"Sam, that family won't worth savin'. I've known them for Tories back as long as I can remember, I wouldn't tell you now if the war wasn't over. But you did exactly what General Jones wanted you to do," said Dudley.

"But everybody knew Hamilton was a well-known Tory," added Turner.

Dudley explained.

"He was also a very influential man. The Council of Safety felt that this was the best way to git him outa town. If he had been thrown in jail, there would have been a heap of bad feeling right here in Halifax. General Jones knew that you'd never let anything happen to Josie Hamilton. ---so he let you save her and solve his problem at the same time."

"And he never said a word to me. All these years I thought I got away with it," said Sam, shaking his head.

"Well, Sam, I reckon that's the reason General Jones was a general and you were a private at that time." Dudley laughed as he spoke.

"What did you do with all that silver you collected in Halifax, Dudley," asked one of the men.

"Let me clear this thing up. Sam and I were the ones who took the silver to Edenton and traded it for gunpowder. The soldiers here were supplied with gunpowder that they wouldn't have had if it hadn't been for me and Sam."

"I understand that Jonathan Lawson took you you for twenty shillings, Dudley," said a red headed man at the counter.

"He paid me back with interest.," said Dudley. "Sam can tell you about it one day when y'all ain't got no news to tell."

"Sam, you'd better be glad you've got a friend like Dudley. What he says carries a heap of weight among us here," said one of the men.

"I carry a heap of stuff to drink, too. That's what give me so much power," added Dudley.

The men began to talk among themselves and Sam was no longer of any concern to them.

"Hey, did you get any good news yesterday? You took the letter away before I got a chance to read it."

"It was a letter from Josie. She's in New Bern. I'm hoping she'll be coming to town on the next stage."

"You know, I wouldn't of give you two much of a chance before the war, but now things just might work out. Seems the war has sort of changed the differences between you two. At least you won't have to contend with John Hamilton. He shore done his part for the British. The way he kept the Tories stirred up. He won't satisfied just to fight. He had to be a leader. He got to be Colonel before the war ended, I understand."

"The last I heard tell of him, he was in Georgia."

"I hear most of the people in the South thought the British won the war when Cornwallis left Guilford Court House and moved to Wilmington."

"That's what I heard. They turned on Harnett and Ashe and put 'em in jail. I heard they were beaten and only given enough food to keep them alive."

"Everybody says they were treated worse than any of the other prisoners," agreed Sam.

"That's what killed them, Sam. To be treated that way by your own kind."

"We never would have made it without Harnett, that's for sure."

"He's the one who kept us all together. It's a shame he couldn't have lived long enough to hear about the surrender," said Dudley.

Sam was thinking how the atmosphere at Dudley's Tavern had returned when a small, thin, red faced man rushed into the tavern and everybody turned toward him. He hurried to the counter and held up his hands.

"General Jones and Colonel William R. Davie are coming down King Street to the courthouse. They want all the people to come as quickly as possible to the common."

The men began to move from the tables as Dudley untied his apron. Sam watched the last two men walk toward the front door and Dudley came from behind the counter.

"Hey, you fellows, wait----hold on----y'all shore have got some manners. Won't even wait for a man to close his business."

"We'll ask General Jones to wait for you. You know he ain't 'bout to start 'til you git there, Dudley," kidded the last man to leave.

Sam waited with Dudley while he locked the front door. He watched the people moving toward the courthouse. Market Street would soon be so crowded the stage would have to stop on King Street to let the passengers off. Realizing this, Sam left Dudley --fumbling with the lock.

CHAPTER TWENTY-SEVEN

Sam hurried along Market Street and made his way against the crowd of men, women and children who were headed for the courthouse. When he reached the town common, he stopped and could see a carriage with General Jones and Colonel Davie coming down King Street. There were two soldiers on horseback riding ahead of the carriage and two riders behind the carriage.

Beyond the cheering crowd, the stage had stopped about half way down King Street.

Sam saw a young lady step down from the stage. She paused and looked about as if she were expecting to see someone. Sam waited, then looked again, not believing his eyes. She was dressed in pale blue outfit and held a dark blue parasol over her head. Realizing that no one but Josie could look so beautiful; he quickened his steps and ran to her

"Hey---Josie---over here," called Sam waving and pushing through the crowd. Even though she was only a short distance from him, he felt that time had slowed and it was as if he'd could not get to her fast enough.

Josie dropped her parasol and came toward him. They met in the middle of King Street and held each other. The passing crowd hurried toward the courthouse. Sam and Josie were oblivious to the sounds and noise of the crowd and were only aware of their feeling for each other for that wonderful moment.

The crowd had assembled in front of the courthouse as Sam walked with Josie back to the stage. Stooping, Sam picked up Josie's parasol and valise. Josie took his arm. He handed Josie her parasol and they turned to walk toward the courthouse. They moved among the people on Market Street until they found standing room near Dudley's Tavern. Sam looked around at the huge crowd and could see Dudley and his crowd standing to his left. The crowd watched and cheered as General Jones and Colonel Davie pulled their carriage to a halt in front of the courthouse. Two soldiers stayed with the horses while two other soldiers made way for their commanders. The two officers were in uniforms. There were still duties required of these two leaders

Standing on the steps of the courthouse, General Jones held up his hand. The crowd responded with immediate silence.

"Your attention----your attention. I am sure all of you are aware that Cornwallis has surrendered at Yorktown and that this war has run its course. We have been victorious on land and sea, but we must now make our country safe for all the people. We must be about the business of building our country. I want you to hear Colonel William R. Davie and be mindful of the responsibilities that shall be yours and mine---if we are to share in the freedom we have won."

The handsome young Davie walked to the highest step of the courthouse and looked to his right where Sarah Jones stood smiling and waiting. Davie smiled back and then looked toward the large crowd.

"Friends and citizens of these United States and all who hear me----I have heard of the celebrations that have been made throughout this state, and by right we should celebrate this great victory over England. We cannot, however, let these celebrations result in lawlessness and destruction of property. We must accept all the responsibility that is ours----to make this state and this nation strong. We must begin now---for we have much work to do. We are Americans now and must honor our state and our nation by being obedient to those laws and regulations that are set forth to guide us in our conduct. If we disregard the laws that have been made by our leaders, we have no hope of success as a nation. We would fare better as British subjects than we would fare in a lawless land. We must now make our allegiance to America and show through our conduct that we are capable of governing ourselves---"

When Davie had finished his speech, he stepped down and walked quickly to Sarah Jones and embraced her. The crowd responded with cheers for Davie.

Sam noticed Dudley had grabbed Zeb Joyner by the arm and yelled ---"Ladies and Gentlemen----I want you all to hear from one of our fellow citizens. You all know Zeb Joyner. Well, Zeb's got a song he wants y'all to hear. I have not heard this song before but Zeb has told me that it's the best song he has ever written. I've heard his other songs and if this is the best--then it has to be special."

Zeb stepped up and smiled at the silent crowd.

"This is called BEYOND THIS DAY. I tried to put words to this song that tell what this fight has been about---I hope all of you get my message."

Zeb began strumming his guitar and then started his song

Beyond this day, we must learn to care
And always seek to share
The burdens we must bear
Beyond this day.

Beyond this place, the pages will unfold
Of all the brave and bold,
Our story will be told,
Beyond this place

Beyond this prayer, will be a brighter day
We'll find a better way
With freedom here to stay
Beyond this prayer

Beyond this dream, Our hopes will always be
All people will be free
Throughout eternity
Beyond this dream.

So take our song and sing it loud and clear
For all the world to hear
Go sing our song.
Beyond this day.

Go sing our song
Beyond this place

Go sing our song
Beyond this prayer

Go sing our song
Beyond this dream

    As Zeb finished his song, the huge crowd clapped and yelled for more. Zeb bowed and waved to his enthusiastic audience.
    Several of Dudley's cronies rushed to the steps of the courthouse and lifted Zeb to their shoulders and paraded him among the people. The crowd cheered as loudly for Zeb as they had cheered for Cornelius Harnett the day he read the Declaration of Independence. The men paraded Zeb to King Street and then brought him back to let him down in front of Dudley's Tavern.
    The large crowd began to break up and Sam could see General Jones coming toward him leading the horse 'Midnight'.
    Josie held Sam's arm tightly and smiled as General Jones came near.

"Josie, I'm happy to see you back in Halifax," said General Jones, as he extended his hand.

"I hope to make my home here, Sir," said Josie, looking at Sam.

"Well, I think I'll give Sam one final order just to make sure you do stay here."

The General turned to Sam.

"Sam, you will be in charge of Miss Josie during her entire stay here, which we hope will be for the rest of her life."

"That's the best order you've ever given me, Sir. In fact, it's one I'll find a real pleasure to carry out."

"Sam, you know I expect you to finish your education at Edenton and I am prepared to pay for one other person to accompany you. You will soon need to decide when you'll be leaving so I can book passage for you two. You'll want to do some other things before you travel to Edenton. I will not be responsible for an unmarried couple traveling together."

Allen Jones shook hands with Sam.

"Sir, you've just asked Josie to marry me."

"I accept, sir," said Josie, quickly.

"Well, Sam, I've been your commanding officer so long I suppose it's got to be a habit---telling you what to do."

General Jones mounted his horse as he spoke.

"Sir, you book passage to Edenton in two weeks and Josie and I'll be prepared to travel in such a way that we'll not be embarrassing you," said Sam, waving to General Jones.

"Thank you for your proposal, Sir," said Josie.

General Jones smiled at the couple as he turned his horse toward King Street.

Market Street was practically clear except the crowd who stood in front of Dudley's Tavern waiting for him to open the tavern door.

Dudley stepped up to Sam and Josie.

"Good luck, Sam. You two know I'm always here if you ever need me for anything."

"Hey Dudley, come on and open the tavern," yelled one of the cronies.

"Looks like you've got a crowd waiting on you, Dudley," said Sam.

"I've been waiting on them for the last twenty years. They can wait on me for a few minutes. I just want to say I have great hopes for you two."

Dudley turned toward the crowd of men.

"As for that bunch, I don't see no hope at all. So, I'll go back to my tavern for the hopeless. There just might be some spirits I can conjure up for them. Since I'm in the business of making spirits high, I'd better go and be about my trade. I can see your spirits are high enough and you don't need me the way they do. Good luck, again, to both of you."

"Thank you, Dudley," said Sam and Josie in unison.

Dudley nodded and quickly turned away. Sam and Josie watched him hurry to the front door of his tavern.

The cronies hastily followed Dudley inside; Josie took Sam's arm and they walked toward Martin's Livery.

When they came to the stables, Sam untied 'Jericho' from the hitching post and Joise again locked her arm to his extended elbow.

Sam turned with Josie and looked back down Market Street. The sun now cast long shadows across the street.

Halifax had cast some shadows of its own these past five years, thought Sam---not shadows that come and go with the rising and setting of the sun----but lasting shadows that would forever shade the thoughts of all earnest men and women who love freedom and liberty.

The End

Maxville Burt Williams

First For Freedom

Money from me he did steal. 2. I had bet my horse, I had bet my house, I had even bet my land. On the cards that I was to get from that crook, which was to be the last hand. Then the candles went out, there was a shot and a shout. And when the candles were lit, alone I did sit. And my

Maxville Burt Williams

First For Freedom

Maxville Burt Williams

Flora

Max B. Williams — *Max B. Williams*

(Chorus) Flo-ra, Flo-ra, you git on home. Or you'll be left here all a-lone.
1. You helped Prince Char-lie at Cul-len-den To es-cape the wrath of the gov-ern-ment men. And the Tow'r of Lon-don could not hold you. But there's Noth-ing here for you to do. So, Flo-ra, Flo-ra, you git on home Or

(Beaut our Pla pie here)

Maxville Burt Williams

First For Freedom

Freedom's Song
Max B. Williams — **Max B. Williams**

1. We have the right to fight for our freedom, Now we must firm-ly take our stand. And have faith and hope in our future, In this free-dom-lov-ing land. We shall be free, we shall be free; In the fu-ture you will

Maxville Burt Williams

Max Williams
Beyond This Day
Williams
Be-yond this day
We must learn to care — And al-ways seek to share — the bur-dens we must bear... Be-
yond this day.
Be-yond this place — the
pa-ges will un-fold — Of all the brave and bold — Our sto-ry will be told — Be-

Maxville Burt Williams

First For Freedom

Maxville Burt Williams

ABOUT THE AUTHOR

Maxville Burt Williams is a resident of Enfield, North Carolina. He is a graduate of East Carolina University with a B.S. degree in History and a M.A. degree in Education. For the past 28 years his book, FIRST FOR FREEDOM, has been produced as an outdoor drama in Historic Halifax. His second novel, STRANGE WIND FROM THE ROANOKE is a sequel to FIRST FOR FREEDOM dealing with North Carolina's role in the adoption of the United States Constitution. Other writings include the plays THE SCHROONCHERS, and THE SCHROONCHERS MEET THE FLIM FLAM MAN. Another one of his plays, TOLERATION, was produced by East Carolina University. He has also written a book of poetry entitled REFLECTIONS. For the past ten years, he has had a newspaper article in the paper each week.

Printed in the United States
44581LVS00005B/55